Qaisra Shahraz is a British-Pakis  and scriptwriter. In 2016 she wo Diversity Lifetime Achiever Award Education, Gender and Interfaith placed in the 'Pakistan Power 100 L.......... nuw or the Royal Society of Arts, her novels *The Holy Woman*, *Typhoon* and *Revolt*, and the classic short story 'A Pair of Jeans', have all been translated into several languages and are studied in universities and schools.

Qaisra is based with her husband and three sons in Manchester, UK, where she has lived since childhood. As trustee of Manchester Multi-Faith Centre and Co-Chair of Faith Network 4 Manchester, she is keen to promote messages of tolerance, peace and community cohesion in the UK and abroad through her literary tours.

www.qaisrashahraz.com

Also by Qaisra Shahraz

The Holy Woman
Typhoon
Revolt

Collection of short stories

A Pair of Jeans & Other Stories

The Concubine
and
The Slave-Catcher

Qaisra Shahraz

HopeRoad Publishing
PO Box 55544
Exhibition Road
London SW7 2DB

First published in Great Britain by HopeRoad 2017
Copyright © 2017 Qaisra Shahraz
The right of Qaisra Shahraz to be identified as the author of this work has been
asserted by her in accordance with the Copyright, Designs and Patents Act 1988.

A CIP catalogue record for this book is available from the British Library.

Supported using public funding by
ARTS COUNCIL ENGLAND

ISBN 978-1-908446-61-9

eISBN 978-1-908446-67-1

www.hoperoadpublishing.com

Printed and bound by TJ International Ltd, Padstow, Cornwall, UK

For my dear nieces:
Sumer, Sophia, Sara, Zarri Bano, Safa, Sana and Alyssa
and to my nephews: Raees, Adam, Ismail and Ayman

We are all strangers in a strange land, longing for home, but not quite knowing what or where home is. We glimpse it sometimes in our dreams . . .

Madeleine L'Engle

Praise for
The Concubine and *The Slave-Catcher*

'An astute and gifted storyteller, Shahraz describes the immigrant experience in Britain with rare passion and verisimilitude' Bapsi Sidhwa, author of *The Crow Eaters*

'A very bold and hard-hitting collection, truly memorable' Lynne Pearce, Lancaster University, UK

'Shahraz's brilliant voice shines as she takes us across four continents and centuries of history in this new volume of stories' Ambassador Akbar Ahmed, Ibn Khaldun Chair of Islamic Studies

'This impressive new collection from Qaisra Shahraz, spanning several continents and centuries, puts the spotlight on the human condition – with each story set against a significant historical backdrop. Powerful storytelling across a culturally diverse literary landscape' Emma Clayton, *Bradford Telegraph & Argus*

'Insightful and culturally diverse, this collection is a timely and utterly essential read. Qaisra's prose enlightens and entrances all at once' Barbara Bos, *Women Writers, Women's Books*

'Shahraz possesses a keen sense of place: her stories devolve to particular locales and yet convey an expansive transnational consciousness' Corinne Fowler, University of Leicester, UK

'Like Buchi Emecheta, Shahraz is passionate about the lives and plight of women and migrants. Like Elif Shafak, she is effortlessly cosmopolitan and has a sharp ear for the voices of the street. Read this sparkling collection if you are interested in migration, in intergenerational tensions' Claire Chambers, University of York, UK

Contents

The Escape

Manchester, UK and Lahore, Pakistan, present day

In the packed prayer hall of Darul Uloom mosque in Longsight, the Imam concluded the Eid prayers with a passionate plea for world peace, and for terrorist activities around the world to cease. Seventy-three-year-old Samir, perched on a plastic chair because of his bad leg, kept his hands raised, quietly mouthing his own personal prayer.

"Please, Allah Pak, bless her soul . . . And let me escape!"

Rows of seated men had arisen from their prayer mats and reached out to energetically hug others and offer the festive greeting, "Eid Mubarak!"

Samir took his time. There was no one in particular he was seeking to greet or hug at this mosque. Most of the men around him were strangers, and of the younger generation, several sported beards – a marked shift between the two generations. His own face remained clean-shaven. Nowadays he prayed at the Cheadle mosque in Cheshire, joining the congregation of Arabs and other nationalities for the Taraweeh prayers during the fasting month of Ramadan. Nostalgia tugging at him, on a whim Samir had asked his son to drop him off in Longsight to offer his Eid prayers at his old community mosque.

Painfully rising to his feet, Samir began the hugging ritual, smiling cordially. Unlike the others leaving the hall, he loitered; he was in no hurry to get out. At the door, he dutifully dropped a five-pound note in the collection fund box.

Whilst looking for his shoes he bumped into his old friend, Manzoor. They greeted each other, smiled broadly and warmly hugged. Outside, in the chilly autumn day, his friend, who lived a street away from the mosque, invited him to his house for the Eid hospitality of vermicelli seviyan and chana chaat.

The smile slid off Samir's face. He was reluctant to visit his friend's house – afraid of the old memories, shying away from the normality, the marital bliss of his friend's home. In particular, he was loath to witness the little intimacies between husband and wife. The look. The laugh. The teasing banter.

Instead he waved goodbye to his friend and stood waiting for his son. "Thank you, but I'm being picked up," he informed a young man kindly offering him a lift home, before sauntering on his bad leg down the street.

"I have all the time in the world," he wryly muttered to himself, savouring the walk down streets he had cycled and scooted along for over three decades.

A lot had changed, the area now thriving with different migrant communities: the Pakistanis and the Bengalis living side by side with the Irish and the Somalis. Many Asian stores and shops had sprung up. The Bengali sari shops and travel agents jostled happily alongside the Pakistani ones and the Chinese takeaway. Mosques catering to the needs of the Muslim community flourished, from the small Duncan Road mosque in a semi-detached corner house to the purpose-built Darul Uloom centre on Stamford Road. The Bengali mosque for the

Bengali community on one corner of Buller Road was only a few feet away from the Pakistani and Arab Makki Masjid on the other corner. Not surprisingly, on Fridays, for the Juma prayers, the street was gridlocked.

He noted that the Roman Catholic church and its primary school on Montgomery Road had disappeared, along with the quaint little National Westminster Bank branch that had been in the middle of Beresford Road with a communal vegetable plot at the back. That had been pulled down twenty-odd years ago. St Agnes' church was still there, however, at the junction of West Point and Hamilton Road and it still enjoyed healthy Sunday-morning congregations.

Samir stopped outside a shop on Beresford Road that had been called Joy Town thirty years earlier. It had been his children's favourite toyshop, especially on Eid day, when they ran to it with their Eidhi money, eager to buy toy cars, skipping ropes and doll's china crockery sets. In its place there now stood a grocery superstore with stalls of vegetables and fruits hogging the pavement area. On Fridays and Saturdays, families like Samir's, who had moved out of the area, still returned to do their shopping, visiting their favourite halal meat and grocery stores, carting boxes of fresh mangoes, bags of basmati rice and chapatti flour back to their cars. The hustle and bustle of these shops always brought out a smile in him.

His son, Maqbool, a well-to-do sportswear manager, dutifully returned to pick him up half an hour later. By that time, Samir was shivering in his shalwar kameez and sherwani, and gladly climbed into the warm car. He had wanted to go to the Sanam Sweet Centre to buy a few boxes of Asian sweets to distribute to friends but he hesitated, suddenly overcome by trepidation.

"Do you want to go somewhere else, Father?" his son asked, as if reading his mind.

Samir shook his head, not wishing to inconvenience his son further, and feeling guilty for already taking up enough of his time.

"No. Let's go home," he murmured, eyes closed.

He had a large five-bedroom detached house – but with his wife and family gone, all the joy of living in it had fled. He kept himself in the master bedroom, hating to enter the other rooms in the house, especially the one containing his wife's clothes. Only when the grandchildren visited did he unlock some of the doors. These days, he spent his time in his new favourite spot, the chair at the dining table next to the window and radiator, where he would sit, leafing through *The Times*, the *Daily Jang* and *The Nation*, watching the traffic go past on the busy road.

His son dropped him off at the door with the words, "I'll collect you in an hour's time." Samir nodded and watched him drive away before letting himself into the house. Another hour to kill. He shrugged. Oh well. It was better here on his own, with the TV and the newspaper keeping him company, than politely waiting around at someone else's house for dinner.

He felt hungry, but the dining table in front of him lay dismally bare. On Eid days it was normally stacked with bowls of delicious food: boiled eggs, seviyan, chana chaats and a hot tray of shami kebabs. And these were just the breakfast starters, heralding a busy festive day of eating.

Last year his entire family had been there. If he closed his eyes he could see his children helping themselves to the food, with him happily beginning the Eidhi money-giving ritual. Five-pound notes for the little ones, ten for the older teenagers, and crisp twenty-pound notes for his daughters and daughters-in-law.

In the steamy warm kitchen with the noisy fan purring away at the window, the smell from a pot of pilau rice and trays of roast lull in the lively conversation he ventured to inform his family, licking his dry lips carefully, "I want to tell you something."

They turned to stare. His daughter, Roxanna, hushed her little girl sitting on her lap with the words, "Abu-ji is speaking, shush."

"I want to go back home to Pakistan," Samir announced. "To visit my family – stay there for a few months . . . It'll be good for me. It's the right time, with your mother gone . . . I need a change of scene and I've plenty of time now," he explained, smiling. "It would be lovely to visit some places that belong to my old life. And it would be a chance to spend some time with my sister, brother and their families."

Complete silence greeted his words.

"A few months! Are you sure about this, Father? We'll miss you." His eldest daughter had found her tongue.

"You'll all be fine without me. Anyway, you can phone me every day. You've all got busy lives and families, so it won't be that bad to have me disappear for a few months. I'll hardly be missed, will I? This trip will be good for me – I need to go," he said, his voice petering out, giving them a glimpse of the abyss inside him. He had only just stopped himself from saying, "I need to escape."

Discomfited and not knowing what was the right thing to say, his children prudently ended the discussion. Their father had always made his own decisions – very rarely paying any attention to other people's opinions. Their mother had battled for years to influence him, and died having never quite succeeded.

"Where will you stay? Lahore?" his youngest daughter, Rosie, boldly asked.

"Yes! In our family ancestral home of course, with my brother – where else?" he replied sharply, annoyed at his daughter's question and semi-hostile tone.

7

Rosie did not bother answering. Instead she exchanged a pointed look with her sister, which their father neatly intercepted. His face tightened. "You need to understand, Rosie, that just as this is your family, I've the same back home . . . They care about me and want me to spend time with them." His tone was harsher than he had intended.

The words 'back home' had just slipped out of him again. How curious. For a few seconds, Samir was lost in thought. Why did he say that? Was Manchester not his home? After all, he had spent nearly fifty years of his life in this city. The other place was just his birthplace, his country of origin and reminder of his youth. Surely these facts should make Manchester his home?

He shrugged these thoughts aside, willing his mood to lighten. He now had a goal: to occupy his mind with tasks, and he loved tasks above all. The big task facing him now was what presents to take for his family and his two college friends in Lahore. He promised himself that this time the three friends would indeed treat themselves to a walk through the elegant Victorian corridors of the Government College of Lahore where they had studied.

Three days later, Samir had flown out from Manchester airport, arriving without any warning at all and taking his 'other family' in Lahore by surprise. They gushed with greetings, hurriedly composing their shocked faces even though, inside, their thoughts were running amok. What was he doing here, all of a sudden? How long was he going to stay? Which other relatives was he visiting – and for how long? These questions battered simultaneously in all their heads.

Samir's face fell, and he quickly averted his eyes, astutely picking up the telltale signs from their faces and body language. Two days later, after visiting the local Anarkali Bazaar, taking a leisurely walk down the famous Mall Road, and spending time with his sister's family in her villa in the Defence area, he headed for the village where his parents were buried. There he was amicably greeted by his host, a second cousin, who gave hospitality to all relatives visiting the family graves.

After some refreshments, Samir headed for the cemetery on the outskirts of the village. Well maintained, it had tall tanglewood bushes growing around it, keeping the wolves out. Eyes blurring, Samir gazed down at his parents' graves. His father had adamantly made it clear that he did not want to be buried in the overcrowded city cemeteries. "I want fresh air, the shade of a tree and plenty of space around – and make sure you leave room for your mother. Don't just throw us in any hole!"

As obedient sons, they had honoured their father's wish, and duly visited the village of his ancestral home where they bought a plot of land for the graves. Thereafter, Samir's sister and brother made annual journeys to the village, to offer a feast and hatham prayers for their parents' souls.

Samir perched himself on the low wall circling the plot with his parents' graves. The tranquillity around him had him thinking about his own burial place. Of course it would be Manchester's Southern or Cheadle Cemetery. He could not imagine his children traipsing back to Pakistan to visit his grave in a land that was foreign to them. He now understood why his father was insistent on keeping a place for his wife. Remembering his own Sabiya, Samir bowed his head. The loneliness crushed him. Two years ago, they had both been here, sitting at the same spot.

He watched a herd of milk buffaloes being shepherded back to the village. Feeling a tiny stinging sensation, he looked down at a line of ants running down the brickwork. Laden with small scraps of leaves, the ants were zigzagging around his feet. He moved his foot away and glanced over his shoulders at the brick-making quarry and kiln, spotting a group of peasant men pushing trolleys stacked with bricks. Two women were carrying small baskets loaded with baked bricks on their heads. Feeling sorry for them and the hard work that the women had to do in order to feed their families, Samir was reminded of the second mission that had brought him to this village – his wife's charitable work in supporting widows and their families. He had to visit one widow with three teenage daughters.

He glanced down, taking his fill, tearfully etching the picture of the graves in his head. Was this going to be his final farewell? Standing over his mother's grave, soft sobs shook his large body. It was a strange world. To be buried continents away from one's own parents. Why was he crying? For his parents who had died decades ago or for his beloved Sabiya?

"Life is a cycle," he mused aloud. He was in his seventies but still demurred from being called 'old'. God only knew where the rest of his ancestors were buried – most probably in India, before Partition. People were born and slid through the cycle of life and then disappeared, with some leaving no trace.

"Samir," he told himself, "stop thinking like this – it's morbid!" And he raised his hands to say a final fervent prayer over his parents' mounds.

His host family had gone to a lot of trouble in their offer of hospitality. The two young women had begun scurrying around the courtyard the moment he arrived. A hen had been snatched from the chicken coop in the far end of the courtyard and quickly dispatched to the cooking pot. The rice for the lamb biryani had been soaked. The pink custard powder was energetically whisked in an earthen bowl. Not content with the home cooking for their special velati, foreign guest from

'London', the host had enlisted the help of Rahmat, the village cook. It was widely said that people always licked their fingers after eating his tasty chicken soup, shorba.

The women had happily obliged. Mina, the daughter-in-law, was seven months pregnant, expecting her first child, and hated squatting on the floor whilst cooking on a pedestal stove. As well as that, her pregnancy was causing her a lot of embarrassment. She was *huge*, everyone kept telling her. And maintaining her modesty by keeping herself well draped in her chador in front of the male guest was proving to be quite challenging.

With a last lingering glance at his parents' graves, Samir followed the path to the village central square with its old majestic-looking minar tree where his driver was resting under its shade. His brother had kindly loaned both their driver and the car for his use whilst he used his motorcycle.

Ahead of him Samir saw a young man pulling a suitcase and dragging something else. Samir stared wide-eyed, temporarily transported to another time and place. He still kept his bedroll canvas bag in his garage in England, never having had the heart to throw it away. Too many poignant memories were attached to it. The frayed brown leather suitcase, stuffed with all his important documents, including his British nationality, was still kept under his bed.

There are special moments etched on people's minds. For Samir it was the one of him pathetically lugging a big bedroll and a large suitcase from Victoria coach station through the streets of London – a memory he found deeply mortifying to this day. How his arms and fingers did not fall off still amazed him. Tired, hungry and harassed, he and his friend stumbled thankfully into a Victorian house with a Bed & Breakfast sign; two Pakistani migrants from the North of England wanting to try their fortunes down south in London.

It was actually his friend's breezy confidence, smart use of English, cocky winsome smile and flirtatious winks that had successfully got them a room late at night, winning over the elegant old lady with her purple rinse. The purple hair colour of many older women in those early days fascinated him. Why did they like such a strange colour?

Samir shuddered, tasting the raw fear he had felt then as they desperately sought a place for the night. *What if we don't find a room? Where will we go and what will we do?* he had silently agonised, panicking at the darkness falling around them. It was his friend's optimism and high spirits that had saved him from making a fool of himself. There was one moment when he was ready to give up – to squat on the pavement and shed bitter tears, bewailing his stupidity in leaving a warm room and a cosy bed in Blackburn.

Sharing a double bed with his friend capped the humiliation of that day further. His friend had joked at their sleeping quarters and went soundly to sleep. Samir had sidled to the edge of the bed, shivering in the thin, coarse blanket making his face itch, afraid to pull it over himself and of waking his friend. In the end, he had got up and taken his own five-inch-thick Pakistani quilt from the bedroll.

His love affair with the English capital was both doomed and short-lived. The city was not for him – too anonymous and intimidating with its huge buildings and mad evening traffic. He knew no one and felt shy and uncomfortable wherever he went, stumbling and stammering over the carefully chosen English words and phrases he had mastered to buy bus tickets, packets of Benson & Hedges or order something to eat. He perked up and smiled widely when he saw brown faces, mainly of Sikhs and Indians. He did not come across many Pakistanis.

After taking some souvenir photographs with an expensive camera he had brought from Pakistan, posing in his smart suit in front of one of the Trafalgar Square lions and outside the Queen's Buckingham Palace gates with the guards, Samir had happily fled. He wished his friend well with his love of London. Years later, when he came across the same fellow again, he laughed aloud. His friend had become a true Londoner, right down to the cockney accent.

For Samir, London was simply too much, overwhelming him and stripping away his self-esteem. Lacking his friend's easy-going manner and ability to make new friends, Samir lasted only a fortnight, after which he had escaped, happily dragging his bedroll and his brown leather suitcase with him.

Back in Blackburn, another friend welcomed him with open arms, letting him join two other tenants in his two-bedroom terraced house. Apart from the kitchen, all three rooms were used. Even the front room had a single bed, hogging the area near the window. That was the owner's room. The kitchen, with its big coal fire warming the room, was the hub of their communal life, where they took turns cooking meals, smoking and chatting, lounging on hard wooden chairs around the small kitchen table. Three of them had young families in Pakistan.

Samir stayed put, intent on earning money to support his family back home by doing overtime and long shifts. Keema lobia, minced meat with white kidney beans, became his favourite dish. He developed into a good cook, very proud of his culinary skills. His first chapatti, painstakingly made using an empty milk bottle as a rolling pin, was a good try. His three fellow housemates praised him heartily, rewarding him with the teasing words, "Your cooking is better than our wives' back home!"

His landlord found him a job in the cotton mill, after he was dissuaded from taking a job in a special nursing home in Darwen.

"You will be working with mentally ill people! You'll become mad yourself," his fellow tenants had cruelly scoffed, frightening him into scurrying into the reception room and leaving a note to resign from the job before he had even started.

In the Darwen textile mill, the huge dark machines dismayed him, but he quickly mastered the skill of working with and around them. It was dull and demeaning work. With his good education behind him, he often heard himself thinking, *If Abba could see me doing this, he'd have a fit!* His father had forked out a lot of money for the fees for a top college and had expected him to do a white-collar office job, not take on a job in some 'grotty' mill, as his youngest son once termed it years later.

The pay packet and its contents, however, had kept him smiling. The thrill of counting the banknotes through the little top corner, and feeling the angles of the sixpences and threepenny bits through the brown paper, along with the occasional half-crown – small sums, but mighty big pleasures they provided then.

In those frugal days, Samir and his friends felt duty bound to keep each other in check; the talk then was always about 'going back home'. They were not here to waste money on luxuries or on themselves. Exceptions were only made for gifts for their children. Samir had not only his wife and one daughter to support, but also his father to appease, for he had never forgiven his son for leaving their home in Lahore to do a menial job in 'Velayat' – a foreign country – in this case, the UK.

The only thing that could win over his father would be the building of a new house, to illustrate his economic well-being and to support his younger brother's family. Three years later, having had enough of textile mills and with his family having joined him, he escaped to the big city of Manchester and started his own business. It was a time when knitwear manufacturing was a booming industry in the north-west, and the area of Ardwick had become a manufacturing hub. Many Pakistani migrants entered this trade and competed with each other. Samir, too, purchased an old factory for his knitwear business.

It was also a time of social and communal uncertainty and skinheads. Enoch Powell had done his bit, frightening the host community with his racist speech citing 'the rivers of blood' and leaving the migrants in fear of being thrown out of the country. When the Ugandan refugees started to arrive in the mid-1970s, after their expulsion by Idi Amin, his friends were very dismal about their own fate in the UK. For some, the mission or the next urgent goal was to build houses back home to return to if things really got bad in England and they were thrown out.

Samir, however, had strong faith in the British justice system. He never for one moment believed that something similar could ever happen in Britain. Unlike some of his friends, his savings went not into a villa in Lahore, but in gradually working his way up to a better standard of living for his family in England, progressing from a terraced house to a detached house in a good area like Cheadle in Cheshire. He concentrated on his children, their education and careers. And the decades simply slipped by, melting away his youth and gradually severing the links with his homeland. His retirement was forced on him; he did not welcome it.

Samir nodded pleasantly at the young man with the suitcase and turned into the village lane to pay that special call. In the widow's home, there was panic as the youngest of the three girls whispered to the others that a man from Velayat was standing outside their door. When their mother spotted the foreign visitor she nearly fainted, but recovered soon enough. Bursting into sobs, she stared at the husband of their benefactor, hiding the lower part of her face behind the fold of her long shawl, and uttering the welcome greeting: "Bismillah! Bismillah!" In the name of Allah!

She owed a lot to this man's wife.

Her three teenage daughters had rushed ahead into their bethak, their living room, to make the place presentable for their guest, mehman. The crochet-edged tablecloth was quickly straightened, the mirrored beaded cushions on the leather settee hurriedly plumped up and the pair of knitting needles and women's magazine snatched and shoved under the table.

Red-faced and brimming with pleasure, the widow led their very special guest into their humble living room, with the walls lined with their best china propped on wooden shelves. It was a quaint sight for him, reminding him of the old days when his father would take him to tour some village for a taste of the other life and warm hospitality of the rural people.

Samir did not know what to say to the women; he was both touched and embarrassed by their humility and behaviour.

"Please don't bring any refreshments, Cola or Mirinda bottles or such – I've a bad stomach," he glibly lied, saving them the bother and cost of purchasing the bottles from the local village shop. "I just wanted to see how you all are – and how your daughters are doing. I know my wife always visited you, as she did with the other homes she sponsored . . ." He stopped, eyes filling up, his Sabiya in front of him once more.

The widow, seeing his tears, burst into loud sobs. "We are so sorry about your wife's death, she was such a wonderful soul and so good to us! We miss her so much, and she phoned us every month – calling us to the butcher's house to chat with us

16

over the phone . . . always checking that we had enough money for my daughters' expenses and enough flour in our grain pots."

"Yes, my Sabiya was an angel, a good soul. And we all miss her." Samir lowered his head to hide his tear-swollen eyes. The widow, touched by his grief, stared in wonder, mouth open, showing her row of uneven top teeth and two missing lower molars. She quickly closed her mouth self-consciously when he glanced up.

Samir noticed the girls shyly peeping at him; his sobbing had caused their eyes to fill up too. They had been used to crying from an early age. Their mother had become a crying machine and often they ended up aping her. Today they found the sight of this older man from England, crying over his wife, very poignant. He himself was thinking, *My wife has made such a difference to these wretched girls' lives!*

Sobering, he wiped his cheeks clean with a tissue proffered timidly by the eldest daughter. As if reading his mind, the widow told him, "Your wife got my oldest daughter married because she helped us with the dowry. Here's that daughter — she's visiting us at the moment." Then her gaze switched to her other daughters. "Who will now finance these girls' weddings?" Poverty had forced her into straight talking, to unabashedly appeal to the good nature of well-off people like him.

Samir had thought ahead. His pension, even if he did not touch the rest of his savings, would be enough to support this household — an ideal way of honouring his wife and her dying wish. Her last words and appeal to all her children and to him had been, "Do not forget all the families that I've been supporting in my life — earn their heartfelt prayers by helping them. Don't forget to keep my register of widows safe. Don't let anyone die of poverty or ill health. Display your humanity and offer generously your zakat, your alms-giving."

His eyes on the four heads modestly draped with dupattas, Samir meditated on one possible way for these girls to get out of this poverty trap.

"Sister," he said, "please educate your daughters. Send them to any colleges that you like. I'll pay all their fees and other costs."

The girls' eyes lit up in wonder. The velati man would do that for them! Pay for them to go to the town college?

Their poignant looks and glowing faces cut Samir to his very soul. His own children, including his two daughters, had been well educated to the highest degree level and had had access to great opportunities. Did these poor girls not have a right to the same? He was suddenly struck and dismayed by the inequality of life. How some had everything, whilst others simply worried about where the next meal was coming from.

The youngest girl moved away from the doorway as Samir's village host, who had followed him to the widow's house, entered the room. Catching Samir's eye, the host signalled to him that dinner was waiting.

Before rising from the settee to say his farewells, Samir hastened to add: "Don't worry about anything, sister. I'll take care of your financial situation and make sure that you get your remittances on time. You have our numbers. Please phone for any extra financial help needed. I shall pay for the furniture for your three daughters' dowries just as my Sabiya did for your eldest girl."

He felt in his jacket pocket and placed a three thousand-rupee note in the youngest girl's hand, lowering his gaze sheepishly in the face of their gratitude.

"I have to go now, and may Allah Pak look after you all!"

He followed his host out of the small courtyard before turning to look back at the girls bashfully gazing after him from their door. "This is their humble world," he mused. "And I live in a large house all by myself." The thought appalled him.

He smiled politely at the other villagers whom he passed in the lane. However, there was no one he recognised and no welcoming reciprocal look of sudden recognition. And why should there be? he chided himself. He was over seventy years old – and so far, he had not seen a soul of that age group in the village.

That night he returned to Lahore to his brother's family, afraid that if he stayed the night here, his village hosts would incur the cost of breakfast and afternoon dinner the following day. He was familiar with their excellent hospitality. Already they had spent a lot on his behalf. Until the entire dining table was covered with plates of cakes, pastries, boiled eggs and parathas they would not be satisfied.

In his brother's home there was no element of guilt – no waiting upon ceremony. They knew what he liked, and so for breakfast his brother would fetch some warm kulchas from the local bakery and the tea would be supplied by his sister-in-law.

Drinking a cool glass of village lassi, Samir instructed the driver to take him back to Lahore, the city of his birth, the old Mughal capital of India. He wanted to call on the way at the famous Data Gunj Darbar, a favourite shrine of his mother. In his childhood days she eagerly took him to pay homage to the saint buried in the tomb, visited by thousands every day from all over the world.

Outside in the Darbar courtyard, the daig men were fast at work, serving food from their big pots to the needy and to those keen to take the tabark, food offerings, home for their family. When the man distributing bags of pilau rice touched him on his arm, Samir was lost for words and nodded, taking the bag of rice with him inside the building. In the large hall amidst the crowd of male and female devotees, peering through the open windows at the tomb draped with a green and gold embroidered sheet, Samir offered special prayers for his wife's soul, tears gushing out of his eyes. Then a prayer for himself, during which he repeated the word 'escape' again.

As he sheepishly entered his ancestral home, the mouths of his brother's family fell open. They had not expected him back that night. In fact, they thought he was touring another city – and yet here he was, large as life. Both parties energetically avoided eye contact. His brother's family recovered first. They had been lounging around on sofas. It was eight o'clock and a popular drama was about to be broadcast. The wife and daughter began panicking. Was their guest fed or did they have to scurry to the kitchen to rustle up a meal for him? Reading their minds perfectly, Samir held up the bag of rice in front of him.

"I got my meal from the Darbar, I'm sure it's delicious. Don't worry about me, just carry on watching. I'll go up to my room and have a shower." With those words, he excused himself and tactfully left them to their drama.

"Yes, please do," his sister-in-law swiftly offered with a toothy grin and orangey sak-stained lips, sitting down to enjoy the drama with her daughter.

He came down precisely after 9 p.m., having given them time to finish watching their serial. In that time, he had showered, eaten the rice from the bag with his fingers and started to gather his belongings. They were expecting him and hurried to greet him, his niece standing up.

"Are you sure you will not want a meal?" his brother asked, unhappy at Samir not eating.

"The Darbar daig rice was wonderful," Samir told him. "It's good to eat tabark sometimes. It reminds us gently what life is all about – our stomachs. Getting food into our bellies is what we work for, don't we?"

Samir's brother nodded cynically. A former director of a firm and now retired, he still had two daughters whose marriage and dowries he had to arrange. It was not just a matter of food for him. He envied his brother for having all his children wed and settled. No worries, only sadness at having lost a wife.

Aloud he instructed, "Bano, go and make tea for your uncle!"

The eldest daughter obediently left for the kitchen, whilst everyone else watched the news.

"Tomorrow morning, I will check flight times." Samir slipped in the information whilst sipping his tea. Heads turned, TV forgotten, surprise written on their faces.

"What, brother! Already? You've only been here for just a week!" The sister-in-law rushed to speak.

"I think a week is enough – it's time to go home," he replied, a gentle smile spreading across his features as he remembered his daughter Rosie.

Dumbfounded, they stared back at him, but did not challenge or question him further as to why. *He must be missing his children*, his brother thought to himself. Once more, all heads turned back to the TV screen. As the eldest daughter got up to take the cups back to the kitchen, she smiled at her uncle, asking if he wanted some more tea; it was the first full smile she had accorded him since he had arrived. Then she surprised him and her parents further with her kind offer.

"Uncle, please give me your laundry. I will see to it before you leave."

"You stupid girl! Your uncle is not going yet," her father chided, red-faced. "He was only saying it. We are not going to let him go yet."

21

His wife quickly echoed the same. "No, brother, you are not going yet."

"Don't worry, Bano. I'll get my clothes washed at home," Samir said, surprising himself. Twice he had used the word 'home'. Was not this his home, the place where he was born?

Chastened and the smile deleted, the eldest daughter took the tray of crockery back to the kitchen. In the lounge, her uncle from England had already decided. He stayed up for some more polite talk and then went up to his air-conditioned room. Picking up the remaining items littering the dressing table, he threw them into his suitcase. His love affair with the city of his birth was over.

On the plane, he found himself sitting next to a man called Mohammed, of his age group and size, both men overweight and uncomfortable with the economy seats and the narrow leg space in front of them. After exchanging polite chit-chat they soon got into serious talking and were onto the question as to why they were visiting their country of birth and youth, their homeland.

"Homeland . . ." Samir ruminated over the term then shared his thoughts aloud with his fellow passenger, who had similar home circumstances, including being a widower.

"By that, do you mean the one that you have just visited, or the one that you are returning to – the place where you have spent most of your adult life? Which homeland are you referring to, or escaping from?" Samir elaborated, making the man's forehead groove into three deep pleats, as he reflected on his situation.

"Escape?" Mohammed asked, disconcerted by the term.

Samir went on to explain. "I am escaping back to the UK – and to a new home."

"New home?"

"Yes. Want to join me?"

The man looked blankly at him, wondering whether this was a joke. Chuckling, Samir enlightened him.

Samir returned home, not having met the two college friends or walked down the tall nineteenth-century corridors of the Government College of Lahore built by the British. Strangely, it really did not matter to him.

Two weeks after his return, Samir had moved into an elderly people's home, leaving his five-bedroomed detached house to his four children but keeping his savings and shares to see to the needs of the family he had promised to support. He made a new will, instructing his solicitor that when he died, one of his children would carry on supporting that widow and her daughters; he asked his eldest daughter to phone the widow, to reassure her that he had not forgotten his promise. Social and cultural parameters had to be maintained. He was a man and would keep his distance from the widow and not compromise her honour, her izzat.

When he phoned his brother on arrival in Manchester, he was asked when he would return to his homeland. After a pause, a bemused Samir repeated, "Homeland? Which homeland? I'm at home now." An awkward silence followed. Then he added, laughing, "You can visit *me* next time."

A week later, the friend he had met on the plane arrived with his daughter, who was carrying his suitcase. Mohammed took the room three doors away from Samir's, his gales of laughter echoing down the corridor. Pure joy raced through Samir, lifting his spirits as he rushed to show his friend around the home, enthusiastically explaining and reassuring, introducing him to the other house guests he had befriended.

23

"It's the right decision," he reassured Mohammed. "You won't regret it. Wave goodbye to loneliness and heartache . . . We're the new English babus, living in an old people's home like the ones we used to ridicule once upon a time . . . We have worked so hard – time to enjoy ourselves now, hey? From now on, it's Meals on Wheels all the way!"

The Malay Host

Malaysian jungle, 1990

Eyes on the crisp banknotes, Aziza Hamat tiptoed into the living room. Reaching the table, she grasped the woven jute money-basket, pulled her shawl over it and turned. Then froze.

From the doorway, Abdul was observing her coldly. Clutching the small basket against her chest, Aziza glared back.

The sound of car wheels crunching to a stop on the gravel outside had her turning to the balcony window. Abdul Hamat took his chance and leapt forward, startling her, and he snatched the basket from her tight fist. Foreign banknotes fluttered down to their feet. Hissing abuse in Bahasa Malay, he squatted on the floor.

"Kitchen!" he ordered, grasping a handful of colourful notes with different motifs and numbers and stuffing them back inside.

Tearfully, Aziza stumbled out of the room and went down into her soot-stained hot kitchen and blazing cooking fire. Swiping her wet cheeks with the end of a kitchen towel, she gazed, fascinated, at the hungry flames licking the simmering pot of meat. The slamming of the car door decided her. *It's now or never!* she vowed, biting her lower lip.

"Ibrahim! Ibrahim!" she called out quietly, tapping the soot-plastered wall with the wooden ladle.

A burning log fell from the fire, just missing her foot. Aziza jumped back, knocking over the three-legged stool behind her. The hessian sack propped on top of it fell off, rice grains spilling out of it onto the floor.

"This is it! It's the last straw!" she shrieked under her breath.

It had taken her weeks to nurse the other blistered foot. Grabbing the smoking log from the floor, she left by the rear kitchen door and ran down the wooden steps. Tall rubber and palm trees heavily flanked the three sides of the house. Like many other rural Malay houses, it was built on a raised wooden platform, standing on eight sturdy wooden stilts and overlooking the jungle.

Turning the corner, Aziza called again: "Ibrahim!" Then, ducking her head, she slid under the platform.

At the front of the house a car door was slammed shut. Aziza crouched, hiding behind a stilt. The smouldering log grasped firmly in her hand, she glimpsed two pairs of sunburnt legs, the gravel crunching under their feet. They were the seventh lot of white legs entering her home today. The hairy ones belonged to a man dressed in blue knee-length shorts. The hem of the woman's floral cotton dress reached above her knees. Then another pair of masculine denim-clad legs and brown feet slid into view.

A thudding sound from the room above made Aziza lift her head – heart still, lips parted.

"Ibrahim?" Her hands shook, imagining the key turning.

Out in the sunshine, the Tamil driver turned to his passengers. Wiping the sweat from his forehead with a clean cloth, he announced, "Sir, madam, here we are for our next spot of sightseeing – a very special place, a Malaysian country house."

He beamed with satisfaction, looking up at the quaint wooden building that he visited daily. He loved both the house and the wily old host with his receding, grease-scraped-back hair, gracious manners and fantastic command of English.

Margery and Robert, a retired couple on a tour of South-East Asia, stared in awe at the black and white painted house standing on its platform. The facade was indeed impressive, with tall trees, a mass of other foliage and pots of colourful orchids and hibiscus bushes strategically lining the sides of the wooden steps leading up to the entrance.

"It's a Malay version of a Welsh country cottage," Margery marvelled, feasting her eyes on the picturesque scene before them. "An opportunity to see a real Malaysian house – how enchanting. Aren't we lucky, Bob?"

"Look." Robert nudged her on the arm.

An elderly Malay man stood on the porch – beckoning graciously for them to come up. Something was digging into Margery's heel. She bent down to remove her sandal, and it was then her startled gaze levelled with that of Aziza's, squatting under the platform, half hidden behind the stilt. Margery smiled and waited. But the Malay woman didn't smile back. Instead she treated her to a pointedly hostile stare.

Disconcerted, and with the smile slipping from her face, Margery stood up to follow her husband into the house, whispering to him, "Bob, there's a woman hiding under the house!"

Their host stood in the middle of the room, a warm look of welcome spread across his narrow face. "Salaam. Welcome to my home, lady and gentleman," he greeted them jovially, charming the couple with his genteel accent.

"Thank you," they echoed together, curiously looking around the large, tidy room. Its four wooden shuttered windows were thrown open, allowing a warm, humid breeze to flow through the room.

"It's as if we are standing in the middle of the jungle," Margery voiced in awe.

The host's brown face split into a wide smile, making his line of greyish-black moustache more pronounced, and gestured for them to sit down.

Margery uttered her thanks as he gallantly drew out a chair for her. Then she suddenly faltered, remembering the woman down below.

"This is my house," continued the Malay host, sitting down on another chair. "Please make yourselves at home and feel free to look around."

His European guests shyly let their eyes fan over the rows of greying sepia and black and white family portraits in glass frames hanging on the two walls. Getting up, their host proudly pointed to one picture of a young man in a military uniform.

"This is me, when I was young. And this is my mother . . . She got married at fifteen and had me at sixteen," he explained, nervously laughing, expecting them to look shocked. "Come and look. It's all right — you're welcome."

Robert and Margery peered at the photographs.

"Is this your wife? She's very beautiful, Mr . . .?" Margery stared at the picture of a young woman dressed in traditional Malay clothes and with a serene expression on her face.

"I beg your pardon, madam!" Colour flooded his cheeks, making them a shade darker. "I haven't introduced myself properly. I am Abdul Hamat and you are . . .?" His eyes bore into Margery, the wide smile fixed firmly in place.

"Margery, and this is my husband Robert," she volunteered, sitting down again.

"Welcome to Malaysia, Margery and Robert. This house belonged to my father – that man there." He pointed to the portrait of another male. "He opened our home to the public forty years ago. Since then we have had thousands of foreign visitors, thanks to this friend of ours here." He gestured at the driver, then went on: "They come from all over the world. Are you from the UK, madam?"

"Yes – Wales actually."

"Right, Madam Wales. Let me show you something special." He padded in his soft sandals to the far corner of the room. Robert and Margery turned to look.

"This is our bridal seat, where the bride and groom sit together when they get married. Please Madam Wales, would you like to sit on it and have a photograph taken with your husband?" he wheedled, seeing her gaze drop. "You can pretend that you are a Malay bride. All my guests love having their photos taken in that corner. Come, madam, you must try it!" he coaxed with his beaming smile.

Exchanging a nervous glance with her husband, Margery got up – worried that the swing seat would not take both their weights.

"You sit down, Marge. I'll take the photo," Robert offered sheepishly, explaining to the host: "I don't think it will take us both, Mr Hamat. We are big people, as you can see, and we really don't want to break your family heirloom."

Abdul Hamat openly giggled. "Yes, you westerners are tall people – probably just your wife then."

Margery gingerly squatted down on the cerise quilted-satin padding of the seat under the attractive canopy drapes. Smoothing her dress over her legs, she glanced up at their smiling host standing beside her, whilst Robert snapped away with his digital camera. *I wonder how many other foreign women have been made to sit in this ridiculous position*, she cattily said to herself.

Their host then ushered them through a door leading to the rest of the house with the words, "Mind your head, you tall people."

The Tamil driver remained behind at the table, reading a newspaper.

A scraping sound against a door and a heavy grunt made Margery and Robert look questioningly at their host as they stood in the shadowy little hallway between two rooms. His smile slipping and his head turned the other way, Abdul Hamat explained in a low voice, "The room on the left is our private room, the only one we keep closed to the public. This is where my family – our women – can gain some privacy."

He had now stepped into the other room on the right.

"This is our bedroom. Come in, please." His eyes averted, Abdul Hamat stood beside a bed. There was a square wooden table with a cotton floral tablecloth and a chair. Another open door led out onto a balcony at the side of the house.

Ducking their heads to enter through the low door, Margery and Robert cautiously stepped on the polished wooden floor.

"This is our bridal bed. Used to be my parents'. Of course, it's a bit small by your standards . . ." He halted as another thudding sound had his guests looking round.

Behind them, Aziza peeped from the door, half in and half out of the room. Margery stared. It was the woman from under the house. All three looked at Aziza and she glared back with her coal-black eyes.

Wanting to communicate her thanks for being allowed into their home, Margery smiled at her.

Abdul Hamat's fists, however, tightened at his sides.

"Ah, this is my Aziza," he offered with false brightness. "She can't speak English." Then he abruptly turned his back on her, signalling with his hand from behind for her to disappear.

"Key!" she hissed in her language.

"Later!" he snarled under his breath in Bahasa Malay.

Panicking, Aziza's poise faltered – her eyes on the two guests staring back at her. Then she withdrew. Margery was left admiring the woman's native dress with its long green and turquoise crêpe de Chine tunic, matching ankle-length skirt and a scarf tied tightly around her head and draped over her shoulders.

The visitors were now shown the balcony. "Oh, this is heavenly!" Margery exclaimed in delight. "I can see the jungle from far beyond. Wow!"

"Yes, Madam Wales," the host said proudly, standing by her side, delighting in her childlike response. "We are very lucky to have a jungle for our garden." His face brimmed with a wide grin. "Isn't it lovely, madam? This veranda is very important for our women. We are Muslims, as you know. Here, at the side of the house, our women can have some privacy to enjoy both the sun and the breeze. Also, it is safe here, away from the snakes from the jungle. Oh, don't worry, madam, there are no snakes in this house," he hastened to explain, seeing the look of horror on her face.

"My mother always sat here," he went on. "It was her favourite spot in the house and she told us stories in the afternoons whilst preparing vegetables for the dinner. You see, there's always a cool breeze up here. Madam, come and sit on this stool, close your eyes and imagine that you are in my mother's days. Is my English OK? Come, madam, you won't fall." He patted the stool. "It's strong. Don't worry – it will not break. Women of all sizes have sat on it." He chuckled again, this time with his body doubled over. "There was this big American lady . . ." Then he stopped himself, drawing in his cheeks filled with silent laughter, remembering his manners.

Margery frowned, not relishing hearing about the incident of the unfortunate American woman; instead, she gazed at the huge flapper-like leaves of the tall trees. Robert placed his arm protectively around her shoulders.

Aziza tiptoed back into the room and watched them for a few seconds – praying that they would not dawdle too long in the house. Abdul Hamat did not see her pull a small parcel tied in an old rag from under the mattress of the bed and then scurry to stand outside the other door, softly calling: "Ibrahim – soon! I will get the key."

Still on tiptoe she went down to the kitchen and dropped the two small parcels containing money and jewellery into an aluminium pot and propped it near the door.

Hands trembling, she waited, listening to their footsteps.

On the balcony, Margery wrinkled her nose. "I can definitely smell wood burning, Robert."

"That, Madam Wales, is our Aziza cooking the dinner down below," their host was quick to inform her. "Come and see our kitchen. I'm sure it's quite different from yours. We still like to use wood as in the old days; in this house we don't like modern cookers. Our food tastes much better cooked this way . . . You can taste our special stew later and see for yourself."

Margery reluctantly got up from the stool. "I could sit here all day, Bob," she sighed, wanting to savour the scene for a few more minutes.

They followed their host down the wooden steps to the kitchen on a lower level. Margery wondered how it would feel, to have strangers inspecting their house in Bangor like this. The thought disconcerted her.

From the steps, their eyes skirted over the sooty paintwork, the kitchen items dangling from the walls and the open fire with its cooking pot on top. The kitchen furniture consisted of two wall cabinets crammed with crockery, a stool and one old wooden chair.

Aziza stepped into the kitchen from the other little door — her face paling at the two visitors staring curiously down at the piece of burning wood in her hand. Her face breaking into a polite smile and eyes steady, she put the burning log back under the cooking pot.

Abdul Hamat addressed Aziza in Malay. Keeping her eyes on the fire, she muttered something back. Margery and Robert were unable to understand but could feel the tension in the air.

Their amiable host turned to them, pinning a bright smile to his face.

"Here, sir, take a picture. You can show your friends back home what an old-fashioned Malay kitchen looks like."

Margery now wished to be gone. The body language, the expression, and the look in the woman's eyes spelt to even the dimmest that they were intruders and had no right to be patronisingly surveying her kitchen and taking snaps.

Margery caught her breath. *We have stepped into a domestic volcano!* flashed the alarming thought. Immediately, she dismissed it as her imagination running away with her.

Aziza was puffing air into the hearth to fan the flames.

"Does it take a long time to light?" Tight-faced, Margery coldly asked, now disliking the host. It wasn't he who had to cook this way!

"Oh no, Madam Wales. Only a few seconds," Abdul Hamat replied breezily. "Come. Let's go back to the main room upstairs."

33

As they set off back up the steps, he commanded Aziza in Bahasa Malay: "Our visitors are going. Please bring them some soup and bid them goodbye."

"To hell with them! I've said goodbyes to thousands already – what difference will it make today if I don't? Anyway, I'll do it later and in style, just you wait and see. Now give me the key, and get them out of here – or you will regret it!" she warned, her voice ice-cold.

Abdul Hamat's poise didn't falter, but his body had stiffened. He would deal with her later, he thought viciously. He followed the guests back into the dining room. The driver was still sitting with his head bent over the newspaper.

"Please, let me offer you some refreshments. You must taste our warm hospitality. Aziza!" Abdul Hamat called from the door.

"Please don't bother," Margery said hurriedly. She coloured, hastening to add, "We already had a good lunch before we came," not wanting to see the woman again or taste her soup.

"If you are sure?" Abdul Hamat looked relieved.

Margery nodded her head vigorously.

"OK then. Would you mind signing our visitors' book?" He held up a pen and a thick register with frayed edges which had evidently passed through many hands. Abdul Hamat proudly rifled through the pages, blotted with hundreds of black and blue signatures and addresses. "You see? I get visitors from all over the world and they all sign it."

"We will do the same and with pleasure, Mr Hamat." Robert quickly obliged with his signature and then passed the book to Margery, exchanging a knowing glance, as their host discreetly placed a small money-basket full of currency notes on the table. Abdul Hamat peered over Margery's shoulder, pleased with her comment. With the register signed, he pointed to the money-basket.

"These, as you can see, are kind donations by people like yourself who visit my home." His hand was now in the basket, shuffling through the notes from different parts of the world. Then he felt the tissue paper underneath come into his hand instead of banknotes. Anger shot through his wiry body – he would definitely be dealing with her today!

Margery and Robert hid a smile. From what they could see, their Malay host was doing very well indeed.

Robert took out a ten-pound sterling note from his wallet and placed it on top of the pile of other notes. The taxi driver smiled appreciatively, for he would be getting his cut. The host was now politely looking away – out of the window, while the money was being produced. Then he held out his hand to them. Margery was unsure whether to shake hands with him or not. As a Muslim, he would not normally be shaking hands with a woman.

Instead she said, "Thank you for sharing your lovely home with us. It has indeed been quite an experience."

"My pleasure, madam. I hope you have a safe journey back home."

"Please thank your wife for us," Margery added, watching the host's face with interest. Abdul Hamat politely inclined his head, smiled once again and waved them off.

"You know, Margery," Robert began as they reached their taxi, "I don't know how that woman can manage in that kitchen of hers. The smoke – I can smell it from here."

"I told you, Bob."

They turned to the patter of feet running from behind the house. It was the woman. Ignoring them, Aziza ran up the steps and stood in front of a highly embarrassed Abdul Hamat. Muttering and shaking her head at him, she shoved her hand into his trouser pocket. He grabbed her tightly by the wrist.

She pulled away and ran down to the driver, speaking to him in rapid Bahasa Malay.

"Please help me! I must get him out. The key – I need the key."

Mouths parted, Bob and Margery looked on.

"Key? From where?" the driver asked.

"Look!" She pointed to the wooden platform. The driver's eyes widened in shock.

Then Aziza rushed back to Abdul, this time managing to pull the key out of his pocket. She then ran into the house with the driver sprinting behind her.

"Ibrahim! Ibrahim!" Panic-ridden, Aziza fumbled with the key in the lock. It turned. Throwing open the door, she ran to the man lying on the floor in the small bedroom over the kitchen.

"Please help him. He can't walk," she urged the driver as he gripped the man from under his armpits to pull him up into a standing position. Placing his arms around their shoulders, they managed to hoist him up and get him out of the house and down the steps to safety.

Abdul Hamat looked on, horrified.

They laid the man on the dry grass, away from the house. Aziza cradled his head in her arms, tears streaming down her lined cheeks.

"Aziza!" Abdul Hamat yelled from the porch.

"Come and take a last look at your precious show house, Abdul Hamat!" Rising to her feet, she jeered in return.

"What are you saying, you mad woman?"

Body shaking with hysteria, Aziza pointed to the house.

Abdul Hamat scrambled down, two steps at a time.

"What have you done!" he cried, peering at the flames licking the sides of the building. His worst fear had been realised. She had threatened to do this – to burn his house down and today she had done it!

"Quick! Water! It'll all go up. Aziza!"

She looked on, not moving. Abdul Hamat rushed to the water pump at the back of the house and soon reappeared dragging a bucket of water.

"It's too late," she said, as she watched him throw the water on the burning wall. "The kitchen is on fire too – I made sure of that."

Bob and Margery remained rooted to the spot. Unable to speak or move. Should they run and help their host? The woman had indeed gone mad.

Abdul Hamat was back with another bucket. They stared helplessly at the flames greedily licking away at the front porch, coiling around the plant pots. The driver took the bucket of water and threw it on the flames.

"Bob, that man was inside the house!" Margery at last managed to exclaim.

Her husband nodded, bemused, looking around and then staring down at the woman squatting on the ground and muttering into the man's ears.

"Ibrahim! Are you all right?" Aziza tenderly brushed strands of his grey wet hair from his face.

"Why was he locked up?" the driver whispered in Malay, standing beside Aziza.

"He locked him up!" Aziza accused, pointing her dainty finger at Abdul Hamat.

"Your husband? Why?"

"No! The one locked up is my husband – Abdul is my brother. He locks Ibrahim up every time visitors come. He's ashamed of his disability – he has done it for the last thirty years." Aziza's dark eyes darted fire.

"For thirty years?" the driver ejaculated. "He's a man – why does he let himself be locked up?"

"Because he's mentally challenged. He . . ." The words jammed in her mouth, as she pointed once again at the host. "He – he married me off to Ibrahim so that he could have this house after our parents died in an accident."

Dazed, Abdul Hamat was watching his home go up in flames. The fire now gripped the upper level of the dwelling.

Enraged, Aziza dashed up to Abdul Hamat, poking him hard in the chest. "You've robbed me of my home, youth, freedom – my life, in fact. Made us prisoners of your greed and tyranny. Well, look . . ." The voice shook with tears and hysteria. "Now you can have it all! The ashes!"

Shaking his head in disbelief, Abdul Hamat winced when he saw her pull out a thick wad of banknotes from her tunic pocket and swish them in front of his eyes. "The money from the basket – that you made from our misery!"

Her eyes large in her worn face, she was now giggling like a child. "I'm taking it all with us. Finally I am escaping from you. You stay and watch the home burn that you turned into a museum and a fortress for me and my husband."

"This is government property! And you've destroyed it – you stupid, mad woman! You'll be jailed for this."

"I don't care." Standing on her toes to be level with him, she sneered the words into his face. Then she marched back to the driver and spoke in her native language. "Please take my Ibrahim to hospital. Please help me – I'll pay you."

"You've gone mad!" Abdul Hamat shouted, running to her and pulling at her arm. She pushed him back and bending down, she cradled Ibrahim's head in her arms once more.

"Ibrahim, my darling, we're free my darling . . . I won't let anyone lock you up ever again. You'll always sit out on the veranda with your drink of Coke, the way you like it, I promise. All day — if that's what you want. I'll see to it, my dear husband." She wept over him, eyes tender.

With a wobbly smile, Ibrahim gazed up into her loving eyes. Aziza pulled him up and let the driver help to put him into the car.

Robert and Margery stepped aside. Too afraid and embarrassed to say anything or to ask. They had simply become invisible.

"Is no one going to put out the fire?" Robert finally ventured to croak as he saw the driver get into the taxi.

"It's too late, sir. There are no fire engines in this area. In any case by the time they arrive, the whole thing will have disappeared." The driver looked at the burning building through his car mirror. Then he said, "Do you mind if I take this lady and the man to the hospital? He needs seeing to."

"Not at all." Margery quickly got into the car. "Come on, Bob."

"But the host, Margery — we can't just leave him behind. Not like this! What's he going to do?"

"Shush — just get in, Bob." She tugged her husband into the car and waited for the driver to explain. It was all too surreal for them.

The driver was in no mood to divulge anything, however. The woman, Aziza, had suffered enough indignities in her life already, without having to share them with these western tourists.

Ibrahim was belted into the front passenger seat. Aziza stiffly sat next to Margery. The two women had exchanged a quick nervous smile before Aziza turned to gaze out of the car window. The driver addressed his other passengers. His eyes not quite meeting theirs in the rear-view mirror, he asked, "Sir and madam, would you want to try the scorpion farm now or the Batu Caves?"

Before replying, Bob and Margery turned to look back. Their Malay host stood stooped against the tree, staring at the remains of his house.

"Don't worry, sir, I will go back for the host later," the driver reassured them.

Three miles down the road en route to the hospital, Bob murmured to his wife, "Did we do the right thing, leaving that poor man?"

In reply Margery whispered, "Did that really happen, Bob, or did I imagine it all?"

Her husband was staring at the wobbling head of the passenger in the front seat, before nodding his own head.

"Yes, I rather think it did."

Not for the first time that day, they both felt a very long way from Bangor.

A Pair of Jeans

Maryam slid off the bus seat and glanced anxiously at her watch. They were coming! And she was very late.

Murmuring goodbye to her two university friends, she rang the bell and waited for the bus to reach her stop. Once there, she got off and waved goodbye to her friends again. Then she pulled her leather jacket close to her body, feeling self-conscious about her jean-clad legs and the short vest she wore beneath it. It had, unfortunately, shrunk in the wash. All day long she had kept pulling it down to cover her midriff. Yet these were just the type of clothes she had needed to wear today for hill walking in the Peak District. Here, in the vicinity of her home, she felt very nervous.

As she crossed the road and headed for her own street, Maryam hoped that she would not meet anyone she knew. She tugged at the hemline of her vest, which had ridden up yet again. With the other hand, she held onto the jacket front as it had no buttons.

It had been a wonderful day, but her legs ached after climbing all those green hills – still it was worth it. Her eye on

41

her watch, she quickened her pace. It was much later than she had anticipated. She remembered the phone call of yesterday evening. They had said they were coming today. What if they had already arrived? As soon as she got home she must make her way discreetly to her room and quickly get changed.

Just as Maryam reached the gate of her family's semi-detached house, she heard a car pull up behind her and swept round to see who it was. On spotting the familiar car and the person behind the wheel, her step faltered, colour ebbing from her face. On the pretence of opening the gate, she turned away and tried to collect her wits. Too late! They were already here. Her heart was now rocking madly against her chest and the clothes burned her. She wanted to rush inside her home and peel them off. She clutched at her jacket front again, to cover the bare skin.

Then she braced her shoulders, accepting the inevitable. She could not scurry inside. That was not the way things were done, no matter the circumstances. Calmly she let go of the gate and turned to greet the two people who had by now stepped out of the car and were surveying her. She didn't realise that she had let go of her jacket too. It gaped open, revealing the short vest underneath. Their eyes went straight to the inch of flesh at her waist. The woman was her future mother-in-law, a slight, frail figure dressed in shalwar and kameez with a chador around her shoulders. The elderly man, who had been behind the wheel, was the woman's husband. He seemed to tower over his wife.

Maryam found herself unable to look either of them in the eye. A hesitant smile played around her mouth. She did not know what to do, or how to act. Her cheeks burnt in embarrassment; her poise now very much lost. And these were the very people she wanted to impress. All she was aware of was the surreptitious glances they darted at her. In fact, not at

42

her as Maryam, but at the figure, the appearance she presented, clad in a pair of Levi's and a skimpy leather jacket to top it off. This was not the Maryam they knew, but a stranger, a western version of Maryam. She immediately sensed their awkwardness. They too were caught off guard and did not know what to do with themselves, particularly with their eyes. The father-in-law was bent on avoiding eye contact with her by studiously looking above her head.

He pushed the gate open and in two strides had crossed the driveway and was now solidly knocking on the front door. Maryam stepped aside to let the woman pass, silently walking behind her husband. Maryam followed them in a semi-daze. As she closed the gate behind her she remembered with mortification that while the woman had accepted her mumbled greeting of "Walaikum Assalam," the father-in-law had ignored it. That was not like him at all.

Maryam's mother, Fatima, opened the door to her expected guests, beaming with pleasure and warmth as she beheld them. She had not expected Maryam to come with them, however. When she saw her daughter hovering behind the two guests, Fatima received a shock. Never before in her life had the girl witnessed such a dramatic change in her mother's face. Normally Fatima wouldn't have batted an eyelid if her daughter had turned up at her door at eleven o'clock at night, as long as she knew where she was and with whom, and at what time she was returning home. Today she was viewing her daughter's arrival and appearance through a different set of lenses – in fact, through the lenses of Maryam's future in-laws. And the view didn't look very good.

The jeans, which wouldn't normally have aroused her interest, today stood out brazenly on Maryam's body, tightly moulded against the entire length of her legs. Her eyes were

43

fixed on Maryam's exposed midriff. Heat was now rushing through Fatima's cheeks. A whole inch of her daughter's flesh was visible! With her mind reeling and a strong urge to usher her out of sight, Fatima desperately signalled with her eyebrows, urging her daughter to go up and change into something more respectable. Maryam understood and was only too glad to oblige.

Squeezing past her mother and out of sight of their guests who had now entered the living room, Maryam ran up the stairs to her bedroom. Once there, she shut the door behind her and exhaled deeply. Her earlier feeling of tiredness and exhilaration from the hill walking had vanished – discontent had taken its place. A mere two steps into her home had led to another world. The other she had left behind with her friends on the bus. She shrugged aside the feeling. What mattered now was the two people downstairs. And oh, how they mattered. Her whole future lay with them.

Removing her jacket, the vest and the tight pair of jeans, she let them fall in a heap on the woollen carpet and looked down at them with distaste, her mouth twisted into a cynical line. "Damn it!" her mind shouted, rebelling. "They are only clothes. I am still the same young woman they visited regularly – the person that they have happily chosen as a bride for their son in their household."

"Deny it as much as you like, Maryam," her heart whispered back. "It's no use. They have seen another side of you – your other persona."

The 'other persona' had apparently – either by sheer accident or mere contrivance – remained hidden from them from the very beginning. When they first saw her at a party, she was dressed in a maroon chiffon sari, and on each subsequent occasion she was always smartly but respectably dressed in a traditional shalwar kameez suit. Never at any time had they glimpsed a jeans-clad Maryam with a bit of midriff showing! In fact, judging by her mother's expression and lack of composure, it must have been a nasty shock! For now they were seeing her as a young college woman who was very much under the sway of western fashion and, by extension, its moral values. Muslim girls did not go outdoors dressed like that, especially in the short jacket, which hardly covered her hips, and a skimpy vest, showing her waist.

She had heard stories of in-laws who were prejudiced against such girls, for they weren't the docile, obedient and sweet daughters-in-law that they preferred. On the contrary, they were seen as a threat and portrayed as rebellious hoydens, who did not respect their husbands or their in-laws. Maryam was all too familiar with such stereotyped views of women.

From her wardrobe, she pulled a blue crêpe shalwar kameez suit off a hanger. As she put it on, her rebellious spirit reared its head again. "They are only clothes!" her mind hissed in anger.

She could not deny, however, that by having them on her back, she had embraced a new set of values. In fact, a new personality. Her body was now modestly swathed in an elegant, long tunic and baggy trousers. The curvy contours of her body were discreetly draped. With a quick glance in the mirror, she left her room. It was a confident woman gliding down the stairs. She was now in full control of herself. There was to be no scuttling down the stairs; her poise was back. Her long dupatta scarf was draped around her shoulders and one edge of it was over her head.

Once downstairs in the hallway, outside the sitting-room door, she halted for a moment, her hypocrisy galling her. She was acting out a role, the one that her future in-laws preferred. The role of a demure and elegant bride and daughter-in-law —

dressed modestly, with her body properly covered. Yet she was the same person who had earlier traipsed through the Pennine countryside in a tight pair of jeans and walking boots and who was now dressed in the height of Pakistani fashion. The difference lay in what her in-laws regarded and termed as an acceptable mode of dress.

Was she the same person? She didn't know. Perhaps it was true that there were two sides to her character. A person who spontaneously switched from one setting to another, from one mode of dress into another – in short, swapping one identity for another. Now, dressed as she was, she was part and parcel of another identity, of another world, that of a Muslim-Asian environment. Ensconced now in the other home ground, her thoughts, actions and feelings had seamlessly altered accordingly.

Her head held high, Maryam entered the living room. Once inside, she felt four pairs of eyes turn in her direction. She stared ahead, knowing instinctively that apart from her father's, those eyes were busy comparing her present appearance with her earlier one. It was amazing how she was able to move around the room at ease, in her shalwar kameez suit, in a manner that she could never have assumed in her earlier clothes amongst these people. She sat down beside her mother, acutely aware of her future mother-in-law appraising both her appearance and her movements.

After a while, the conversation flagged. Fatima was doing her very best at entertaining and trying to revive a number of topics of interest to the other couple. The two guests, however, were not interested in any of the topics, particularly the one concerning their children's marriage in six months' time. This was so unlike their usual behaviour. Fatima was now quite anxious. From the moment her guests had stepped into her home, she had sensed that something was wrong. She was ready to discuss the subject with them. But first she asked her daughter to bring in some refreshments. The dinner had already been prepared and laid out on the dining table in the kitchen.

Maryam was only too happy to leave the room; behind her a hushed silence reigned. She pottered around the kitchen, collecting bits and pieces of crockery from the cupboards. Her own hunger had vanished. The appearance of those two people had done a miraculous thing to her appetite.

She was arranging the plates and glasses on the tray when she heard voices in the hallway. It sounded as if the guests were saying goodbye to her parents. Surprised, Maryam hastened and picked up the tray. Were they going already? They hadn't eaten anything! The table was laid for dinner.

She called out, "Auntie," addressing her future mother-in-law, who turned and smiled. They were in a hurry to get home, she said, because they had guests staying in their home.

That is a lousy excuse, Maryam thought. *If they had guests at home, why did they bother to come in the first place?* She returned to the kitchen and dumped the tray back on the table. What a waste of time!

The two prospective parents-in-law walked to their car in silence – both lost in their own thoughts. The silence continued during their journey. There was no need for communication. They could read each other's minds fairly accurately.

On reaching home, the so-called guests to whom Begum had referred earlier had apparently gone. Their elder son, Farook, was not yet in. The younger one was upstairs, studying for his GCSE examinations. They could hear the music from the CD blaring away. He loved listening to songs as he revised.

Ayub shed his jacket, hung it in the hallway and went straight to the living room. Begum followed behind, also taking off her coat and outdoor shawl. Switching on the television, Ayub sat down in his armchair. Begum hovered listlessly near his armchair for a minute, looking down at her husband – waiting. Then mechanically folding her woollen shawl into its customary neat folds, she left the room and went upstairs to her bedroom to place it in her drawer. For a few moments she stood lost in her thoughts, looking out of the bedroom window. Mrs Williams had another car, she noted – the third in ten months. What did she do with them all? Then she heard her husband call her name, his voice supremely autocratic.

With all thoughts of Mrs Williams and her love of cars put aside, Begum returned to the living room and sat down on the sofa opposite her husband, waiting for him to begin. Her heartbeat had automatically quickened. The seconds were ticking away into minutes, and her husband still had made no move to say anything, his gaze on the newscaster. She picked up the Urdu national newspaper, the *Daily Jang*, from the coffee table, and began to read it. More precisely, she was pretending to read it; the words were a blur in front of her eyes.

Ayub stood up at last, stretching out his legs. Striding across the room, he switched off the television. Returning to his chair, his pointed gaze now fell on his wife.

"Well!" he began softly.

It was now her turn to play; she pretended not to hear him or understand the implication of his exclamation. Now that the moment of reckoning had come, she absurdly wanted to prevaricate – to put off the discussion.

"Well, what?" she responded casually, buying time, peeping at her unsmiling husband over the edge of the newspaper.

"You know very well what I mean! Don't pretend to misunderstand me, Begum," he rasped under his breath, not at all amused by her manner, tone or her words.

Begum calmly examined the harsh outlines of her husband's unsmiling face. She did not know what to say, or how to say it. Thus her lips would not open; she simply stared at him.

"Well, what do you think of your future daughter-in-law? I thought you told me that she was very 'sharif', a very modest girl. Was that naked waist what you would call modest?" he shot at her.

"I am sure she is," Begum said defensively, feeling hedged in. After all, she was the one who had originally taken a liking to Maryam.

"Huh!" Ayub grunted. "Sharif? Dressed like that? God knows who has seen her. Would you like any of your friends and relatives to have seen her as she appeared today – would you, Begum?" The voice was cutting.

"But she's a college student – they do dress like that. Haven't you yourself joked about tatty jeans-clad university students?" Begum boldly persisted. She wanted to excuse Maryam's mode of dress to herself and to him; she knew she was not going to make a success of it, however, because at heart, she very much agreed with her husband.

"Tell me, in those clothes of hers, would you be proud to have her as your daughter-in-law? I know I would not. You talk about her being a university student. Well, have you any idea what sort of company that she might be keeping with that lot? You've only seen her at odd times, and always at home. Do you know what she is really like? Have you thought of the effect she could have on your household? With her lifestyle, such girls also want a lot of freedom. In fact, they want to lead their lives the way their English college friends do. Did you notice what time she came in? She knew we were coming, yet that had not made any difference to her lifestyle. Do you expect her to change overnight in order to suit us?"

He cleared his throat before going on. "People form habits, Begum, do you understand? Are you prepared for a daughter-in-law who goes in and out of the house whenever she feels like it, dressed like that – and returns home as late as that? Don't your cheeks burn at the thought of that bit of flesh you saw? Imagine how our son will feel about her. Shame, I hope! And what if she has a boyfriend already – have you thought of that? What if she takes drugs? What if . . . what if . . . so many questions to ask ourselves. Are you aware that we do not know this girl at all, Begum? Can you guarantee that she will make our son happy?"

He paused strategically, waiting for her to say something. Begum, bemused, had nothing to add. The talking had become his arena, not hers.

He continued: "You know of a number of cases where the educated, so-called modern girls have twisted their husbands around their little fingers, and expected them to dance to their tune. Are you prepared for that to happen to your beloved son? To lose him to such a daughter-in-law? Have you the heart for that?"

Begum just stared, listening quietly to her husband's angry lecture. Deep down, she agreed with much of what he had said. However, rattled by his tone and his words, she was reluctant to voice her agreement. After twenty-five years of marriage, she could read him like a book. His words, their nuances, the tilt of his eyebrows, the authoritative swing of his hand, the thin line of his mouth . . . spelled only one message.

She had already jumped ahead and had guessed correctly the conclusion, the outcome of this discussion. Her own thoughts had run in a similar direction. When she had seen Maryam standing near the garden gate with her jacket open, similar thoughts had whizzed through her mind too, although she would not have voiced them in such an uncompromising way. Her perception of what her daughter-in-law should be like did not tally with the picture that Maryam had presented to them, nor to the clear picture that Ayub's words had conjured up. "Oh, why did that stupid girl have to wear those jeans and that vest today of all days?" she angrily groaned inside her head. "And why did Ayub, of all people, have to see her like that?"

She had always reckoned on a conventional sort of daughter-in-law, the epitome of tradition. Definitely not one who was so strongly influenced by western forms of dress and culture – and probably feminist ideas – as Maryam. The mad girl had no qualms about blatantly showing a part of her naked body in a public place. Begum shuddered.

What about Farook, their son? How would they deal with him? Luckily, it was not Farook who had initially befriended Maryam, but she herself. A glimpse of Maryam at a mehndi (henna) party had tugged at Begum's heart. From the first moment, she had fitted the vision of what her future daughter-in-law should be like – young, beautiful and well-educated. The girl had just obtained three A-levels at high grades from school, and was now doing a geography degree at the university.

Begum had liked the way Maryam had behaved – ever so correctly and gracefully. Above all, she had liked the way she dressed herself. How ironic that assumption was after today's event. It was the way the black chiffon sari had hugged her slender figure, and how her hair was elegantly wound up in a knot at the top of her head – just perfect. She was neither over-dressed, nor over-decked in jewels, nor overly made up as some of her peers were wont to be. Nor for that matter was she boisterous or making a spectacle of herself as some of her friends did. In short, Begum had viewed her as the epitome of perfection, everything that was correct and appealing. She definitely had stood out amongst the other girls.

Looking back now, two years later, Begum was sure that she herself, not her son, had fallen in love with Maryam at first sight. And not just that, her name 'Maryam' wove a magic spell around the older woman. It had a special ring to it and she had loved using it.

And there was more. Begum had taken a real liking to Maryam's parents too, especially her mother. And liking one's child's in-laws, particularly the mother, was an important part of the equation. She knew of cases where the two mothers-in-law hated each other's guts. Begum and Fatima met for the first time at the same mehndi party. After that, they became warm friends and were seen to be going in and out of each other's homes. With the subject of their growing children's futures looming on their domestic horizons, the two mothers had, as a matter of course, discussed and dwelled at length on the subject of their son and daughter's marriage prospects.

Farook and Maryam had also met each other soon afterwards. Often accompanied by their parents, they, too, took a liking to each other. They found they were very compatible in their interests and personalities, and had a lot to laugh about – often giggling together. When their parents suggested the idea of marriage, both heartily agreed. Farook just couldn't help grinning all over his face. Maryam was struck with sudden shyness, her cheeks burning. Soon afterwards, an engagement party was held for the two. In order to let them complete their respective courses, the wedding was postponed for eighteen months.

That was a year ago. Today, Farook's parents had gone to Maryam's home in order to discuss the arrangements for the forthcoming wedding in six months' time. They were to decide on the date and discuss possible venues for the two receptions. Instead they had returned home, without even mentioning the word 'wedding'. Yet their thoughts were very much centred on that subject. But more importantly on Maryam herself – her clothes and her body!

"Well?" Ayub's cold prompting brought his wife to the present.

Begum turned to look at her husband once more and waited for him to finish what he was going to say. There was a speculative gleam in his eyes.

"What are you going to do?" he rasped.

This time she could not pretend to misunderstand him.

She faced him squarely – poised for a battle. Yet as she was about to utter the words her heart sank. She saw her Maryam fast disappearing from the horizon. But then as she tried to hold onto her image in her mind, there arose that one of her in that silly pair of faded jeans, and that ridiculously short vest. There was no alternative. It had to be. It was better to face the matter now than regret it later.

The problem was how she, Begum, was going to deal with it. She did not have the courage to play the role demanded of her, the one that she inevitably had to assume in this drama. Knowing her husband, she was sure that he would leave it to her to sort out the situation with the two parties: her son, and Maryam and her family.

Once again, she looked her husband directly in the eye.

"You truly don't want the wedding to take place then?" she asked, still desperate to hold onto Maryam.

Begum's gaze fell as Ayub glared at her.

"I thought I had already made myself clear!" He was enraged and he let her know it.

"I suppose I agree with what you say, but how are we going to go about it?" Begum stammered, the boldness gone, now very much resigned to both her and Maryam's fates.

"I leave that entirely to you – especially as you were the one who was so hot on the girl. I'm sure we can find lots of other women for our son, women who have a more discreet taste in clothing and a good understanding of female modesty. Similarly, I'm sure her parents will find a man more suited to her lifestyle than our son – a man who has the capacity to tolerate her particular mode of 'dressing', for want of a better word."

Just then, they heard the front door open. That must be their Farook. They stopped talking and stared at each other. Begum's heart was thumping away, dreading talking to him about Maryam. She felt like a traitor. Quickly getting up, she went into the kitchen to get his dinner. Ayub picked up the newspaper and began to read it.

Maryam had just got in from university when she heard the phone ringing. She dashed down from her room to answer it, then faltered – it was Aunt Begum. She quickly obliged the woman in her request to speak to her mother. Then, setting down the phone, she went into the living room and switched on the television.

Fatima left the meal she was preparing and went to speak to Begum. They talked for nearly five minutes. There were several moments of awkward pauses on both sides. By the time the conversation ended, a pinched look had settled around Fatima's mouth. Begum had nervously said her 'Salam', but Fatima had quite literally forgotten to return the greeting at the end as she silently replaced the receiver.

At the other end, with her head bent over her legs, Begum thanked Allah that it was over and done with. She sank down on the stairs, leaning against the banister. She felt bad, oh God, terribly bad. She had hated herself every minute of that conversation and the role she had been forced to play. Putting herself in Fatima's position, she realised how painful it must be for her. How would *she* feel if she had found out that her daughter was to be jilted at the last minute?

Mechanically, as if in a daze and with her hand held against her temple, Fatima went into the living room and sat down on the sofa next to her daughter. She absent-mindedly pushed the cushion aside and stared in front of her, at the fireplace.

Maryam did not notice anything unusual about her mother until she realised that Fatima had not said a word since she entered the room. "What did Aunt Begum say?" she asked quietly.

"I . . . I . . ." Fatima stalled as she sought to answer her daughter's question. She was not yet ready to divulge what she had learned – still reeling from the shock herself. What would it do to her daughter? She turned her face away from the girl.

"What is it, Mama?" Maryam felt a sense of dread. "What did Aunt Begum say?"

Unable to control herself any longer, Fatima bitterly burst out with, "She said that your engagement had to be broken off!"

Maryam paled. "But why?" She was amazed at how clearly her mind was functioning, although a buzzing sound was vibrating in her head.

"She said that they came yesterday to inform us, but found it impossible to get around to doing so. Begum says that her sister insists that her daughter was betrothed to Farook. That they were well matched together. She says she's very sorry and apologises, but apparently her sister comes first."

Liars! That's just another lousy excuse! Maryam's mind screamed, but she uttered not a word. Instead, she left the room. She ran upstairs to her bedroom and closed the door behind her. Standing in the middle of the room, she drew in a deep breath.

Where had this sister come from? Why was it she had never been mentioned before?

"So I'm not to marry Farook," Maryam said to herself. Why, only yesterday she had been planning how they were going to lead their lives together. Deciding in which area they would purchase their first house, after they got married and had jobs.

Her mouth twisted into a line of anguish. In her heart, she knew. From the first moment she had seen them that night in her tight jeans and shrunken vest, she had had a dreadful premonition. She had known – although she had denied it emphatically to herself – that something was wrong or bound to go wrong. Their faces, their body language had told the whole story.

The buzzing sound was still hammering in her head. Going to her wardrobe, she pulled it open and looked inside, rummaging through the clothes and the hangers until she found what she was seeking.

She pulled off from the hanger the repugnant-looking articles and threw them on the floor, as if it would scorch her to hold them. Then with her foot she gave them a vicious kick. Her uni friends would never believe her if she told them the trouble those jeans and the vest had caused.

The shabby-looking and much-worn pair of jeans and the shrunken vest lay nonchalantly near the end of the bed, blissfully unaware of the havoc they had created in the life of their wearer. Maryam stepped over the jeans and looked at herself in the long mirror on the wall. Eyes focusing, she scrutinised her face and body for any telltale signs of her inner turmoil. Her face looked haggard. The mouth, which was normally full-lipped, was still a thin line. There was a certain stiffness and air of strain about her, as if carrying her body was an immense ordeal.

Angrily, she stormed away from the mirror and went to the window to look down at the lawn and flower beds in the back garden. Thoughts jolted and formed in her head, each vying with the other for attention. One idea, however, lodged itself firmly in her mind: Farook and his parents weren't going to get away with it!

They can't do this to me! her mind screamed. She didn't know whether Farook knew about this development, but she was going to make sure that he definitely did – and there was only one way of finding out if he didn't! She noticed that the flowers below were in full bloom. The colour of those roses reminded her of the bridal bouquet she was planning for herself. All of a sudden, her body relaxed and she felt a certain calmness descend over her as she closed her bedroom door behind her.

There was no rushing. She simply glided down the stairs and had begun to dial Farook's phone number on her mobile by the time she reached the hallway. As the phone bell pipped away at the other end, her heart skipped a beat for a fraction of a second. What if his mother or father picked up? What would she say to them? She shook her fears aside. So what if they answered the phone! She would deal with them and the situation as it arose. To her dismay, nobody answered the phone at the other end. She tried again, defiantly letting it ring for two minutes – somebody was going to answer it one way or another.

Her mother came out of the kitchen and saw Maryam with her mobile phone held fast to her ear. Fatima shot her a questioning glance. Who was she ringing? A worried look crossed her face.

At last, somebody picked up the receiver. The ringing stopped and the word 'hello' was audible to Maryam's ear.

Relief shot through her. It was her Farook. She greeted him first with 'hello' and then with the Arabic "Assalam-a-Alaikum" – Peace be upon you! She then reverted to speaking in English.

"Farook, it's Maryam." She tried to keep her voice steady.

"How are you?" he asked.

"I'm fine." She frowned. Fatima was desperately signalling to her to end the call. Ignoring her mother's gesturing hand and turning to look instead at the picture of a landscape on the wall opposite, Maryam concentrated on what she was saying.

"Are you alone at home, Farook, or are your parents with you? If they are there, I want us to meet in the Student Union," she said brusquely.

"Usman is with me. Mum and Dad have gone out. They'll be back soon though. Did you want to speak to them?"

"No, it's you – I wanted to speak to you, Farook." She paused for a few seconds, her heart thudding, and then continued, still in control: "Have you heard anything about us?"

"Us? No. What do you mean?" He was now quite intrigued.

"Just as I thought." Her voice hardened, a bitter laugh echoing in her head. "It's probably too soon for them to break it to you. They are no doubt deciding what to do and how to put it to you."

"Maryam, you've got me all puzzled now. Come on, girl, what's going on?" He laughed nervously.

"I'm sorry, Farook – just talking to myself. I know it's all in riddles to you, isn't it? Look, I can't say much more over the phone, but can I come and see you at home, and then we can talk together with your parents?"

"Of course you can, but really, you've now got me all worried, I must say."

"It's nothing to fret about. I'll tell you in a short while. Allah Hafiz." Her voice and thoughts were calm again.

Maryam switched off her phone and faced her mother. Fatima noted the distinct mutinous line of her daughter's mouth. She struggled to say the right thing but did not want to bruise her daughter's ego further. She had a duty, however, to advise her as a mother, but the right words just failed to spring to her aid. Finally, she softly offered: "Maryam, that wasn't the right thing to do or say."

"The right thing to do?" Maryam ejaculated, stung. "Do you think Farook's parents have done the right thing by me?" she hissed, her betrayed eyes darting an angry look at her mother.

Fatima realised her blunder. It was a mightily wrong thing to say under the circumstances. Of course her daughter had the right to feel as she did. So, Fatima attempted to placate her with her next words.

"I'm sorry, Maryam, I didn't mean that. It's just that I thought that instead of you contacting Farook, it should be us, your parents, doing it in the first place – that is the seemly thing to do."

"Oh Mother! There you go on again about 'seemly' things. There's nothing 'unseemly' about me contacting my own fiancé." She laid extra stress on the word 'own'. "After all, I'm engaged to him, am I not? Or have you forgotten that too?" Her cheeks were red with anger.

"No, I haven't forgotten! And there's no need for your sarcasm," Fatima snapped back, also now quite flushed, beginning to get irritated with her daughter and the situation in which she presently found herself.

"I just mean that your father and I should go firstly to visit Farook and his parents to discuss the matter. Do you think that we don't care about you – about how they have jilted you, and on what grounds? After all, it's a matter of our izzat, our honour, the way we are being treated so shabbily – that our daughter is dropped like a sack of potatoes. I was under a great deal of shock when I listened to Begum earlier today on the phone, but now the shock has worn off, and like you I am very, very angry," she ended passionately, hoping to clarify her own feelings and position to her daughter.

Maryam shrugged. "You can sort that out with Father, Farook and his parents, but I am going to see Farook personally – and right now, Mother!" Hoping that Fatima had understood the message, Maryam turned and ran upstairs to her bedroom.

Fatima stared after her daughter helplessly – she was in a real dilemma. She wanted to advise Maryam that she shouldn't meet Farook until they themselves had discussed the situation with his parents. At the same time, she felt deeply for her daughter and wanted to support her in any way that she could. Never before had she felt the gulf between Maryam's generation and her own so keenly. At the moment, it appeared as wide as the ocean. She had never done this sort of thing in her youth. Unthinkable! No matter what happened, the parents saw to everything. It was they who resolved problems; children did not take matters into their own hands.

Pakistan was so far from Britain; it was another place and she was thinking of another time. As her daughter had said, it wasn't a matter of what was the right thing to do convention-wise, but it was time for positive action. If Maryam thought she had a right to consult Farook about this matter, then she, as her mother, would support her! Times had indeed changed. They lived amidst different traditions and cultures. Above all, the world was quickly changing around them.

Returning to the lounge, she stood indecisively in the middle. It was a pity that her husband was not in. He would have seen to everything. What would have happened if, instead of her, Ayub had picked up the phone? she wondered wryly. Would Begum have dared to say the same thing to him that she had said to Fatima? Probably not, she thought.

Inside, her blood raged, and she felt so terribly bitter. What had their daughter done, to deserve to be treated in such a fashion? It was a great insult for all of them.

She herself had liked Begum so much. Up until this evening she had prided herself on gaining a good kourmani, a mother-in-law for her daughter. They had also become good friends over the time they had known each other. And now this!

She heard her daughter's steps on the stairs – light and jaunty. When Maryam entered the room. Fatima's eyes widened. Then her gaze met Maryam's and was held there. Fatima registered her daughter's challenging look and accepted it wordlessly. The girl held herself tall and erect, determined and confident.

"I'm going to see Farook, Mother," she informed her and then waited, giving her mother sufficient time to say something. But Fatima said nothing, and her gaze dropped. Maryam then turned and left the house.

Fatima moved to the window, which looked out onto the front garden and its driveway. She saw her daughter shut the garden gate behind her. Then, placing one hand in the pocket of her faded pair of jeans, while the other held the short jacket tightly against her chest, Maryam began to walk away.

The Slave-Catcher

Boston, USA, 1839

"The slave-catchers' big ship from South Carolina is in the harbour!" exclaimed Molly, a stout, middle-aged seamstress, to Mrs Lucinda Huddersfield, the thirty-one-year-old lady of the house. She had impatiently waited to impart this dreadful news until Ayanna, the young black maid, had carried the silver tea tray out of the drawing room.

Then, her round eyes shining, Molly proudly untied the string on a parcel of garments from her drapery workshop and reverently placed the items on the table beside the couch where Mistress Lucinda lay resting her sore back. The cuirasse bodice corset – the very latest fashion – was offered first for inspection, followed by a white woollen petticoat and an elegant silk camisole top. Then there was a calculated pause before Molly presented the final hand-stitched article of clothing.

Molly had a moral and professional duty to show off the intricate lacework trimmings on the long underskirt that Becky, her eldest, nimble-fingered daughter, had laboured well into the evening to complete. First had come the crocheting, followed by a pedalling away on the Singer sewing machine to complete the onerous task of attaching those yards of broderie anglaise lace onto the garment. Molly craved to please this generous, god-fearing and extremely beautiful mistress who was unfortunately unable to conceive a child.

"What ship is that, Molly?" enquired Lucinda, gracefully lifting her head of russet curls and treating the visitor to a vision of her porcelain cheeks and gorgeous hazel brown eyes before lowering them to inspect the pretty lacework on the underskirt. She averted her gaze from the unsightly black mole with sprouting hairs on Molly's upper lip and, while she took a dainty sip of the freshly brewed tea, wondered why the other woman did not simply pluck out the ugly, unwanted hairs.

"Why, it's the slave-catcher ship, Missus Lucinda!" Voice raised, Molly was intent on titillating Lucinda's imagination, aware of her deep preoccupation with the welfare of 'black' people.

"Oh no!" Lucinda gasped. "The Dogs!"

"Yes, they are right here in town, tracking runaway slaves and their families. But what else could we expect, now that they've been given permission from the government."

Lucinda sat up, holding tightly onto the china cup, her full bosom rising and falling behind the smocked bib of the ivory silk blouse.

"Our Tobias told us about the ship," Molly continued merrily. "Remember, my son is a junior cook, making fish stews at the No Name Restaurant overlooking Boston Harbour. He's a chatty, friendly kind of a lad and has been talking to these 'Dogs' and the slave owners whilst serving them. He's around the harbour all day long. Says he heard a lot of screams the other night and when he went to look, he saw with his own eyes, coloured folks chained and dragged onto the vessel. That ship there is heavily guarded all the time by tall, sturdy men – and she's armed to the teeth, Missus Lucinda, with guns and rifles." The seamstress drew in a breath. "There's to be no loitering allowed anywhere near the ship. She's due to set sail, I think, in the next couple of days."

Colour ebbing fast from her rosy cheeks, Mistress Lucinda put her china cup back on the table.

"I did not know about the ship, Molly."

"You need to be careful, ma'am," Molly hastened to advise. "I know how much you care about Ayanna. You don't want to lose her, do you? The slave owners from South Carolina plantations are now, as I speak, scouring Beacon Hill and the Quincy area, knocking on doors, seeking the black fugitives. They've done their bit in Cambridge and the Salem area, I've heard." She lowered her voice. "Two doors away from us, they lost a black employee. Can you believe it, Missus Lucinda? An educated, well-read young man, helping with administrative chores in their law firm."

"Why, that's terrible. What will that poor man do on a South Carolina cotton plantation? His home is here in Boston. He's a free Bostonian for God's sake!"

Lucinda was now highly distressed, and her breathing grew ragged. "So, the Fugitive Slave Law has become a brutal reality. Congress is actually allowing the repatriation of all the runaway slaves and their descendants back to the South. It's a human disgrace, Molly." She burst out: "May the Lord Jesus help us all and forgive those who sin!"

"I know, Missus Lucinda. This is what Abolitionists like you say. But the Dogs will say they are just doing their duty, ma'am, and the slave owners, of course, reckon they are rightly 'claiming back' their property. So, who is right and who we should believe is a bit difficult for ordinary folks like me."

Lucinda was indignant. "But my dear Mrs Samuels, you know that slavery has been abolished in Boston. Most of the coloured residents in Massachusetts have been born here. Like our Ayanna, for example. They are free people, descendants of Robert Small and other families, who escaped from the chains of slavery in the South."

"I know, ma'am, how this must hurt you. Your family has supported the Abolitionist movement from the outset. Why, your father furnished one of the classrooms at the Abiel Smith School for black children. You and Master Cape are truly very kind to Ayanna and her family."

"Molly, please go ahead and warm yourself," Lucinda offered, catching her visitor's gaze straying towards the blazing hearth. "With all that snow last night it's quite chilly outside. I'll go to my boudoir and try on these items you have lovingly stitched."

Molly was only too glad to oblige. After the lady of the house had departed from the drawing room she sidled over to the open fire, lifting her petticoat to warm her frozen feet and taking the opportunity to ogle the framed sepia photographs of Missus Lucinda and Master Cape's fine-looking family members which stood on the mantelpiece.

"With the snow, I did not want to risk going out, in case I slipped," Lucinda explained, returning to the room. "Thank you for coming to measure me up. The corset fits perfectly, like everything else."

"So glad, Missus Lucinda. And I was pleased to come here. It's lovely to visit you, as always." Then, recalling the primary reason for her call – to collect the money for the garments – Molly pointed to the daisy motif on the petticoat in Lucinda's hand and said, "Look, Missus Lucinda, I embroidered that for you last night. I know you love pretty things. Did you like the puffed sleeves on your silk blouse?"

Lucinda laughed, slowly rising to her feet and smoothing down her ankle-length velvet skirt. "Yes. Thank you, Molly. I'll call Gwen to pay you for all this."

Later, in the study, Lucinda put her novel down when her housekeeper Gwen entered, thinking it best to inform her.

"The slave-catcher's ship is in the harbour, Gwen."

"They are a determined lot," the other woman marvelled, eyes widening. Then, shrugging her shoulders, she added, "I guess they think they've a right."

"*Right*? What right? To chain free men back into slavery?" Deeply offended, Lucinda sharply reprimanded her long-time employee and friend, her faithful shadow since they were both fifteen.

Blushing, Gwen said, "It's costing them time and money, isn't it, and so the owners are not going to go back home empty-handed, are they?"

"Has everyone forgotten the day when all the church bells of Boston rang to celebrate the end of slavery in the North? What do the politicians expect – that we'll turn the other cheek and smother our consciences? And all for what? For cotton and trade with the South!"

Mouth pinched, Gwen politely looked down, unable to echo her mistress's passion for politics and idealism. The picture was very clear to her: without the slaves, the cotton-picking businesses would suffer and stand still – both in the North *and* the South. Freedom for the blacks yes, but the economy and the welfare of the whites came first in her opinion.

"Be careful," Lucinda instructed her housekeeper. "Don't let poor Ayanna open the door or go out anywhere until the ship has left. And make sure you send Benjamin with her when she goes home this Saturday. We are responsible for her safety, remember."

Nodding her head and bristling, Gwen neatly switched the topic. "Do you fancy an apple and pumpkin pie for supper, ma'am?"

"Not tonight, thank you. Remember we're dining at the Union Oyster House tomorrow, where I'll be treating myself to Lazy Man's Lobster and their delightful Indian pudding. My poor wisdom tooth could not cope with sugary stuff for two consecutive days."

Her good mood now soured with images of the ship crammed with fugitives, Lucinda pushed the black feather back between the pages of Nathaniel Hawthorne's *The Scarlet Letter* to mark her place. She had reached an exciting point: poor Hester Prynne facing the wrath of the Puritan community of Salem and a public shaming for her adulterous act, hugging her illegitimate daughter Pearl to her bosom with the scarlet letter 'A', standing for 'Adulteress', pinned to her dress, whilst her husband Roger Chillingworth looked on, determined to exact his revenge.

Back in the kitchen area, Gwen warned Ayanna about 'the Dogs', the Federal Marshals, ending with the earnest advice: "You must go home with Benjamin this Saturday, Ayanna. Or better still, tell your family to go into hiding until the ship has sailed out of the harbour."

The tall, twenty-year-old black maid was polishing the rusty corner of the cast-iron stove with the black wax, pushing her linen cap back in place on her neatly braided head. She smiled at the housekeeper, grateful for her concern. Gwen returned the smile, her eyes twinkling with pleasure at the gleaming appearance of the stove.

Ayanna was a good worker, an amiable and extremely cheerful companion. Much to Gwen's delight she took to scouring the pots, with hardly a frown on her face. All the copper and aluminium pans in the larder were forever shining, thanks to Ayanna. She was always eager to help with the baking, the pounding of sugar loaves, the sifting of flour, the shelling of the nuts, and she kept an ever-watchful eye on the stove flue, to maintain a blazing fire all day long. Ayanna had recently braved the icy winds, digging and shovelling away the thick layers of snow and stubborn slush from the garden path.

Above all, the girl never said no to any request, always respectfully replying, "Yes, ma'am," and "Yes, sir!" Obedient to her very soul. And she was fun too, often sending Gwen into stitches of mirth with her lively mimicry of the elder African folk, the goings-on at her Sunday church sessions and the African Meeting House in Joy Street on Beacon Hill.

"I've skinned the fish for the clam chowder, ma'am," Ayanna informed her now, feeling Gwen's affectionate touch on the shoulder. "The black beans are ready too."

"Thank you, dear. What are your folks saying about the slave-catchers? I mean, they must be really worried."

"Yes, ma'am. Pa tells me that our Uncle Jacob has gone into hiding – I guess either into the woods or further up north heading for Canada." Ayanna pushed her cap back from her forehead, rising to her feet, the soot from the stove dusting her dark brown cheek. "And Pa was telling all of us to be very careful. In fact, our community leaders have started to hide some of the older folks in case they are recognised by the Dogs."

"But how many will they be able to hide, Ayanna? And hide where? Field Marshals are active everywhere."

69

The girl shrugged. "There must be urgent meetings going on but I don't know what else is happening, as I've not been back home yet."

Later in the afternoon, Gwen had reached the top of the mahogany staircase with a basket of newly pressed bed linen in her arms when she heard heavy-booted footsteps coming down the narrow staircase from the attic. Quickly, she stepped back, hidden from view, heart pounding.

When Master Cape passed by without seeing her, Gwen waited – then headed for the storeroom down the corridor, where she put the linen away in a chest. On the way back, she paused near the little staircase leading up to Ayanna's room, lost in thought.

The next minute she had lifted up the hem of her petticoat, to ease her wide-hipped body up the narrow wooden stairs, feeling claustrophobic between the two walnut-brown panelled walls.

At the top, she stood in the semi-darkness on the small landing then pushed the door open and peered inside. Ayanna was standing near her wooden cot with her back to the door, the afternoon light streaming down the roof window onto her head, with its rows of three-inch-long braids of hair. Her cap and dress were lying on the floor at her feet.

Hearing a floorboard creak, Ayanna whipped round and gasped, caught with her left hand tucked between her legs, wiping herself with her underskirt. The two women's gazes clashed. Letting go of her shift, the girl reached for her shawl to cover herself, draping it over the brown globes of her breasts.

Nausea flooded through Gwen and she stumbled down the narrow staircase, heart thudding – but not with the fear of tripping and falling.

Upstairs in the attic chamber, Ayanna felt faint, whilst the heat of shame flushed through her body. Once back down in the scullery, she headed straight to the water pump to sluice her flushed, cherry-brown cheeks. Gwen, chopping parsley, peered from under the fringe of her frilly cotton cap. Ayanna remained standing against the sink, vigorously scouring the dirty clam-chowder soup pot. And waiting for the storm to break, for the words of abuse to rain down on her.

Her stiff back to Ayanna, Gwen was now quartering potatoes, hitting the wooden board hard with the large chopping knife.

"You were warned, Ayanna," she hissed. "I warned you!"

Ayanna trembled. She did not recognise the voice – heard and felt only the rage.

Silence.

Then: "He came . . . Master Cape followed me upstairs . . . Master Cape insisted . . . I could not refuse." Ayanna's voice faded away, the stain of shame spreading across her pretty features.

He insisted with me too . . . Gwen silently echoed, remembering that precise moment when duty and fidelity for her mistress made her drop the china washbasin on the attic chamber floor, in a bid to hurriedly flee from the master's reach. Armed with a complaint about her slipping down the narrow staircase, she got Mistress Lucinda to change her sleeping quarters to the storeroom near the mistress's room. Cape Huddersfield could not and would not enter there.

"But he's the master," Ayanna wailed pitifully, in a bid to defend herself.

Red-faced, Gwen swept round, her tone harsh. "And she's our kind, wonderful mistress! Fighting for you coloured folks! There are some orders you don't obey, you stupid girl," she scoffed.

"Ayanna," Mistress Lucinda called from the other room.

Ayanna paled, her eyes growing large. Her mouth fell open, revealing a row of white teeth. As well as the kitchen chores, it was her duty to see to little errands for Mistress Lucinda. Normally, she would have rushed out to the study room, where her mistress was writing the draft of her first novel about a runaway slave.

The housekeeper stared at the maid, and much to her annoyance found her eyes straying to the shape of Ayanna's breasts thrusting through the bodice of her dress. The image of the master's broad, greedy hand near them had Gwen squeezing her eyes tight and wanting to run from the room.

"I'll see to Mistress Lucinda." Gwen pointed to the simmering stew on the blazing stove. "You see to that." Gaze hostile, she wiped her hand on her apron and strode out of the kitchen area.

In the study, Lucinda sat on the chaise longue, massaging the painful muscles of her neck with her slender fingers. She had opened the top collar button of her blouse.

"Here, mistress, I'll do it for you," Gwen said. "You should not write your novel until your back is fully recovered."

She helped her mistress to lie down. Once Miss Lucinda was comfortably settled, Gwen gently lifted the heavy, russet-brown curls and laid them over her mistress's right shoulder. Last night, she had pinned them up for her with rag strips. Marvelling at their scented softness, Gwen wanted to run her fingers through them again. A smile transformed her face, adding colour to her pasty white cheeks.

"Gwen, I desperately need your massage, my neck is killing me. Here, let's try the almond oil for a change. It's over there." Lucinda pointed to the bookcase.

Gwen found the pretty little blue bottle. Slapping some drops onto her coarse palm, she began to massage the back of her mistress's neck.

Her hand moved slowly round the creamy white throat to the front, pushing aside the heavy curls to the back. Lucinda began to relax; she opened three more buttons at the top of her blouse and let Gwen ease it off her shoulders. The housekeeper heard her mistress's heartbeat, her eyes on Miss Lucinda's full bosom thrust up by the tight corset, the curves rising with each breath. Gwen's fingers tentatively reached down, lightly brushing the soft, plump flesh with her chapped fingertips.

Lucinda closed her eyes, her cheeks glowing with pleasure.

"Does this feel good, mistress?" Gwen asked breathlessly.

Lucinda murmured, her mouth parted. "It's beautiful. Please don't stop . . ."

"Mistress," Gwen suddenly heard herself saying, her voice urgent, "you must visit the doctor that the minister's wife recommended. Please get yourself checked again. You need to be with child. It's not fair to you."

Silence greeted her words. Gwen hung nervously over her mistress.

"I know, dear. Thank you for reminding me. I promise I will. Once my back is better I'll go and see this doctor, but Gwen," she whispered, "what if it's *him* – your master – who has the problem with his seed?"

Gwen stiffened, heartbeat stopping, on the point of uttering, "It's not him, mistress!" But she stopped herself in time.

"I've always cared about you, Miss Lucinda, ever since we were young – the time when my mother worked in your father's home. It's the reason why I've followed you from Cambridge to Framingham, in order to work for you."

73

"Yes, I know, Gwen. I also know that you gave up the chance to marry because of me. I'm so sorry. You could still find a husband. "

"At thirty-one? When women normally get married before they're twenty? I've no regrets nor any wish to marry, Mistress Lucinda. I'm just happy to serve you. That is what gives me the greatest pleasure."

"Still . . ." Lucinda was not convinced.

"Please don't fret about me," Gwen said tenderly, gaze falling. "I'll be here with you till my dying day. Now close your eyes and I'll carry on. Sorry that my hands are so rough."

"They're good working hands, Gwen . . . they're wonderful!" Lucinda sighed dreamily, her eyes still closed.

"Do you like me massaging you like this?" Gwen softly asked.

"Of course, Gwen! What a question!" Lucinda giggled like a little girl.

Gwen forgot all about Ayanna and the scene in the attic as her hands carried on with their loving task, warmth and rapture spreading through her body.

Ten minutes later, the outside doorbell rang. Gwen immediately pulled her hands away from the soft flesh, shifting the blouse back in place. Lucinda sat up reluctantly and fastened her buttons while Gwen excused herself.

"I'll go and open the door. It will be Master Cape," she mumbled, eyes averted.

Gwen woke up suddenly in the night, for the temperature had dropped and she was cold. Tucking the coarse blanket tightly under her feet, she was reaching for the glass of water on the floor when a creaking sound made her halt. It was the top attic step.

She slid off her narrow cot onto the icy cold floor, quickly putting on her house slippers. Then, tiptoeing across the room, she stood by the door, opening it just wide enough to look through. She waited, her mind swamped by images. Only her numb legs and frozen feet signalled to her that she had been standing there for a long time. Rays of morning light had begun to filter through the slit of the window drapes.

The same creaking sound made her heart thud and she drew back. She listened to the feet coming down the attic stairs then reaching the carpeted area of the hallway. When it was safe to pull the door fully open, she put her head through and caught sight of her master disappearing into his bedchamber, returning to his four-poster bed and a sleeping wife.

Three words thudded in Gwen's head: *For how long?* How was it that she had not noticed anything until yesterday afternoon?

Then she trembled. Her mistress was barren, but Ayanna with her warm, welcoming womb was not.

"O Lord Jesus help us!" Standing in the dark corridor, she debated. Would she, Gwen, for the sake of her beloved mistress, have to get the local midwife to poke Ayanna's shame out of her? She could not stop herself. In the early-morning darkness, she felt her way up the narrow attic steps for the second time in twenty-four hours, heart thumping as she stepped on the loose floorboard that creaked outside the half-open door.

Gwen peered into the room, eyes going straight to the narrow cot where Ayanna lay.

The girl sat up, one hand held across her pert, youthful breasts. "Master?" she said, her voice meek and hesitant.

Gwen hastened back down the attic steps, heart thudding. The image of a light brown, mixed-race child suckling at those brown breasts had her heaving.

In the roof chamber Ayanna continued staring at the door, mouth open, pearly beads of sweat gathered on her forehead. She could neither lock nor bar her door from the inside. Just as she could not bar herself from the master's strong arms, lewd gaze, his wandering hands, his honeyed words or the little bags of sweetmeats and small trinkets from Quincy market that he often smuggled to her. She wondered who had been there behind the door. Was it Gwen? Ayanna pulled the blanket over her naked body, trepidation gathering inside her as she lay on the narrow old cot where Gwen had once lain – and where she herself had conceived. The girl knew that she had betrayed not only the mistress but also the trust of her companion, Mistress Gwen the housekeeper, who had categorically warned her to stay out of the master's way.

Gwen was getting the breakfast tray ready in the morning when Ayanna entered the parlour carrying a heavy copper coal bucket, preparing to light the fire. She waited until Ayanna had left the room before pouring the black coffee, not trusting her trembling hands.

Later, Gwen gazed out of the drawing-room window at the rear garden, its lawn freshly carpeted by a four-inch layer of snow. Sparrows hopped over the tree branches, dislodging showers of white powder. This was the family's seventh winter in this large stately house. They had all seen quite a bit of winter snow and April daffodils. Gwen had only gone back home for Christmas once. The occasional letter was her only means of contact with her few remaining folks. Mistress Lucinda's home was her home, too. But after today, would she see another year in this house? Only time would tell.

"Please get me out of this monstrosity, Gwen," Lucinda begged, sitting on the edge of the four-poster bed, her back to her housekeeper, holding up the silver hook tool. She was waiting for Gwen to unhook her corset and pin up her hair in curls with the old rag strips for the night.

Gwen swiftly got down to work. "There, mistress," she said. "You're free now."

"That's much better." Freed from the tight corseting and lacing, Lucinda rose to her feet, stretching out her slender frame. Gwen smiled, glad to be of help.

"Gwen, my dear, I envy you your comfortable loose drawers. These darned rows of hooks and tight laces drive me mad with pain at times."

"I know, mistress."

"Sorry for wasting your time. I know you're still busy with preparing the plum marmalade mixture."

"The syrup is ready. It can wait. Mistress Lucinda, I enjoy doing things for you."

"Yes, I know. You are a good, faithful and trustworthy companion." Lucinda had turned around, her bosom rising then falling as the corset was whipped away. She sat naked down to the waist. Gwen looked away, embarrassed. Lucinda laughed, startling her companion.

"Why so bashful, Gwen? You know every part of me."

"Well, not quite, ma'am," Gwen shyly clarified, a blush rising into her cheeks.

"You've washed me all over during my illnesses in the past, remember?"

"Yes, you are right."

Lucinda was about to pull her nightgown over her head.

"Shall I massage your back, ma'am?" Gwen asked. "The whalebones must have been hurting you all evening."

"Yes, dear. I could do with the soothing touch of your kind hands."

Lucinda lay down on the bed with her naked back to Gwen, the new lacy underskirt covering her lower body and her face turned to the side. Gwen went to the chest of drawers for the oil bottle.

"But what if the wider corset increases my waistline?" Lucinda's back twitched with the cold oil drops.

"What?" Gwen's hands began their circular movement.

"The new crinoline dresses and corsets. They are wider."

"Your waistline will always remain beautiful and trim. Not like mine — a bell shape."

A shuttered look descended on Lucinda's face. "This beautiful waist hides a barren body, Gwen."

"No, mistress!"

"Yes, Gwen. Time is running out for me. I have to face the facts."

"You must seek medical help soon, mistress. Otherwise . . ."

"Otherwise he'll take another wife or a mistress. Or divorce me," Lucinda quietly finished for her. Gwen felt the body tense beneath her hand.

They heard the master's steps outside the room. Gwen sat back, reaching for the oil bottle again.

Cape Huddersfield stared at the two women, taking in the full scene. As he moved into the room, shedding his woollen waistcoat, Gwen hastened to explain.

"The corset was hurting Mistress Lucinda's back again. I won't be long, Master Cape."

"Take your time, Gwen." He had now pulled off his outdoor boots and, barefooted, walked on the polished wooden floor to the china washbasin and jug to rinse his hands.

"Is Ayanna around?" he asked. "I've not seen her today."

Gwen's hand went still on her mistress's back. Lucinda opened her eyes.

"Gwen told me earlier that Ayanna had to go home today," she told her husband. "Apparently, her father came to collect her and hide her until the ship has left the harbour. We know it's not going to go back empty."

Master Cape stood lost in thought. "I must see Ayanna's family," he decided. "We should get them smuggled out to Canada."

"Yes, Cape, please do something. We must protect them."

"Right – I'm going there now."

"It's late, sir," Gwen meekly advised, gaze lowered, hand still on Lucinda's back.

"I'll be gone an hour or so, Lucinda. If I'm late, please go to sleep."

"I'm normally asleep by the time you join me on most nights, Cape, anyway," Lucinda reminded him, smiling.

"Yes, you sleep like a log. Nothing wakes you up."

"Gwen, you've stopped. Please continue."

"Yes, do continue, Gwen. My wife's always in a better frame of mind after your massages, no longer fretting about other matters."

The master expected Gwen to understand and she did, politely nodding. She was paid to keep her mistress happy and was happy so to do.

Pulling his boots back on, Cape Huddersfield left the two women, closing the door behind him.

The bottle of oil poised in her hand, Gwen asked, "Are you ready for the front, mistress?"

"Yes." Lucinda lay on her back, cradling her arm shyly across her breasts, eyes closed. Gwen began her soothing strokes on the soft flesh of her mistress's belly button area, before reaching for the sides and massaging upwards under the breasts. Lucinda normally discreetly covered herself with a small towel. Today there was no cloth nearby.

Lucinda opened her eyes and saw what she always saw. Her arm gently fell to the side, hand reaching for her muslin night shawl fallen on the floor. Gwen dropped her gaze, heartbeat quickening. Lucinda steadily stared into Gwen's face as the housekeeper poured oil on each breast and then with gentle strokes covered every bit of the area methodically, including around the pink nipples.

"They are beautiful." The words were out before Gwen could stop herself. She bit her lip, feeling embarrassed.

Smiling, Lucinda nodded. "Thank you. I'm sure yours are too."

Another embarrassed smile and eyes evasive. "That will do for tonight, Gwen."

"Oh . . ."

"Thank you. And once my back is fine, it'll no longer be necessary . . . You're very busy as it is," Lucinda said kindly. "Anyway, I think it's about time that your master took on this task for a change. I'm sure he won't mind!" She ended with brittle laughter.

Gwen's face fell. She rose to leave – then as she reached the door, she remembered Ayanna and the kitchen chores piling up since the afternoon.

"We'll need to get a new scullery maid, Mistress Lucinda. An older one would be best."

"Why an older one?"

"There should be no temptation, mistress. In this house."

"Temptation?" Lucinda frowned.

"Why do you think the master has gone to enquire about Ayanna at this time of the night?"

"What do you mean?" An expression of distaste streaked across Lucinda's face.

"Don't worry, mistress. Ayanna won't be back. She'll soon be on her way to South Carolina."

There was a stunned silence. Lucinda sat up, draping her shawl over her body. "What? You have not . . . *Gwen!*"

The seconds ticked away. There were no words. Gwen's hard, unapologetic eyes said it all. Lucinda would not read the message in them.

"I did it for you, mistress!" Gwen finally bewailed, her voice breaking into a sob.

Mistress Lucinda's beautiful eyes were large with shock; her body trembled.

"She had to go, mistress!"

"You've handed her to the slave-catchers," Lucinda choked, barely able to get the words out of her mouth.

Gwen nodded defiantly, mortified by the look of horror and condemnation on her beloved mistress's face. Watching Lucinda holding a hand across her eyes, shunning her, she cried out: "I told you – I did it for you, Mistress Lucinda! Did you want to raise your husband's brown baby? For that child is probably already growing inside Ayanna's shameful womb!"

There was no reply.

Face flushed, Gwen stepped out of her mistress's bedchamber. Head held high.

In her bed that night, Gwen relived the scene that afternoon when Mistress Lucinda and Master Cape were out of the house. And only she, Ayanna, and the young errand boy were at home.

"No, Gwen! Please save me!" Ayanna had screamed as the Field Marshal, one of 'the Dogs', dragged her out of the house. He manhandled Ayanna as she slipped on the slush made by the carriage wheels, badly grazing her hand and squealing in pain; her clothes dripping with icy, muddy water.

Holding onto his tall hat, the man pushed her roughly from behind, keeping a vice-like grip on her wrist. Two other tall and formally dressed 'Dogs' with rifles in their hands stood waiting beside the carriage, ready for action if required. Ayanna had thrown another desperate look over her shoulder at the closed door of her employers' house, unable to believe what was happening to her. That Gwen the housekeeper had let the men into the house to drag her away when the kind Mistress Lucinda, who fought so hard for the black folks, was absent from home.

Benjamin, the twelve-year-old errand boy from the house, who had been sent by Gwen to collect a parcel of tablecloths from Molly's drapery shop, ran up to the man.

"Hey! Where are you taking our Ayanna? Leave her alone, you Dogs!"

"Mind your own business, you little brat. We're following the law. Need to return these coloured people to their rightful owners. Anyway, we were invited into your home."

"What?" Benjamin looked aghast, unable to believe his ears. This was the home of Mistress Lucinda, who was fighting to protect black people.

"Benjamin – run! Go and find Master Cape!" Ayanna told him, hope gathering in her face. The young boy nodded and sped off.

Ayanna looked imploringly at the door of Mistress Lucinda's home again, before being pushed into the carriage. Her screams of distress and betrayal became indistinct, smothered by the rag tied roughly over her mouth. Weeping, she sank in a huddle on the cold floor of the horse-driven carriage.

Peeping guiltily behind the curtains of Master Cape's home, Gwen watched as the carriage was driven away. Benjamin slammed his fist on the door. Gwen ran to open it.

"Gwen, what's happening? Where's Master Cape? And why are they taking Ayanna? She's not a slave! She belongs here, with us, Gwen. Stop them, Gwen! Please, please stop them!"

Gwen's answer was to clip him hard on the head and pull him inside, bang the door shut.

"Stop shouting, you stupid boy! Ayanna stole what did not belong to her and had to pay the price."

"Stole! Money?" His young face creased in disbelief.

Ignoring the look on his face, Gwen wrenched the door open again and ran out, nearly slipping on the slush outside the door, watching the Dogs' carriage disappear into a side street as Ayanna's muffled screams continued to ring in the chilly air.

Later that evening, Gwen waited in the parlour for her mistress – the household chores forgotten. The money tucked in her bodice, she had listened to Mistress Lucinda's languid account of the meal and the people she and Master Cape had met at the restaurant.

That night, Gwen turned on her side in her wooden cot, face pressed into the lumpy pillow to suffocate the screams in her throat, echoing Ayanna's screams of earlier. Then she reached for the dollar bills hidden under the pillow, clutched them in her fist then threw them up into the air. For a second they floated, before drifting down to lie scattered on the bare wooden floor – her reward money for handing their Ayanna to the Dogs for the South Carolina's slave-catchers' ship.

An Evil Shadow

Punjab, Pakistan, present time

Robina Bibi, the sweet-maker's wife, had just been to see her pir, her spiritual guide, in the next village. Glowing with happiness, she couldn't wait to meet her best friend Neelum and tell her the good news.

Getting off the bus on the main GT road, she walked on the narrow, dusty path with cotton fields on one side and sugar cane on the other. Just ahead of her, she spotted one of her neighbours, Zakia, carrying a basket of goods. Hastening her pace, she called out to her.

The woman stopped. "Assalam-a-Alaikum, Robina Bibi," she greeted her with a smile. "How are you?"

"Walaikum Assalam, with God's blessing, I'm well. And your family?" Robina enquired in return.

"We are all well, mashallah. Have you been visiting your relatives in the city?"

"No. I've just been shopping and before that went to visit my pir in the next village."

"Is there anything in particular that prompted you to visit your pir, Sister Robina?"

"Yes." Robina held up her bulging shopping basket – her tokerry – and lifting the lid, she revealed the fluffy blue balls of wool inside.

"Who are they for – the knitting, I mean?" her friend asked curiously, giving her a knowing glance.

Robina smiled, her face creasing into fine lines. Unable to contain her joy, she burst forth: "We've been blessed, Sister Zakia."

The neighbour understood immediately. It was a known fact in the village that Robina had been desperate for a grandchild. Married for five years, up till now her son and daughter-in-law had not produced a child.

Robina held up her hands in prayers to Allah and thanked Him. Her friend followed suit.

"So pleased for you, Sister Robina. How many months have passed?"

"Oh, just three."

"Is everything all right with the pregnancy?"

"So far, yes. I've sent her to the city to be checked over by a special doctor and have stopped her from doing any physically demanding work – and of course I've forbidden her from going to any houses with 'chillah' – other women in confinement – and those where a miscarriage has taken place. My pir has advised me not to let her go into a house where there's a likelihood of perchanvah, the Evil Shadow, being present, and to protect her from any physical contact with a woman who has miscarried and whose perchanvah might affect my daughter-in-law."

"Oh, don't worry, Sister Robina, your Faiza is a healthy young woman and you'll soon have a fine young grandson." Zakia gave her friend a generous embrace.

"My pir says the same. He's sure my Faiza is going to have a son. And I believe him," said Robina, hugging her friend in return.

The two women walked on together, engrossed in a conversation about their children, neighbours, pirs and weddings.

In Robina's home at that time, Faiza had just finished washing the marble-chip floor of the veranda and the central courtyard. Their maid had already helped with most of the household chores. Her mother-in-law had stopped her from doing any work in the house apart from cooking. Today, however, Faiza decided to wash the floors herself, particularly as her mother-in-law wasn't in.

When the outside door facing the veranda creaked open, Faiza looked up, expecting to see her father-in-law on his return from their sweet shop.

Salma stood awkwardly in the doorway, not knowing whether she would be welcomed inside or not. Nervously her eyes scanned the courtyard to check whether anybody else was around. On seeing her best friend, Faiza was disconcerted at first and then, with common sense asserting itself, she welcomed her with a smile.

Salma gestured with her hand to ask if there was anyone else at home. Faiza shook her head and then called her in, feeling guilty nevertheless, as if she was committing a crime. In trepidation, Salma stepped forward, also feeling guilty, knowing that with her history of miscarriages she shouldn't be visiting her pregnant friend. If Faiza's mother-in-law, Robina, should find out or see her, there'd be big trouble!

Faiza got up from the floor to go and hug her friend. As she was halfway across the courtyard, her sandal skidded on the wet floor and she fell with a thud on the hard surface of the marble floor. Shocked, she cried out in pain.

Horrified, Salma rushed to her friend's aid, muttering, "Allah Pak. Are you all right, Faiza?" She helped her friend to sit on the charpoy on the veranda. "Oh God, you shouldn't move so fast in your condition, particularly on a wet floor."

"Yes, I know." Faiza moaned again in pain. 'My mother-in-law is always telling me to be careful. I thought that as she was out today, I would wash the floors myself. I don't know why, but I seem to have a craving to do household chores."

"Are you sure you are OK?"

"I'm just bruised around my thighs. I'll feel better soon. How are you, Salma? You know you shouldn't be here. If my mother-in-law sees you, she'll be furious — you are aware of that."

"Oh Faiza. You don't believe in all that crap, do you? It's an old wives' tale. I'm your best friend and I would never mean you any harm. It's not my fault that I have had three miscarriages. All that perchanvah rubbish is a superstition that we've inherited from ancient times. It has no place in the twenty-first century. How can an educated, modern young woman like you believe in it?"

"I know, but surely all women can't be wrong? They really believe those superstitions. It's no use arguing or reasoning with them. Our pir has been feeding the same ideas to my mother-in-law."

"But it's not fair, Faiza. How would you feel if you were in my shoes? I'm discriminated against and victimised. Do you know what it's like, to be shunned from any contact with pregnant women? I'm being treated as if I was an evil spirit. They think that my mere shadow will harm them. One pregnant woman even refused to eat the pudding that I had prepared the other day. It's as if my perchanvah had infected the pudding. Can you credit it? The whole thing is stupid." She sighed tearfully. "How could my miscarriages possibly affect another woman?"

"I don't know, Salma. It's just the way this myth has been perpetuated over the centuries."

"It's not fair to those women who've miscarried. I feel as if I am unclean." Salma wiped away a tear. "I can't begin to describe to you the suffering I've undergone, not only at the loss of my beloved babies, but also at the way other women like your mother-in-law have treated me. Instead of offering sympathy, they reject me."

"So sorry, Salma. I'm just as guilty as my mother-in-law. Anyway, I haven't seen you in over two months. Was there something you wanted to talk to me about that made you risk coming round?"

"Yes. I've some good news . . . I went to Peshawar two days ago to see a lady doctor, a gynaecologist. She told me that the reason I have miscarried is that I have a loose womb of some sort, making it difficult for me to have full-term pregnancies. She suggested a drug treatment for six months. After that, everything will be all right. I'll be able to have a normal healthy pregnancy."

"Oh, I'm so glad for you, Salma." So saying, Faiza's natural love for her friend made her grasp the other young woman by the shoulders and warmly hug her.

It was at that very moment that Robina Bibi entered her home. She stopped dead on seeing her daughter-in-law locked in an embrace with that girl. Blood thundered through her veins. The bulging tokerry with the wool fell out of her hands. She was so furious that she just froze, glaring at the two friends.

Faiza was the first to spot her. Her face as white as a sheet, she jolted away from Salma. Shocked by her friend's action, Salma too looked round and reddened, noting the anger shooting out of Robina's eyes and the fallen tokerry, spilling its contents on

89

the wet floor. Salma sensed the danger of the situation and the predicament in which she had found herself.

Should I apologise? But for what? she thought. *For visiting and touching my best friend? But I've done nothing wrong!* She was distressed by the look of horror on Robina's face, as if the woman had expected her to murder Faiza.

Deeply offended, and not wishing to taste Robina's wrath, Salma stepped away from Faiza and walked out.

Robina remained standing, staring at Faiza, who came forward to scoop up the balls of wool from the floor. Seeing the blue wool, Robina broke the silence.

"That girl is after us! How many times, Faiza, have I told you to have nothing to do with her. Salma has now shed her perchanvah from her recent miscarriage in our house. How could you be so stupid? Don't you care for your baby? If you don't, we do. We want this baby badly."

"Of course I do, Auntie. It's just that I couldn't turn her away from the door. It would have been cruel and inhuman. She hasn't been here for the last two months. And she's my best friend," Faiza ended petulantly.

"I don't care whether she's your best friend or not." Robina cut her short. "Friendship doesn't come into it. What matters is your health, silly woman! Until you've had the baby, I want you to have nothing to do with her, or any other woman with the perchanvah. If you don't care for your child, at least consider our wishes. I want a grandson. Our pir has said that you will have a son. How's that?"

Faiza's cheeks glowed with delight. Boys were always traditionally welcomed. It would be a great honour indeed to have a son first.

"Now we've got this perchanvah of Salma's in the house, I'll have to do something about it." Her mother-in-law walked

90

briskly into their kitchen. Taking a pinch of red chillies from a container, she returned to the courtyard and ordered Faiza to stand in front of her. Ritually she circled the air over the young woman's head and shoulders with the three red chillies still between her fingers. Then she checked Faiza's neck for the amulet with some holy verses from the Holy Quran copied by the pir. The amulet was to ward off the evil eye.

"I think that from now on, I had better stay at home the whole time," she said. "I don't trust that girl. If she sets foot in our house again, I'll . . ." she stopped, mid-sentence.

"You'll what, Robina Bibi?" her husband asked, returning from the mosque. He had overheard what she'd said.

"Nothing," she said defensively, her face reddening.

"You women! You were talking about Salma. Why can't you stop victimising that poor girl? And when will you stop your primitive ways and customs? Do you really think that swirling chillies over your daughter-in-law's head will ensure her good health? Huh," he laughed.

Robina kept a tight rein on her anger as she confronted her husband. "You always find it so amusing, don't you? You delight in belittling our beliefs!"

"I find it utter nonsense. It's against the teaching of Islam – and it's inhuman. How would you feel if Salma was your daughter, and somebody treated her the way that you treat her?"

"Bah! You men! You don't understand anything. Let me tell you what my pir has told me," she said, with a smile.

"What did your pir tell you this time, Robina Bibi?" he asked, loathing the spiritual influence that the old man had over his wife and other women.

Robina looked at him gloatingly. "He said that we're going to have a grandson. He had a dream and a premonition."

"Oh well, that's great, if he said that. What will you do if it's a girl? Will you return it to him?" He chuckled.

Exasperated, Robina turned away from him. It always ended like this. Her husband invariably managed to nettle her, which only made her stronger than ever in her beliefs.

The next day, early in the afternoon, a lot of guests arrived unexpectedly at the sweet-maker's house. It turned out to be a very busy afternoon for both Robina and Faiza, as they fed and entertained the guests, and prepared the hookah for the two elderly male relatives.

It was while she was making chapattis in the kitchen in the evening that Faiza felt herself get wet down her legs. Her heart stood still. The chapatti in one hand remained poised in mid-air, while another on the tava or flat pan was burning.

"Oh Allah Pak," Faiza moaned under her breath. "This is not supposed to happen." She was three months pregnant and therefore shouldn't be menstruating. It could only be one thing! Her mind refused to think further.

Leaving the kitchen, she headed for the bathroom, feeling her thighs getting wetter and wetter against her linen trousers.

"Oh God, help me," she prayed. To get to the bathroom, she had to cross the courtyard. The guests, along with Robina Begum and her husband, were sitting on cane chairs and enjoying the evening breeze. Faiza drew her clothes around her body, letting her shawl drape down to her ankles, to cover the wetness of her shalwar.

In the bathroom, her hand trembled as she worked on untying the string holding the shalwar in place around her waist. She glanced down at her body, and closed her eyes, feeling faint. It was what she had feared. What did one do in this sort of situation – go to the doctor or lie down? For a few minutes, she stood leaning against the bathroom wall with her eyes closed. She didn't want to spell it out to herself that she was losing her baby. It couldn't be. God couldn't be so unjust!

Then Faiza remembered the guests.

Swiftly showering and changing into fresh clothes that happened to be hanging on the towel rail in the bathroom, she returned to baking the remaining chapattis. When she finished, she went into the courtyard and whispered into Robina's ear that she was tired and wanted to lie down.

"Of course, my dear. You should have told me earlier, Faiza darling. I could have made the chapattis." Robina looked at her daughter-in-law indulgently. The look cut the girl to her soul.

Oh God, she doesn't know and wants the baby so much. Please God, help us.

Quietly Faiza slid away to her room. Putting an old sheet on the bed, and an extra layer of quilt padding in the middle, she lay down and waited. She continued to feel wetness.

When her husband, Ali, returning from his work in the city, came to visit her, Faiza pretended to be asleep. He went away. Returning later, he lay on the single bed in the adjoining room and went to sleep, after having switched off the lights.

Through the window, Faiza watched the stars in the sky. Two of the guests had wanted to sleep in the open in the courtyard on charpoys, especially as it was so warm. One elderly gentleman was still puffing away at the hookah, its base making a gurgling noise in the silence of the night, as he half reclined on his charpoy. The other, in the nearby charpoy, was snoring away.

Faiza tossed and turned on her wooden palang bed. Then at about three o'clock in the night, her abdominal wall somersaulted into action with a strong spasm. Her high-pitched scream broke the silence of the night, awakening everybody with a start.

She clamped her hand over her mouth, but it was too late. Lights were switched on everywhere, and the shuffling of feet could be heard. The first person to appear at her bedside was her husband, and then her mother-in-law, standing near the bed. "Are you all right, my dear? What's the matter?" Robina's voice shook with fear.

Faiza pointed to her lower body. Robina's eyes widened in horror, her mouth dropping open, one hand held against her chest. Then collecting her wits about her, she told her husband and son to leave the room. After they left, she stared pointedly at Faiza's pain-racked face.

With trepidation, Robina lifted the quilt off Faiza. Then she dropped it as if it had burnt her. She stepped back. Then right before her eyes, Faiza's body doubled up with pain, and she screamed again.

Through clenched teeth, Robina asked her son to call the dhai, the village midwife.

Perched on one corner of the bed, Robina rocked herself back and forth as if in a trance. Then she collected herself and gently began to massage Faiza's shoulders to soothe her.

Cradling the girl's body against her own, Robina began to cry as the reality of the situation dawned on her. All her hopes and wishes had gone to the clouds. There would be no grandchild. Faiza too began to cry. Not so much for the baby, but for her mother-in-law's loss and feeling of devastation.

When the midwife arrived, Faiza lay in Robina's arms, her eyes closed, her body weakened by the contractions of her womb. Birkat Bibi, the midwife, began to work diligently, while expressing her sorrow at this misfortune. Normally she found her role as the local midwife very rewarding, particularly when she delivered healthy, bouncing boys. It meant that her own payment would be topped up by lots of other presents, and she would be personally congratulated on her work.

On occasions like this, however, she kept a low profile, and often felt guilty about receiving any payment for the care and treatment that she provided to women miscarrying or delivering a stillborn child. She was saddened by this mishap. Like everybody else in the village, Birkat Bibi knew how important this baby was for the family.

With Faiza refreshed and resting in another bed, Birkat Bibi accepted some tea and halwa. It was then that she asked Robina what had happened and why Faiza had lost her baby.

Robina was hovering in the room, lost in her sorrow. At Birkat Bibi's words, her head shot up, struck by pain, like a bolt of thunder.

"That charail, that witch, Salma! She's been after Faiza ever since the day she learnt of my daughter-in-law's pregnancy."

"What? Which Salma, Robina dear?"

"Salma, the baker's daughter, who still lives with her parents," Robina said contemptuously. "She has miscarried three times, as you well know, in the last two years that you have seen to her. She has not left my Faiza alone. Just yesterday she was here and actually embracing our Faiza. Can you believe it, Birkat Bibi? Everything in this house is now soaked in her perchanvah."

The midwife tactfully kept silent. She knew what Salma's problem was. She herself was the one who had suggested that Salma see a gynaecologist in the city. At the same time, she knew all about some village women's beliefs and superstitions. She herself didn't believe in them, but as she had to work with these women and was generously rewarded by them financially, it wasn't in her best interests to argue with them. However, she often found herself irked by her forced pandering to their whims and superstitious beliefs. As a midwife and local nurse, her credibility would be in question if she started to perpetuate any of those same beliefs.

She felt sorry for Salma, for being made the scapegoat in this miscarriage. She had already found out why Faiza had miscarried by asking her whether she'd fallen. Faiza had affirmed that she had slipped on a wet floor, but had also pleaded with her not to tell her mother-in-law. Birkat Bibi promised to maintain her silence and left.

For the rest of the night Robina kept vigil near Faiza's bed. Her eyes were filled with anger and sadness. When her husband came into the room in the morning, she gave him a bitter, crooked laugh.

"You thought I was crazy. That it was only an old wives' tale. See what has happened? We've lost a grandchild within one day of that woman being in our house. You think that I spout nonsense. You ridicule me and my rituals. I suppose you're going to say it was all a matter of coincidence. Isn't it strange that our healthy daughter-in-law suddenly miscarries the very next day after embracing a woman with a perchanvah. You think I talk nonsense, Javed-ji?" She raised her voice as she said his name.

Her husband didn't reply. He was very sad and also bemused by what had happened in his home. He didn't believe his wife, but on the other hand, it was all so strange. Were these women right, after all, about amulets and so on? Shaking his head in sorrow and disbelief, he quietly left the room.

The guests, although they didn't discuss the matter openly, knew what had happened in the middle of the night and they were both saddened and disappointed. They had come to spend a few pleasant days in Javed Salman's house and taste the special sweets he made in his shop. Now a cloud of doom hung over the household. Everybody sat around the courtyard in hushed silence; the only sound was that of the black crows pecking on the fruit from the jamun tree.

By nine o'clock, after supervising the breakfast prepared by the woman helper for the guests, Robina could wait no longer. With her outdoor chador draped around her shoulders, she collected her best friend, Neelum, from next door and headed straight to Salma's house.

When she arrived, Salma's mother Zeinab was clearing away the breakfast dishes in the kitchen while Salma was busy sweeping the veranda floor. The sudden thudding on the outside door made mother and daughter exchange surprised looks, wondering who could be calling so early in the morning. The postman had already passed by.

Zeinab opened the door with the word of greeting, "Bismillah," on her lips, and let the two visitors in. She was immediately taken aback by the sight of Robina standing stiffly in the middle of their small courtyard with a forbidding expression on her face.

"Khair hey, Sister Robina? Is everything all right?" she asked.

"No, everything is *not* all right!" Robina exploded, taking advantage of the cue offered by Zeinab's question. "Our Faiza miscarried last night." She pinned her glowering gaze on Salma.

"Oh, I'm so sorry, Sister Robina. Really I am." Like everyone else, Zeinab knew how precious the baby was for Robina's family.

"So you should be, Zeinab." Robina deliberately omitted the complimentary word 'Sister'. The omission was not lost on the others. "Your daughter has been after my Faiza since the day she conceived. Just because she keeps miscarrying herself, she made sure that our Faiza couldn't have a healthy baby either."

"What utter nonsense! What has my Salma got to do with Faiza's miscarriage? Miscarriages are a medical, physiological

97

matter, you stupid woman. In Faiza's case, it had to do with her body and not my daughter. I've tolerated your superstitious ways and whims about perchanvah and chillah, but this is ridiculous. It goes beyond the pale of reasoning and rationality." Zeinab ended her outburst, her cheeks reddening with anger.

"Hah! Sister Neelum, listen to this woman. She says it has nothing to do with her daughter. Don't you think that it's a great coincidence that I saw Salma in my own home, embracing the life out of Faiza, and the very next day my daughter-in-law loses her baby? I suppose you think that I imagined all that? Didn't you go to our house yesterday, Salma?" Robina turned her angry gaze once again upon Salma, who was standing near one of the pillars supporting the veranda, her mouth dry and her heart racing.

"Well – did you, Salma?" her mother screeched.

"Yes, Mother," Salma affirmed quietly, utterly distressed by the whole affair.

"You see? If I were you, I would keep your manous, ill-fated daughter under lock and key until the right amount of time has expired, rather than let her go gadding about and spreading her perchanvah on healthy pregnant women."

And so saying, Robina swished her chador shawl over her head and shoulders and made a dramatic departure with her friend Neelum scurrying behind her, totally embarrassed by her friend's behaviour and words.

Mother and daughter remained standing on the spot as if turned to stone; they were both overcome by Robina's cruel remarks and accusations. At last, Zeinab sank down on the charpoy on the veranda, looking at her daughter, who seemed to have shrunk against the pillar. Zeinab was livid, but also hurt and upset on her daughter's behalf, knowing what she must be feeling.

"Salma, Salma, how many times have I told you not to have anything to do with your friend until she's had the baby. I know that we don't believe this perchanvah rubbish, but these silly women do. They have brainwashed themselves with those outrageous beliefs of their pir. No amount of argument or reasoning will persuade them otherwise — least of all that witch, Robina. Why oh why did you go yesterday? And why, of all things, did you have to embrace Faiza? You've just played right into Robina's hands."

"It wasn't me, Mother, it was Faiza. She embraced me . . . She slipped on the wet floor and fell yesterday, right before my very eyes."

"What? Why didn't you tell Robina?"

"I was too afraid to tell her. And I'm sure that Faiza hasn't told her mother-in-law."

"But this is an outrage!" Zeinab shot up from the charpoy. "Allah Pak, that woman is going around spreading rumours that you've caused her daughter-in-law to miscarry, when it was her fall that did it. I'll not let her get away with this. Come on, my girl, fetch your chador. Robina will not victimise you any more. I'll see to it!"

"Where are we going, Mother?" Salma's lips quivered; she was unwilling to be drawn into the unsavoury limelight further.

"We are going to Robina's house to sort out this matter, once and for all."

A few minutes later, mother and daughter left for Robina's home. Zeinab's wiry body was emboldened with rage, whereas Salma, since learning of the miscarriage, had lost all confidence in herself. She recalled Robina's vindictive word manous — evil — as she had called her. Perhaps if she hadn't gone to see Faiza, the latter might not have slipped and thus lost the baby. Perhaps there was something, after all, in the concept of perchanvah.

Perhaps it did affect women. And how could her mother persuade the woman to believe otherwise?

When Zeinab and Salma entered Robina's courtyard, all the people assembled there turned to stare at them. Her cheeks burning with embarrassment, Salma hid behind her mother.

On seeing them, Robina's eyes widened in disbelief. Zeinab calmly and with an unwavering gaze stared back at all the people in the courtyard. There were men and women, both young and old. All of them looked in her direction. A hushed silence descended. Everyone now speculated as to what was going to happen next, surprised that Robina didn't issue a welcoming greeting or stand up to receive the two women.

Zeinab, too, had dispensed with the customary greetings and social etiquette. Drawing herself up to her full height, she stood there in the middle of the courtyard, mirroring the stance that Robina had taken a short time earlier in her courtyard. Now it was her turn.

It was Javed, Robina's husband, who broke the silence, irked by his wife's rudeness.

"Welcome, Sister Zeinab. Come and sit down." He drew out a high-backed chair for her under the tree. "If you've come to see Faiza, she's resting in her room."

"Thank you, Brother Javed. It's not Faiza whom I have come to visit. For you see, Robina has forbidden us from doing that." She enjoyed watching the expression of irritation pass over his face. "I've come to see Robina, and Robina's spiritual guide, the pir."

"Oh! What about?" he asked, bristling at the mention of the word pir.

His wife interrupted him, demanding, "Why do you want to see my pir, Zeinab? What has he done to you?"

"Oh, he has done a lot. He's the one who has stuffed silly and gullible women like you with sheer nonsense and made my daughter into your scapegoat for Faiza's miscarriage."

For once, Zeinab didn't care about mincing her words. After all, Robina hadn't minced hers. She had almost accused her daughter of murder. She felt no shame in talking about miscarriages, a taboo subject like sex and pregnancy while in the presence of men. Today wasn't a normal day, however, and she didn't feel normal. Everything had been taken out of proportion.

Javed, the village sweet-maker, had been perturbed for years by the influence that the pir had on his wife and some other women in the village. He therefore welcomed this speech, even though it was an insult to have his wife called 'silly' in front of all these people. Then anger rose in him as he realised that his wife must have done Zeinab and Salma a very great wrong, to make this most gentle, pleasant and dignified woman behave and speak in this most uncharacteristic way.

Light dawned. "Robina, what have you done? Have you been blaming the loss of our grandchild on that innocent child? This is ridiculous. You cannot go around doing that." He was now livid.

"Trust you, Javed, to delight in me being insulted and ridiculed!" Robina could hardly speak – her own anger was choking her.

"It's not a matter of ridicule," Zeinab continued. "It's a matter of religious and social debate. Where does it say in the Holy Quran or Hadith about perchanvah? For aren't those the books and sources of our faith? Anything else is shirk. Where has the pir got his ideas from? Is he a woman? Is he a doctor? Is he an authority on all female health matters?"

"We all know that you do not believe in pirs. That doesn't give you licence to ridicule ours." Robina stressed the word 'ours', hoping that her husband would support her. However, from Javed's expression, it appeared that the contrary was true. In fact, he was visibly gloating, for here was his chance to discredit her pir. Robina felt very much alone.

"No, it doesn't. You are right, Robina," Zeinab replied steadily. "I respect holy men. People like us need them, to guide us in all religious and spiritual matters. It's their lack of knowledge in female matters and meddling with superstitions passed through the centuries that I abhor. You have yourself told all of us that your pir said that a woman who was expecting should avoid contact, or even the presence, of someone who had miscarried.

"With some of you women, that has meant that you not only shun but also offend women like my daughter, who has had the misfortune to miscarry on more than one occasion. It's not a disease that you can catch. Some of you have even refused to eat food that Salma has cooked and put in front of you. All this I have bitterly observed and tolerated, but what has been the outcome of your superstitious ways? You've harmed young minds and the sensibilities of women like my daughter. You've belittled her – in fact, insulted the whole essence of womanhood."

"I'll not listen to any more of your nonsense!" Robina stated, standing up to face Zeinab, her body quivering with rage.

"But I haven't finished yet, Robina. I suppose it's all right for you to come storming into my house and accuse my daughter of witchcraft and virtual murder. You said that my Salma caused Faiza's miscarriage. Well, has your Faiza told you that she fell?" Zeinab waited for the words to register in the other woman's mind.

Robina's mouth went dry as the words did indeed sink in. She stared at Zeinab. "What? I didn't know anything about her falling!"

"Well, why don't you go and ask her?"

Robina headed to Faiza's room. Zeinab, Salma, Neelum and Javed followed her.

In her room, Faiza lay awake. She had overheard everything in the courtyard. As the footsteps approached, her heart started to thud. They all came in and stood around her bed. Faiza spied her friend, Salma, standing behind her mother, and studiously avoided looking her in the eye.

Robina looked down at her daughter-in-law with a message in her eyes that she desperately wanted Faiza to interpret correctly.

"Your friend Salma said that you fell yesterday. Is that true?"

Faiza looked her mother-in-law steadily in the eye. "No."

As she said it, she caught the crushed look on Salma's face and quickly averted her gaze, having just confronted the moral choice of either betraying her friend or allowing her mother-in-law to lose face. She knew well that she had lost the baby through her own fault. She had been warned about wet floors and had ignored the advice. Since she was aware of how much the baby had meant to her parents-in-law, she could not make Robina lose face too in front of everyone.

Zeinab turned to her daughter. Salma, her eyes brimming with tears, had rushed from the room, unable to believe that her friend had lied and had thus made her the scapegoat and sealed her fate with perchanvah.

"Well, apparently your daughter-in-law is not only a liar but a coward too," Zeinab pronounced, returning into the courtyard. Bitterly she turned to look at Robina, who had followed her out.

"Don't think that the matter is now closed, Robina. I'm going to ask Chaudharani Sikandra to invite your pir to come and give his version of the ideas you have perpetuated in our village."

Then, with a dramatic wave of her hand, she pointed around the courtyard and the house, and said: "Moreover, perchanvah is now in your house. Now that your daughter-in-law has miscarried, according to your rules and beliefs, no household with a pregnant woman should welcome her nor will they visit your house. Now it's the turn of your Faiza to be the one who will be shunned. As this is your belief, if anyone miscarries in the next two or three months, it will be due to your Faiza's evil shadow. As you have made the rules, madam, you must now live by them. You cannot have it both ways!"

So saying, Zeinab made a dignified departure. Salma, mortified and wounded to her very soul at her friend's betrayal, had already run ahead.

Robina remained standing in the middle of the courtyard, amidst her guests, her mouth opening and closing. For once in her life, she was at a loss for words.

Our Angel

Abu Dhabi, UAE; Kabul, Afghanistan, present day

The majestic, pure-white Sheikh Zayed mosque in Abu Dhabi was elegantly etched against the clear blue sky. Inside, the Fajr early morning prayers had come to an end. Fazal Karim, a fifty-three-year-old Afghani taxi driver, ritually took his fill of his plush surroundings. First, of the rich texture of the exquisite prayer hall carpet. Relaxing in the splendid inner hall of sanctity, he felt uplifted and spiritually prepared for his daily twelve-hour driving shift, moving passengers around the city of Abu Dhabi and elsewhere.

Outside in the main courtyard, his eyes roamed in awe over the tall marble pillars with their gem-encrusted engravings, gold-leaf patterns and Arabic calligraphic designs.

He was slipping his feet into his leather sandals when his cell phone started to vibrate in the pocket of his white kurtha, worn over his traditional Afghani baggy trousers. Spotting the Kabul number, Fazal Karim's heartbeat quickened; his first thought was his ailing mother. His wife rarely phoned, diligently paying homage to the tradition of wifely obedience in complying with his instruction to wait for his twice-weekly calls.

Determined not to waste money or minutes, Gulchara, his forty-six-year-old wife, dispensed with greetings and raced ahead, eager to reel off the latest family news, and breathless with the excitement of her special request.

"Noorie's Babajaan, please come home!" Gulchara never called her husband by his first name, especially in the presence of others. "I beg of you, don't delay our Noorie's wedding for another year. It'll be disastrous if we do." She stopped there, dreading his answer.

Fazal Karim stiffened, his greyish-blue eyes cold in his sun-bronzed face. He was not at all happy with this early morning request; now he had the whole day to dwell on this matter. However, highly sensitive to the burden his wife was carrying in running their household single-handedly in Kabul, he softened his tone, accepting that she had a justifiable reason for her call.

"But you know, my dear, that I need at least six more months here in order to earn enough for the cost of our Noorie's gold jewellery."

"Then it'll be too late!" Gulchara wailed at the other end of the line, with stark images of her abandoned, sobbing daughter flitting before her eyes.

"What do you mean?" Fazal Karim asked, desperate to hug her and shower kisses on her face.

"That witch Qadsia is dangling her daughter Laila's hand in marriage in Mustafa's household. You know what she's like . . . she has not an ounce of integrity or decency in her bones. This is her chance to exploit our weakness – your absence from home. I'm told by Mustafa's maid that she visits their house regularly with her daughter – and always in the evening. Can you guess why? Simply because our future son-in-law is at home at that time. And their gossiping maid tells me further that the girl is always decked up in glamorous clothes, her cobra-green eyes lined perfectly with dark kohl to make them look even bigger. Wicked women! Mother and daughter have no shame. Fancy flaunting your daughter before strange men!"

After a moment's pause to wipe her eyes, she continued, "Whether we like it or not, everyone says that Qadsia's daughter Laila is very pretty too, and still studying like our Noorie."

The silence at the other end made Gulchara wonder if she had been cut off or if she had rambled on too much. "Hello?" she said tentatively.

"Gulchara!" was all poor Fazal Karim could manage. It was simply too much for him to face a domestic crisis this early in the morning in the serene surroundings of the mosque. Something had to be said, however. And he said it heavily, knowing he was going to disappoint his wife.

"What our Almighty wills, happens. I'm trying my best, my dear," he reminded her sadly. It was he who, for economic reasons, was exiled from his home and family. At least Gulchara slept in their bed and enjoyed the company of their children.

"And right now, I must get on," he told her. "I need to pick up an Englishman from the airport and take him to the oil rigs, Gulchara. Kiss Mother for me, please. Wasalam."

Gulchara barely had time to bid her husband goodbye; the phone was already dead in her hand. Gathering her thoughts, she tried hard to wipe the expression from her face before turning to her daughter, who was hovering anxiously behind her. It was Noorie who had prompted the phone call this morning.

"What did Babajaan say?" the girl asked.

"Your father has promised to come home soon," Gulchara lied, determined to dispel the look of worry from her Noorie's face. And she succeeded. Her next words caused a radiant smile to emerge through the two dimples in her daughter's cheeks.

"Your papa says he'll be back in three months' time."
Gulchara normally did not lie, but she was loath to let her poor
Noorie worry over a possible jilting by her fiancé's family just
before her final teaching exams.

Noorie had two important goals in life: to complete a
teaching course and to marry her fiancé, Ashar, whom she'd
adored since her childhood – her good-looking, charming,
distant relative. Ashar, for his part, had patiently waited
for her to reach her eighteenth birthday before his family
could formally ask for her hand in marriage. The fact that
her father worked abroad made it easier for them. Brides
from families of men who worked abroad were eagerly
sought after for wedding matches, as they were reckoned to
be from wealthier homes and with prospects of migrating
abroad. Splendid wedding feasts and lavish gifts were also
guaranteed.

When Noorie turned nineteen, Ashar's family was keen
to finalise the wedding arrangements. Her parents, however,
insisted that they wait until Noorie was at least twenty years
old and had completed her teaching course. The unmentioned
agenda in Noorie's family was that they were actually buying
time for her father to earn enough money from his work in
Abu Dhabi for the wedding. The would-be groom's family
reluctantly agreed to wait for another year.

What no one had predicted, however, was Qadsia's
unscrupulous nature, and her wicked plan to marry her
daughter to Ashar by breaking off the alliance between the
two families. At first, the young man's family was amused
by Qadsia's blatant efforts in wooing them. Then they began
to take her earnest offerings seriously, particularly after she
started bragging about her eldest brother's offer to sponsor
her family to join him in the US.

Qadsia astutely kindled a hunger in them for the American green card which would enable their son to migrate to the land of plenty with a much higher standard of living and where money could be made. As a member of that family, their son's new home would be in New Jersey, far away from war-torn Kabul and the Taliban.

Family politics, human greed, and female rivalry had introduced a new demon into Fazal Karim's family life. Qadsia, a pernicious relative, was aggressively muscling her way into Noorie's fiancé's world, with the sole aim of marrying her daughter into that household. Moreover, Qadsia was not stealthy in her endeavours. On the contrary, highly skilled in embellishing facts, she had openly mocked her rivals.

"As everyone knows, Fazal Karim is not likely to return for at least another year, or as is rumoured, for probably two years. Can you, my dear relatives, possibly wait that long? Think! Your poor Ashar is already twenty-six years of age. Most of his friends got married a long time ago and I'm sure some have two or three children each by now. What about your son — should he go on waiting, the poor boy?"

It was a well-known fact that Qadsia's family could marry off their daughter within weeks with pomp and ceremony. In addition, the girl Laila was so pretty, with her tall, statuesque figure which she flaunted in many fashionable outfits.

"How can the homely looking Noorie compete with my Laila?" Qadsia had bitchily crooned to her cronies.

One crony had, of course, equally bitchily relayed the words back to Gulchara, sending her into a state of panic. Straight after preparing semolina halwa for her mother-in-law's breakfast and rinsing the old lady's henna-dyed hair in an aluminium tub, Gulchara headed off to their bedding storeroom in the basement of their home. There, perched on a chair in a quiet corner, she had called her husband. Keen to listen to the conversation, Noorie had followed.

After Noorie had left for college, Gulchara moved listlessly around the house. With a heavy heart, she started on her daily chores: the airing of the bedding quilts, sweeping litter from the floor, scrubbing the soup pot and chopping the vegetables for the afternoon meal.

"Will my Noorie actually make it to Ashar's household as a bride?" Gulchara wondered, feeling disheartened as she stooped over the simmering vegetable pot. Only God knew when her husband would return home.

She began to weep bitterly, hating the migration process that had snatched her husband from their lives. The tinkling noise of her mother-in-law's hand bell startled her, made her wipe her eyes and sent her scurrying round the veranda and into the room that Noorie and her grandmother shared.

Sighing, Gulchara philosophically accepted that life had to go on. There were more chores to be completed, and the continuous care of her diabetic mother-in-law who suffered from dizzy spells.

Across the Arabian Sea in the airport at Abu Dhabi, Nigel, a fifty-one-year-old British geologist from the north-east of England, joined the immigration queue of international passengers. After collecting his luggage, he waited for two other men who worked for the same oil company to join him. One was from the US and the other from Italy. Fazal Karim, with his large taxi, had been sent to collect them.

A Tamil worker carrying a placard with Nigel's name greeted him, followed by two men in their late thirties, dressed in European clothes. Nigel politely exchanged handshakes with his workmates with greetings in English and a 'Namaste' to the

Tamil worker. They were led to their taxi where Fazal Karim, dressed in his traditional Afghani shalwar and kurtha suit, put their luggage in the car. Intimidated by the Europeans in their smart suits and the loud voice of the American, he avoided eye contact with them.

Leaving Abu Dhabi city behind, they were soon on their way to the oil refineries. Nigel gazed out of the window at the tall palm trees, his partner Judith's last remark stinging his ears.

"If you go again, then don't be surprised if Tommy and I are not here when you get back." Tommy was her son from a previous relationship.

Did Judith actually mean it? Her semi-teasing and threatening comment had dogged his journey to the Emirates where he was about to resume his six-month contract on the oil rig, for mud-logging work, checking of the volcanic rock and gas monitoring. There was to be a short spell of similar work in Cyprus too. He wondered if Judith would join him there as it was a European country.

Judith was unhappy about him being away for months, as families were not expected to accompany the workers. They both disliked the months-long inevitable separation. Coupled with that, living in the Middle East did not appeal to Judith. He knew of many friends whose wives or families had moved to live in Dubai or flew out to join their men for short weekends. They thoroughly enjoyed what the Emirates had to offer them, with plenty to do, including desert safaris and shopping in the lively malls. Not his Judith, though.

Fazal Karim stole a look at his passengers through his rear-view mirror. His gaze met the American's supercilious look and he immediately averted his eyes. Fazal Karim's once fair skin, now tanned from the hot Emirati sun, turned a deeper shade in embarrassment.

The Italian national was looking out at the old Nepalese man hosing the plants at the side of the road. Nigel, sitting in front, was admiring the large palm leaves, swaying in the gentle breeze. Beyond the palm trees he could glimpse the sand dunes. Their destination – the oil rigs – was still a long way off.

The car suddenly began to shudder, forcing its passengers to turn to look at the driver. Poor Fazal Karim started panicking, but luckily the engine picked up speed again. Fazal Karim promised himself that if he reached their destination safely, he would offer ten extra thanks giving Nafl prayers that night. His anxiety killed his appetite, and he forgot all about the meal his housemates were preparing that evening for the birthday of their Hindu housemate, Prem.

In the pitch darkness of the cool Emirati night, Nigel trod carefully around the large compound with its workers' huts, which housed the South Asian and Far East workers and artisans. He had quickly found that the flip-flops he liked to wear on his feet were not adequate protection against the desert snakes or the black scorpions. Only two days ago, he had seen three Bengali migrant workers bent over a bucket with a coiled sleeping snake inside.

As if reading his mind, Fazal Karim shyly held out his hand to Nigel to guide him in the dark.

"Thank you." The Englishman gratefully took the hand.

They reached his hut. Fazal Karim was desperately praying that he would be spared the embarrassed looks of his housemates and that they would have had the presence of mind to tidy up their main room before opening the door to an unexpected guest. It had been a spur of the moment decision, inviting 'Sir kind Nigel', as he termed him in his head, back to his lodgings. Fazal Karim had really taken to Nigel after the man had given him a very generous tip. Without fully realising the implications of his impulsive action, Fazal Karim had issued the invitation to Nigel to try a curry with him.

His timid knocking on the door went unanswered. Fazal Karim fervently hoped that his friends would be able to understand by the knocking that someone else was standing outside the door, since they knew that he had a key. Unfortunately, the strategy did not signal to his housemates that a white European man standing outside was about to grace them with his presence. No special preparations or frenzied tidying up had taken place for that possibility.

Fazal Karim was so glad that the night's darkness hid his flushed cheeks. Now he truly regretted his impulse in bringing the European visitor with him and letting him trespass into their humble world.

In the dim light, Prem's brown cheeks also blazed red at the sight of the smiling white face behind Fazal Karim's shoulder. His gaze fell as he stepped back, letting Nigel enter their one main room which served as both their living room and bedroom. The other occupant, a Pakistani man in his late thirties called Khalid, dropped the playing cards on the floor and scrambled to his feet from his squatting position on the rug. Feeling humiliated, his condemning gaze shot to Fazal Karim. What was he thinking of, bringing a Gora – a white man – into their shabby shack and without warning! It was most unfair, especially for him. Wearing only a white cotton vest over a crumpled Pakistani shalwar, he was particularly aggrieved at being caught half-undressed.

Irritated and embarrassed, he reeled off his displeasure in Urdu and Hindi, the two languages of Bollywood and understood by all of them, who were from three different countries: Afghanistan, India and Pakistan. Two occupants were Muslims, and one was a Hindu – Prem from Kerala.

"Don't panic. He's a very nice man – and he's only come to try out our curries," Fazal Karim hastened to reassure his two housemates. "Prem, can you put the chapatti pan on the stove, please?" he requested whilst smiling at Nigel, who stood politely in the middle of the room, looking on uncomfortably.

Nodding his head, Prem scurried into the adjoining room, which acted as a kitchen and storeroom, with the occupants' suitcases containing their clothes stacked in one corner. He returned to switch on the TV. The Pakistani man hastily collected together the orange plastic plates and matching glasses they had used for Prem's birthday party meal from earlier in the evening, and hid them behind the three mattresses lined up against one wall and used as beds at night-time. When the mattresses were laid out at night, there were only a few inches of space between them. The men had to hop over each other to go out, either to work or to another hut nearby where they showered and performed their ablutions.

Nigel perched himself on the sofa, which was covered by a white cotton sheet, painfully aware that his arrival had discomfited Fazal Karim's housemates. He now regretted his action in invading the men's privacy, wishing he had reflected on his quest for a curry before barging into their lives unannounced.

He politely smiled at the Pakistani man, recognising him as the chapatti maker in the Asian artisans' communal cafe that he passed to get to his hotel. The chapatti maker had an important job, supplying chapattis all day to hungry artisans who were not so keen on the local bread, especially in the evening when they returned from their long working shifts. So when it came to cooking for themselves at night, the chapatti maker firmly declined to go anywhere near the kitchen stove.

Smiling sheepishly, the younger man Prem was still fiddling nervously with the TV remote buttons, trying to locate the

BBC News 24 channel for their British guest, so that he could listen to English news.

When Fazal Karim returned with a glass of orange juice, Prem mumbled the words, "Excuse me," and disappeared into the kitchen. The Pakistani housemate with his shirt buttons still open followed him, letting Fazal Karim entertain their unwanted visitor.

With the other men gone, Nigel relaxed. Fazal Karim drew a small coffee table in front of him before sitting on a chair next to the sofa.

"Tell me about your family." Nigel was genuinely interested in the Afghan's background. "Do you have any children?"

"Yes, sir. Four! Two daughters and two boys. Boys are big and the girls . . . one is old and the other is young."

Nigel tried to keep a straight face, before correcting Fazal Karim. "Your daughter is now an adult – a young woman, you mean."

"Yes, she – young lady."

"How old is she?"

"She's nineteen. A woman."

"Yes, a woman. You speak English well, Fazal Karim. Tell me, where did you learn it?"

"I was driver with British Council. Madams and sirs speak English. I learn from them. Good for this taxi job – drive people from Europe."

"Excellent!"

"My Arabic is better," feeling confident now, Fazal Karim joked.

"I bet."

"Ah, here's the food," Fazal Karim announced as Prem shyly brought in a tray of food.

Apart from fried vegetable rice, there were two other dishes, a korma and a cauliflower curry, with two chapattis. Nigel tore off bits of the chapatti with his fingers and dipped one piece into the curry bowl to scoop up pieces of meat. Fazal Karim watched with open admiration and was delighted to see him use his hands and fingers – just like them.

With his mouth full, Nigel assured him wryly, "Don't worry, I know how to eat curries with my fingers. See?" They both laughed.

Fazal Karim's housemates, who were peeping from the kitchen doorway, stood there beaming, finding the western geologist's unpretentious manner so endearing. They loved watching him lick his fingers afterwards. Nigel, their special guest, grinned back. The two men standing in the kitchen door now felt confident enough to join them in the room.

"Tea?" Prem, a Keralite from Cochin in India, chirped happily, thoroughly pleased with himself; it was his chapatti that the white babu had eaten.

Nigel gave a hearty nod. Prem then became bold enough to ask, "Masala chai, sir?"

"Yes, why not. Thank you. But please – call me Nigel, chaps."

The men stared, an uneasy look on their faces.

"Not good!" Fazal Karim exclaimed, frowning at the thought. "You are 'sir'."

And Prem, who was in his late twenties, promptly explained, wanting to amplify the cultural point further, "You old!" He then blushed when Nigel laughed.

What he had wanted to explain was that Nigel was older than Prem and thus he could not insult him by calling him by his first name. His cultural upbringing would not allow him to call Nigel by his first name. Only the words 'sir' or 'Mr Nigel' were to be used. Then, blushing again, Prem excused himself, and at the door informed Fazal Karim that he was going for a walk, forgetting about the masala tea he had offered to make.

In their shared language, Hindi, Prem suggested to Khalid that he, too, leave Fazal Karim and his English guest alone. Heartily agreeing with his suggestion, the Pakistani grabbed his outdoor jacket and both slipped away out into the dark night for a long walk.

Alone with his European guest, Fazal Karim shyly asked, "Rice – more?"

Nigel nodded. Fazal Karim went to the kitchen. Nigel glanced around at the cramped surroundings of the room, then followed Fazal Karim into the cooking area. Fazal Karim could feel heat coursing through his cheeks, knowing Sir Nigel was standing behind him as he looked for a fork, the only one they had in the cupboard. They were used to plastic plates and eating curries using their fingers. Spoons were only used for rice. With the wooden cooking spoon, Fazal Karim scooped out the remains of fried rice from the small pot.

"The rice will take some time to heat, sir," he murmured apologetically.

"Oh, that's fine," Nigel quickly assured him. He could spot no microwave in the kitchen. The men probably ate straight after they cooked.

"Sorry, that's all we have at the moment. Our cooking is mainly vegetarian. Today was Prem's birthday – he eats no meat. You like lamb, Sir Nigel . . . will make for you next time." Fazal Karim expected him to agree that lamb was his favourite dish.

"Do you take turns with your housemates?" Nigel asked. Fazal Karim looked puzzled. Nigel reworded his question.

"Cooking? The men who live with you – do they cook too, Fazal Karim?"

"Yes, we do. Apart from Hindu Prem – he cooks vegetables. Too much problem with meat pots, which he not like touch. And we like meat, like you. He makes chapattis. This . . . his pan." Fazal Karim laughed nervously, wondering why he was telling this stranger about their Prem. He remembered the last Hindu housemate, Kishore. How Fazal Karim missed him, but at the end he understood the reasons why he had left their shared accommodation.

It was not just the food question, but also the inherent racism they demonstrated in Kishore's presence, with their thoughtless little jibes at his religious practices, 'pooja' of 'bhuts', his numerous gods and goddesses. Without realising it, they had all indirectly, at some point or other, deeply hurt him with their offensive manner and jokes, including the one, "How can that little bhut merely three inches tall solve all your problems and answer your prayers?"

Big-hearted, and unwilling to hurt them back, Kishore always laughed it away in their presence. Thus no one was any wiser about his inner distress.

In the end, it was Fazal Karim who one day took him aside and asked whether it was worth living with people who were not even aware of their own prejudices and were offending him unwittingly. So, when he met a new Hindu worker from the Indian state of Kerala, who joined the same taxi firm, Fazal Karim introduced him to Kishore and the two men had gone on to share living space.

Nigel returned to the main room, letting his gaze dwell for a few seconds on a photo inside the open wallet that Fazal Karim had left on the table. It was of his family. His wife, head draped with a lace-fringed shawl, was shyly looking down. Two pretty teenage daughters were sitting each side of him and two young men were hovering over his shoulders.

Fazal Karim entered, holding a glass and a bottle of water for him. Putting the things on the table, he held his wallet out to Nigel to have a better look.

"My family," he explained. "When we lived in Peshawar, in Pakistan."

"I thought you were from Afghanistan?"

"Yes, we are, but we migrated to Pakistan many years ago. All my children . . . born there. Then my mother want to return to home country. That's why I speak many languages, like Urdu."

"So you were migrants there too!"

Fazal Karim laughed aloud. "Yes, we all migrants. Now you are one too, Nigel Sir. We all economic migrants."

Nigel could see the sense in that. "Absolutely right, Fazal Karim. Me too. I've joined your lot – I'm an economic migrant too."

Fazal Karim's face fell, and there was an awkward pause. Nigel wondered if he had said something wrong. Looking askance, he forced Fazal Karim to bare his soul.

"I hope not, sir," he said.

"Why?" Nigel didn't really understand.

Fazal Karim sighed. "You'll stay perhaps for few months and then go back – correct, Sir Nigel?" He used the popular word 'correct' he had picked up from his Indian friends.

Nigel nodded. Another pause. Nigel prompted his host to continue. "And you?"

"I've been here for twenty-one years."

"Wow!" Nigel's exclamation did not elicit the reaction he expected. Fazal Karim appeared deeply unhappy talking about this subject.

Nigel put his spoon down and asked, "And when do you go back to visit your family?"

"After two years normally."

"Oh." Nigel was deeply shocked. The thought of separation from his Judith for that long a period was unthinkable. Judith would have left him by now. She had already jokingly threatened to do so if he did not get this bug of working abroad out of his system.

119

I need to get real, he chastised himself. *What did I expect? These men are here for purely economic reasons, to work hard and make money to support their families back home.* That was the brutal truth.

Aloud he asked, his tone serious, "How long do you stay in Afghanistan?"

"Normally for three weeks or a month."

Nigel pushed the plate aside. The stark reality of what the man was telling him hit him. His agile brain was busy calculating the total number of months Fazal Karim had stayed with his family in twenty-one years. At three weeks per year, it amounted to fifteen months in twenty-one years. He closed his eyes.

"You must miss your family very much," he said quietly.

Fazal Karim nodded, struggling with a sob rising in his throat, now feeling quite distressed.

"I'm so sorry," the big Englishman told him, and his voice conveyed his sincerity.

Fazal Karim shrugged his shoulders and said, "That's life, sir. Money . . . more money here in Abu Dhabi."

"Are you going back this year?"

Fazal Karim shook his head.

"Next year?"

Fazal Karim nodded.

"Oh! Why?"

"My daughter's marriage, sir. I need to make more money, for air fares, her dowry and wedding expenses – food, party, clothes, gold presents," he enumerated dully.

"I see." Nigel's eyes had widened. "Is it very expensive? The wedding costs, I mean."

"Yes, sir. Weddings too expensive, for one man worker," he said, lifting his hand to signal that he was the only breadwinner in that family. "My money pay for everything, flour, rice, bills, school money for my children. And doctor money – my mother has sugar. Medicine – too much cost."

"Oh, she's diabetic?"

"Yes. I work hard, but my taxi journeys only make so much money. I get less than half my daily earnings. The car belong to the firm, sir. Sometime nice customers give me good tips. Here life expensive, sir. Big bills. Food. Expensive, sir. More than Kabul. So I work and work. Go home in nineteen months' time."

"I see."

Fazal Karim was now eager to change the subject, humiliated by discussing his financial matters with a man from the land where all looked healthy and young and where it was rumoured medical and education costs were taken care of by the government. What would this man understand about his life and his hardships? His prayers at the mosque to Allah were for his family's well-being and for himself to remain healthy. For he could not afford any more medical bills. His mother's declining health had eaten a sizeable portion of his income and also made the poor woman feel guilt-ridden for years.

"Would you like cola drink, sir?"

"No. Water is fine. Thank you."

"I cooked this rice yesterday . . . Nice, sir?" Fazal Karim asked with pride.

Nigel resumed eating with relish. "More than nice," he said. "Your rice is delicious! You're a really great cook."

Fazal Karim was delighted. "Thank you. My wife speak same." He went on: "Yes, when in Kabul I cook for my wife sometime. We do this quietly! So that my mother does not find out. She be angry with wife, say – my son no cook!"

They both chuckled.

"Your English is truly very good indeed," Nigel said. "I can understand you – that's what matters. They did a good job."

"British Council, sir? Now bad English – forget, sir." But Fazal Karim's chest lifted in pride. He had long recognised the importance of learning English as one way of bettering oneself and getting good jobs. It was the reason why he had insisted on all his children learning it at school. Especially his daughters. He was really ambitious for them, wanting them to become teachers of English. The girls loved learning. When he went home, he didn't speak Pashto or Arabic with them but practised English instead. That night, he had plenty of practice with his English guest.

The next morning, Nigel raised his hand to wave to Prem when he met him on his way from the hotel, saying, "Hi there."

Upon meeting their 'European guest' again, Prem smiled but quickly looked away.

When Nigel looked surprised by the young man's reaction, the suave Italian rigger by his side said helpfully, "A bit of advice, pal. Don't mess with the system here by becoming too friendly with these guys. The workers keep to their side of the fence, as you would say in English. More importantly, our local hosts, the Emiratis, encourage this system of two kinds of workers here – us and them." He jerked a hand at Prem.

"You mean it's a bit like an apartheid," Nigel stated, his tanned cheeks flushed with indignation.

"Of course not. Well, you know, they keep themselves to themselves and we do the same. We have nothing in common," the Italian, Roberto, tried to explain. "I noticed that you went out last night to their shack."

Nigel bristled defensively. "Yes, I did – and it's not a shack!" He said brusquely to Roberto, "I had a fabulous curry meal with them last night. Anyone have a problem with that?"

Roberto shrugged his shoulders and hastened away. Let this British guy sample the wretched lives of these hardworking artisans. He himself was here to work, nothing else and certainly not to get involved in the politics of their employers' treatment of employees from the Third World.

Fazal Karim rushed into the hotel, worried in case something had happened. He hovered in the reception hall, painfully aware of the well-dressed men in formal western suits and crisp white shirts around him. Finally, he went and joined the queue for the reception desk, to ask about the whereabouts of Mr Nigel.

Then his eyes lit up as Nigel entered through the rotating door, his glasses perched low down on the bridge of his sunburnt nose after spending the past two hours examining mud samples under the microscope. Lightheaded with relief, Fazal Karim hurried to meet his new friend.

"Good evening, Sir Nigel," he greeted formally, smiling.

"Assalam-a-Alaikum – thanks for coming, my friend. Shall we go to the cafe area and have a cup of tea?" Nigel said cheerfully.

The smile slipped from Fazal Karim's face; he was unhappy at both prospects, firstly of being offered tea and secondly at having to pay for it, knowing how expensive things were in hotels.

Reading Fazal Karim's mind accurately, Nigel said quickly: "You offered me great hospitality the other day, so please let me repay you, in a little way, by offering you tea and perhaps a slice of cake. How's that?"

"Please, sir. I have drunk tea."

"Then have something to eat if not tea." When Fazal Karim continued to look uncomfortable, Nigel added, "OK. Let's sit down there." He sauntered across the lobby with Fazal Karim trailing behind him to a quiet corner, away from a group of Japanese guests.

Fazal Karim sat perched on the seat opposite Nigel, self-conscious in the plush surroundings of the hotel, embarrassed by his muddied shalwar hemline and the dry flaky skin of his toes visible in his leather sandals.

Very much aware of his guest's discomfort and knowing that he was eating into his working time, Nigel went straight to the point. "I wanted to thank you for your hospitality, Fazal Karim. First, tell me when are you thinking of going back home for your daughter's wedding?"

Taken aback by the question, Fazal Karim looked away, made wretched by the reminder of a topic that weighed on him night and day. "Next year, sir."

Nigel, too, looked down, thinking about what words to use to avoid bruising the man's pride, and widening the cultural differences that separated them and their circumstances.

"Will you do me the honour of taking a gift from me for your daughter's wedding?"

Fazal Karim's head shot up. "A gift, sir?"

"Yes." Nigel drew a thick envelope from his trouser pocket and held it out to him.

"Sir?" Fazal Karim did not know what to say. The envelope stood between them.

"Please," Nigel prompted quietly.

Eventually, Fazal Karim's hand reached for the bulky envelope, wondering what it contained. He flicked back the seal and gasped at the ream of crisp British sterling £20 notes.

"Sir . . .?" He struggled to hold onto his composure.

Nigel's eyes filled. "I was very touched by what you told me about your family. I did not know what to give as a present. Please use this money to buy her what she wants . . . and please go home. That's the present I want to give her – to have her father back at home. Please don't spend another year in your cab on the Emirati roads. Get your daughter married!"

He stopped. Fazal Karim's hand was trembling. Then his eyes widened in amazement when Nigel mentioned the sum in the envelope.

"There are two thousand pounds in there. I think in your country it's a decent sum." He cleared his throat. "I hope it helps you, Fazal Karim."

Good with numbers, Fazal Karim was already converting the sum into his local currency, Afghani. He felt a big lump in his throat. He tried hard to say something, to refuse and to thank the man, but the words would not come.

Nigel came to his aid. "Please accept – I'll not take it back. Here, this is my business card. Let me know how your daughter's wedding goes. I am sure it will be terrific. If you really don't fancy tea then it's pointless me wasting your time – you need to get back to work. I myself am going home to my family. No more separation!" Nigel stood up, holding his hand out.

Fazal Karim rose too, clutching the envelope. Finally his mouth opened, just as Nigel was about to turn.

"Thank you. Allah bless you!" Fazal Karim's cheeks were wet, his mouth quivering. The look of utter gratitude in his eyes would stay with Nigel for years. Inside, Fazal Karim was uttering special prayers in his own language. "May Allah bless you sir, Our Angel." He repeated that phrase over and over again in the next twenty-four hours, including during his long Isha prayers.

That night, he returned to their hut early, hid the money in his clothes and locked his suitcase. He trusted his housemates, but could not let go of his fear of losing it. Instead of two o'clock in the morning he was back home at ten o'clock in the evening and thoroughly enjoyed watching an Indian movie with the others. And for a change, he watched the whole movie as he did not have to rise early. He also offered to cook the meal for everyone, including his special white Kabuli chickpea vegetarian dish for Prem.

Next morning, he visited the travel agent.

In the Abu Dhabi hotel room, Nigel made himself a coffee and looked out of the large window at the grand Sheikh Zayed mosque, where Fazal Karim had said a special prayer for the well-being of his 'Nigel Sir'.

Back in Newcastle in the UK, a few weeks later, Nigel was checking through his morning emails, when one popped up with a Muslim name he did not recognise. Curious, he scanned through its content. Then he sat back, lost in thought. His partner Judith came in and stood behind him with a mug of fresh coffee.

"Presentation finished?" she enquired.

Nigel pointed to the laptop monitor screen for her to read the message. Judith leaned over his shoulder and read the long email aloud.

Dear Sir Nigel,

Hello. I hope you do not mind me writing to you. First I apologise for my bad English. My English is not as good as my sister Noorie. And I have not got her to check my writing this time. As this is a surprise message for her.

Sorry, let me introduce myself first. My name is Ali, I am Fazal Karim's eldest son. You met our father in Abu Dhabi last month

— the man you gave money to for my sister Noorie's wedding presents.

I wanted to thank you!

THANK YOU!

And to tell you how happy you have made us all, by your money gift to us. You'll never know the difference it has made to our lives. We now have our father with us at home, when we expected to see him only next year. My sister's marriage, too, may not have taken place. Because — and this is difficult for me to explain — but her in-laws' family would not have waited for that long, I mean for my father to arrive.

My mader kalan, my father's mother, spends her day kissing my father. My mother now laughs all the time. She thinks she's on holiday, because Father is doing all the shopping and the preparation for the wedding. We do not know how to keep/hold our happiness. Sorry my English is bad.

The only one who is cross at times, is my young brother — he has to stay more at home and study hard, because our father is here to supervise his studies. Before, my brother would boss my mother and run out of the house to play cricket with his friends in the park all evening. My mother always worried about his exam results. This was her extra worry apart from running the house, looking after Grandma and everything else. Now she's leaving almost everything to our father.

Babajaan is taking care of us all.

You are Our Angel. The name our father uses to describe you all the time. And guess what — this is what my grandmother calls you. We now all call you this — I hope you don't mind. We will never forget what you have done for us in funding Noorie's wedding and therefore giving us our father back again!

Thank you, too much, Our Angel, for bringing lots of joy in our life, and for getting Noorie married on time and to the man she wanted to marry!

P.S. Sir I feel shy about asking this but could you come to my sister's wedding? She'll be so thrilled. You would be our very special guest. Then everyone could see and meet Our Angel.

Yours warmly, Ali

By the way I got your email address from your business card that Pader keeps very safe in his wallet.

Nigel and Judith exchanged a charged look, and she reached for the tissue box to wipe her wet eyes.

In Kabul, Ali checked his emails many times on a laptop that he shared with his siblings. The girls in the family were allowed to use the laptop, with a proviso that they would share an email account with their brother. Their father, although worldly wise and very much into women's rights and education, still had to adhere to the tradition of protecting his daughters' honour. He wanted to ensure that the girls did not stray or compromise their family honour by befriending any males over the internet.

Fazal Karim had heard many sorry tales about the immoral things happening over the internet. Who knew who spoke to whom, and who wrote what and to whom? He trusted his daughters, but whilst they were in his care as single women it was his paternal duty to diligently supervise their spiritual and emotional well-being. So Noorie wrote to her female friends from her brother's account. Brother and sister respected each other's correspondence and need for privacy.

The messages from her female friends were never opened by Ali. Noorie, in turn, never glanced at his male friends' messages.

A message suddenly popped up with an English male name. After reading it, Ali shrieked in delight. "Look, everyone!" he shouted.

Her bosom rising and falling behind the layer of her shawl, Gulchara ran into his room and hovered behind him. "What has happened?" she asked, her mouth dry.

"Our Angel is coming to Noorie's wedding!"

His mother and father exchanged quick glances. Then Fazal Karim rushed to his mother, with others following him.

"He's coming to our Noorie's wedding!" Fazal Karim's excited voice sliced across his mother's room.

"Who's coming, my Fazal Karim?"

"Our Angel!"

"What a blessing!" His mother had sat up, pulling her shawl around her shoulders to cover herself well in front of her son. Fazal Karim walked over to his mother's bed and kissed her hard on the forehead.

"Yes, Mother, it's a blessing indeed. Nigel Sir has done so much for us."

Wide-eyed and with glowing cheeks, Noorie stood behind her parents.

In Kabul, after the Nikkah wedding ceremony, Noorie's henna party was in full swing. The women guests in their traditional Afghani party gowns and dresses, with matching richly embroidered gauzy veils, and decked with gold and silver jewellery, including the regal-looking forehead pendants called matikka, were having a great time with their singing and dancing in two large rooms allocated for them in the house.

129

Trays of lemon drinks and platters of cakes and sweetmeats were being served.

The younger women, eager to catch a glimpse of Noorie's trousseau, had settled comfortably on the rugs and bulky cushions on the floor. Noorie's Cousin Halima arrived from Herat and, dressed in the glamorous outfit from her own wedding, was preening herself for the special role assigned to her. She had fought hard with other cousins of Noorie to win the honour of being the mistress of ceremony for the showing of Noorie's trousseau.

Halima stood ready on a carpeted pedestal in the middle of the large reception room: tall, elegantly dressed, face immaculately made up courtesy of a local beauty parlour, and arms heavily laden with gold bangles. One maid was serving the drinks while another served nuts and cakes. Noorie sat with her sister and mother-in-law on the special sofa suite. Most of the female guests in the room were from the groom's side. The close relatives of Noorie's clan had already enjoyed their own 'trousseau trunk opening ceremony' the previous day.

For the women guests, the viewing of the trousseau presents was an exciting part of the wedding celebrations. Halima's job was not only to display the gifts but to provide a verbal running commentary. And if any relative who had contributed to the gifts was there, it honoured that person by having their present admired and praised.

Almost bursting with happiness, Halima opened the heavy lid of the large steel trunk, and, one by one, lifted and held up the bridal items: the elaborately embroidered party gowns, boxes of jewellery, make-up kit, jumpers, shoes, sandals, lingerie items and shawls, as well as the traditional modesty burqa veil to wear outside.

After Noorie's bridal gifts, Halima displayed those for the groom's family, all elegantly packed in velvet boxes. When it came to a purple party gown, Halima raised it above her shoulders and proudly added, "And this, ladies, is from my family. I chose this colour. Look at the work on the front of the gown — is it not superb?"

One lady sneered, holding a hand across her face, whispering, "See how she shows off her own family's present!"

Her friend mischievously smiled in agreement, eyeing carefully the next outfit in Halima's hand, wondering which tailor in Kabul had designed that particular white suit for Noorie's mother-in-law. The design with its fine stitching in different colours was very eye-catching indeed. And she intended on using the same design for her next Afghani suit.

In the other section of the house, the male guests, from young teenagers to grandfathers in their seventies, were patiently waiting for the bride's father to join them. They had been informed that Fazal Karim had gone to the airport to pick up their very special guest — an Englishman he had befriended in Abu Dhabi.

All afternoon, the talk had centred on this special mehman. Some of the guests were quite apprehensive. They had come to enjoy themselves and did not relish the prospect of having the wedding ambience dictated by the presence of an outsider from another race, culture and country.

A nervous silence descended in the room when someone announced, "He's here! Fazal Karim has arrived with the foreign guest!" All rose expectantly to their feet to greet Noorie's father and his guest. But Fazal Karim did not come to their gathering. Instead, he had headed straight to the women's room to introduce Nigel to his mother, who was sitting on a high upholstered chair, her head and body draped in a special shawl designed for her granddaughter's wedding over a beige shalwar kameez suit. "This is my mother, sir!"

Fazal Karim had made special allowance for Nigel to enter the women's domain. Gulchara had been alerted ahead by phone that the two men were visiting that room first. The formal notice gave the female wedding guests time to discreetly drape or rearrange their veils around their bodies and heads. Some, too shy to appear in front of a European male guest, had retreated into another side room. In Pashto, his mother tongue, Fazal Karim proudly addressed his mother.

"This is Our Angel who has transformed our lives. Please bless him."

With tears in her rheumy, grey-blue eyes, his mother shyly raised her wizened hand with two bent arthritic fingers to pat the tall white man. She knew well that it was due to this man that her beloved son Fazal Karim had returned home and their Noorie was getting married that day. Smiling broadly, Nigel ducked his head in front of her, and offered his shoulder for her to pat. Then remembering Fazal Karim's advice about appropriate manners and the etiquette of greeting Muslim women in his household, he reached for her hand, kissed it on the back, and then blushed red, concerned that the old lady might find the action offensive.

Her beaming face reassured Nigel. When Gulchara, too, bashfully stood in front of him with her lowered eyes, offering her greetings with a whispered "Hello", Nigel knew he was indeed being honoured. In arranging for him to meet the women of the house, Fazal Karim had compromised traditional etiquette for his sake.

The fact of the matter was that his interaction with western people for over two decades had enabled Fazal Karim to understand and appreciate their customs. Fazal Karim's conscience had dictated that he had little choice but to present his entire family to Nigel, their benefactor for Noorie's wedding. Similarly, it would have been mean-spirited of Fazal Karim to stop his family from meeting the man who had become their Angel. A man who was so generous and humble in his bearing had to be introduced to all the female members of his family.

"I'm a master in my own household!" Fazal Karim had firmly reminded himself. Even if some male relatives later complained that he was allowing strange men to interact with his female family members, he did not care. It was his family and he, Fazal Karim, would decide what was right or wrong. He would not be oppressed by social pressures nor would he let his women be bullied or oppressed by them. Over the years he had compromised on many social customs, particularly relating to women, and he was very happy at having done so.

Still, he prayed to his Almighty Allah that their generous guest might not become a liability with his wedding guests, especially with the groom's family, as a result of any cultural clashes. Straightaway this concern was laid to rest, as Nigel in his typical suave manner blended in with the environment, the wedding guests, and the occasion.

"He's a man of the world and, of course, knows how to behave. Why was I so worried about him? He's very sensitive about our cultural practices and I know he'll not offend anyone either directly or indirectly," Fazal Karim happily reassured himself.

He was delighted at the way Nigel had taken his shoes off and immediately taken to squatting on a pile of cushions on the floor with the other men and sipping the hot chai whilst munching away on the little sugar rock in his mouth. When a huge platter of Seekhi kebab and Kabuli pulao was placed in front of him, Nigel helped himself using his fingers and with such ease as if he had eaten that way all his life. With great

133

interest, some male guests surreptitiously watched Nigel as he ate. Relaxing and smiling in his company, they continued with their own energetic eating.

Later in the marquee set up in the courtyard of Fazal Karim's home, Nigel had taken part in the high-spirited Afghani Attan dance accompanied by traditional wedding music. The groom, dressed in an Afghani green chappen tunic, and with his elegant Qulay Post hat, also joined in the dancing.

Inside the two-storey house after the wedding dinner, the women too were busy with their lively Attan dancing in rows, after enjoying the entertainment provided by a professional female dancer and singer. Older women were howling with laughter, joining in the clapping to spur the dancers on. Noorie, the bride, watched happily from the bridal sofa.

It was while Noorie was having her meal in her grandmother's room that her father arranged for Nigel to meet her in person, letting him freely gaze at his daughter in her green wedding dress and veil, which showed off her newly styled hair, fronted by the large gem-encrusted matikka. Regarding him as a member of his family, Fazal Karim allowed Nigel to take photos of his Noorie.

"You can sit with my Noorie, Nigel Sir. You are like uncle. Take many pictures, but please not show men. Only you and your family can see. You understand, Sir Nigel?" he asked.

Nigel vigorously nodded his head, happily sitting beside the bride.

Noorie greeted and smiled at their special guest, with her face partially hidden behind a gauzy veil, which upon a signal from her father she pulled aside, letting him see her properly.

Nigel peered into her kohl-lined big grey eyes. "I've come Noorie, for your wedding. Can you believe it?"

"I'm so, so happy to have you here, sir. We are all so very happy. You know why! I am getting married today rather than next year because of you – and I'm so happy to marry my husband Ashar. You made that possible for us, Sir Nigel. Thank you so much, because …" She stopped, unable to share details about the threat Qadsia had posed in trying to poach her fiancé for her own daughter, Laila.

Noorie's fervent tone and the tremor in her voice moved Nigel deeply. He wanted to shake her hand or hug her, but was afraid to risk it. His host family were honouring him by compromising their traditions. He did not want to jeopardise the friendship by unwittingly taking any wrong steps.

"Please, Noorie, don't call me that," he said jokingly. "You can call me Uncle Nigel."

"OK – 'Nice Uncle Nigel'."

They both giggled. Bemused, Fazal Karim looked on, not fully hearing what they had said. In his local culture, this would not be a normal occurrence for him, as the father of the bride, to allow Nigel, an outsider, to sit beside his daughter and pose for photos. But having mixed freely with people from other ethnic groups, Fazal Karim found that his ideas about life and culture had changed over time.

Enjoying his position as the head of his family, Fazal Karim believed that he was entitled to make the right decisions about his children's welfare. He knew that his Noorie would, at times, be openly mixing with men – even with foreign ones – when she worked. So why not let her get used to interaction with other men and build up her confidence in the process, he thought wisely.

Nigel was admiring the rich patterns of the silk rug on the floor of Fazal Karim's reception room. He bent down to trace his fingers over the soft surface.

"Do you like it, sir?"

"Yes, Fazal Karim, it's beautiful!" Nigel exclaimed.

Three hours later, Fazal Karim's eldest son, Ali, appeared with a thick carpet roll on his shoulder. Shyly, Fazal Karim announced, "A present for you, sir, as our guest. A carpet for you to take back home."

Nigel unrolled the finely woven silk rug, marvelling at its elegant design and floral patterns, and thrilled at the prospect of taking it back home.

Three days later, Nigel was ready to return home. He had visited some historical sites of Kabul, those not destroyed by the wars. He had also gone shopping in Kabul's Shahr-e-New Kabul bazaar dressed in a baggy shalwar and long tunic stitched specially for him within twelve hours by Fazal Karim's local tailor master. He was also taken to the countryside where he enjoyed walking in the fruit orchards and munching on peanuts.

Nigel was delighted to accompany Noorie's family for the final showing of the gifts to the groom's family. He carried a platter of chocolates and a basket of fruit that he had purchased as his personal gifts to the family.

In the dining area, he was honoured as a special guest, with Noorie as the bride ritually serving him some rice and korma first. A ritual demonstrating that the bride now belonged to that family. Noorie happily smiled her way through the whole evening with her husband beside her, interpreting for him what their European guest had said.

Nigel had finished packing to leave that evening when he shared his secret business plan with Fazal Karim and his eldest son.

"I really like the carpet you bought for me, Ali. I'm thinking of setting up a business in carpets. My cousin in Newcastle can sell them at a good price. It could be a profitable business venture, you see. You could export and we two could import – and if it works, then you'll never have to go back to Abu Dhabi, to drive another taxi ever again, Fazal Karim. Here, I'm leaving you some money to purchase a few rugs for me. We can talk further about this over the phone later. You can run this business from home where you'll have time to spend with your old mother and family. What do you think, my friend?"

Fazal Karim stared at their Angel, his mouth opening and closing wordlessly. He had only taken the money previously as a wedding gift for Noorie. And he was loath to take more, fearing he would be buried under the debt of gratitude.

Nigel read his mind and dilemma. He understood and handed the cash to his son instead.

"Ali can purchase the carpets for me and send them to Newcastle. Any resultant profit we will share. It's a good business proposition for your family, Fazal Karim, believe me, including for your son. He could open a rug shop himself. I'm determined to have you stay in Kabul, Fazal Karim, and not go back to drive that taxi of yours. It's not charity, my friend, please believe me. This business will give me another reason to return and visit your family. I would like that very much."

Fazal Karim nodded his head, smiling. Put like that, it was all heavenly talk!

Fazal Karim, his two sons, and Ashar, his new son-in-law, saw Nigel off at the airport, hugging him warmly before they let him go. Once inside the plane, Nigel rested his head, his mind with the family back in Kabul and a glorious feeling running through him. The money he had spent on this trip had not made a hole in his bank account; it had merely dented his savings a little. The difference he had made to their lives, however, he could only guess at.

That difference in their lives took the shape of Fazal Karim's elderly mother raising her hands up high to her Maker for a long time, offering her fervent prayers. "Please, Allah Pak, may all your blessings be bestowed on this generous man, Our Angel, who has brought so much happiness into our lives, and his family."

From their bed, Fazal Karim's desire-filled eyes roved over his wife, watching her undress, catching his breath as she peeled off her garments. She was about to get into bed still wearing the chemise.

"That too, Gulchara," he whispered. She shot him a coy look.

"Get used to this," he breathed against her throat. Her reply was a soft giggle and a shy smile, accepting his warm caresses. "We have many years to make up for, my dear wife. I want you here in my arms. In twenty years, I've slept only a few months with you."

"Fazal Karim! At this age! You are shameless!" she teased.

"What do you mean? Are you saying this because our daughter has just got married?" He looked down at her face, grazing her soft cheeks with his beard, as he kissed her again. She then let him recapture the moments stolen out of their years of his life spent abroad.

"You are actually going to stay here for months. I can scarcely believe it," she marvelled, snuggling into his arms, relishing the warm embrace.

Early in the morning, Gulchara was about to slide out of the bed but Fazal Karim stopped her.

"You rest. I'm here now. I'll see to Mother. Don't get up until I wake you." He was out of bed and off to see to his mother's breakfast before his wife could argue.

Gulchara turned on her side and went back to sleep. To her shame, she did not get up until ten o'clock. Her husband had excused her absence with a wink and a secretive smile, as he negotiated the price of the silk rugs with the local carpet seller over the phone — witnessed by his mother, who laid her wizened hand possessively on his arm, her son who had been returned to them by a very special man: their Angel.

An Elopement

Manchester, UK, 1977

The telephone was ringing again. The three women in the living room jumped visibly. They exchanged quick glances, silent messages passing from one to the other.

No one spoke.

The phone began to ring persistently. Two pairs of eyes turned to one figure seated by the window.

Suriya Qureshi knew that her two teenage daughters were waiting for a sign from her. Waiting to see whether she would get up and answer the phone herself.

She disappointed them. By a nod of her head she motioned to her youngest daughter, Farina. Out of her three daughters she was the good conversationalist. She could cope with any situation. Farina, however, drew further into the settee and nudged her older sister Nadia.

"You go," she hissed.

Nadia got up very reluctantly, nearly tripping over her sister's feet as she made a dash for the door and disappeared into the hallway.

In the living room, mother and daughter stared at one another, their hearts literally in their mouths, their ears cocked to the conversation going on over the telephone. In both heads the same thought hammered. *Was it her?* They listened intently, trying to glean information from the nuances of words and phrases that Nadia was using. The mother's head fell back against the sofa.

It was not her. It was not Rubiya. Nadia would not be speaking to her like that. Her words were too polite and stilted. It sounded as if she was speaking to her Aunt Jamila. Oh, not her again. Nadia was talking about Rubiya. Surely Jamila had not found out about Rubiya – surely not! Oh God! She could not bear it. She felt faint.

"I bet she suspects something and is now trying to get the full story from Nadia. She is very good at doing that. Oh God, why didn't I answer the phone and shut her up. Surely Nadia hasn't gone mad and blabbed out the truth?"

For a moment, Suriya did not realise that she had spoken out loud, until she saw her daughter's expression. Ignoring the look on Farina's face, she decided that she must do something. She would go out and have a word with Jamila herself. Just as she got up from her seat, however, she heard the clicking sound of the phone as Nadia replaced the receiver on its cradle. Too late.

Nadia entered.

The others immediately turned towards her, anxiously scanning her face for clues as to what had passed. The girl gave her mother and sister a watery smile, knowing all too well what they were thinking about. She came further into the room and sat down gingerly in the vacant place beside her sister, then addressed their mother.

"It was Aunt Jamila. She wanted to know whether Rubiya would sew a shalwar kameez suit for her."

"What did you say?" Suriya interrupted her daughter quickly.

"I told her that Rubiya was out, visiting a friend of hers — therefore she could not say whether she would be able to do it or not. Auntie then added that she would drop in later this evening or tomorrow afternoon with the suit." Nadia exchanged a significant glance with her mother.

Suriya's heart sank. Oh God, Jamila on top of everything else. She feared this sister-in-law as she did no other person, excepting her husband. Jamila, with her eagle eyes and her sharp mind, was sure to find out the truth. They could not lie to her — not to her. She was sure the horrible truth was written on their faces. Jamila would sense immediately that something was amiss. In fact, everything was amiss. They were not the same, their thoughts and actions were no longer the same. Ever since yesterday afternoon, it felt as if they had entered another world — a theatre in which they themselves were puppets, with Rubiya as the master puppeteer.

The woman still marvelled at the fact that her husband had not found out. It was a sheer miracle that Haji Farook Din did not know that his eldest daughter Rubiya had not been seen in the house since yesterday morning. He had no idea that she had left home and eloped with a young man, God knew where to. A two-minute telephone call from a phone box yesterday evening gave them the most shocking and shameful information. She was going away with this man, she said, and that was all they needed to know.

Suriya Qureshi and her other two daughters had been devastated. Their world turned upside down there and then.

When the phone call had come, Haji Farook was out. Nor was he at home when Farina had rushed in with the unbelievable news that she had seen Rubiya getting into a car with a strange man and then driving off without saying anything. Farina omitted to add that she had seen the man with Rubiya before. At breakfast-time this morning, Haji Farook had not commented on his daughter's absence. He probably thought that she was upstairs somewhere or still asleep. It would not have occurred to him in a million years that his eldest daughter was missing – that she had not slept in her own bed but was out there in the night with some young man.

Why, the news would kill her husband, Suriya thought. He would never recover from the shame. Like the father of the girl in that disgraceful affair they had heard about last year who, long after the affair was over, was in and out of hospital. No, Haji Farook would never be able to hold his head upright again in public, in their community, amongst their relatives and friends.

Had she herself not died a thousand deaths since yesterday afternoon? She still could not believe that this was happening to her, to them. It could not be. It was a long nightmare, from which she must wake up. Oh, Allah Pak, she must. It could not be true. In a few seconds her complacent, happy and respectable – oh so respectable – world had toppled: to be replaced by this wretchedness. Her daughter, surely, could not do this to them. She could not be so cruel. What had they done to deserve this treatment? Her father a Haji too! Shame on her!

They had heard of another such incident some time ago, but had shuffled it aside in their minds. It had no relevance for them. Theirs was a decent family. Neither of the parents could conceive of any of their three daughters behaving like that. They'd felt sorry for the parents who had to suffer the consequences of their daughter's crime. Suriya recalled with bitterness the twist of fate. Once, they had pitied those parents: now they were to be pitied. She couldn't bear the thought. How would she show her face amongst her friends?

What had Rubiya done to them all? How would they survive?

Suriya closed her eyes in anguish, her body rocked by silent sobs. She drew her dupatta over her face in order to hide it from her two daughters, who were watching each and every movement. Rubiya had thrown it all away. Her reputation, that of her parents, her honour – her izzat and theirs – all in one go.

Again, Suriya found it hard to believe that her daughter had left home, perhaps for good, and committed that heinous act. The images it conjured up in her mind left her feeling nauseous. The injustice of it all struck her anew. Every fibre, every cell of her being loathed her daughter. The girl had no right to cause such suffering in their household, to create such havoc in their lives.

At the moment, only she and her two daughters knew about this. She daren't think what would happen if her husband found out, or any of their relatives – especially Jamila, who would never allow them to recover from the incident. On the contrary, she would gloatingly force her point home – that this was what happened if you gave your daughters too much freedom and let them become too westernised. Suriya closed her eyes tightly, wanting to shut out the picture of the outside world. She'd never be ready to confront it again.

For how long could the three of them hide the truth from her husband and other people? Jamila had said she was coming and she was bound to find out that Rubiya was missing. Already, one whole day had passed. This afternoon had given Suriya a taste of what her ordeal was going to be like if her eldest daughter did not return. The unexpected appearance of Neelum, one of Rubiya's friends, calling by at the house, had thrown the three into jitters, and they'd had to resort to excuses and lies to explain her absence. They fidgeted with their rings, their hair, their bangles and their clothes, hardly paying any attention to what Neelum was saying. Their thoughts were all focused on Rubiya and the telephone, willing her to get in touch. The girls could manage only monosyllabic conversation, and they were sure that their nervousness was apparent and would arouse suspicion. They were relieved when their visitor left.

Even amongst themselves, the subject of Rubiya's elopement was taboo. It was too terrible to discuss openly. Farina and Nadia were unable to voice their thoughts, but inwardly both condemned their sister's action. Had she taken leave of her senses? They shuddered at the thought of their sister being in close proximity with a strange man. They tried to put themselves in her place and imagine what she felt and what must have compelled her to do what she did. Their minds, however, shied away from the situation. They knew the man Rubiya was infatuated with. There was no other term to describe this relationship. While Rubiya might have described it as 'love', they would have labelled it as infatuation and sheer madness. Although younger than Rubiya, they knew their limits. They despised their sister's desire to ape their English girlfriends by having a boyfriend. It would never work, they were convinced. The couple would tire of each other soon enough, especially when they couldn't survive in a social vacuum, surrounded by shame and rejection.

Nadia cursed herself over and over again. She was the one to blame. She had known what was going on but had done nothing about it, when she ought to have warned her mother. Now Rubiya was lost to them forever. Even if she came back, their sister would carry the stigma, the stain of her action, for the rest of her days. Worst of all, she had let her family down. The scandal would affect them too, for the rest of their lives.

Rubiya had not only slammed the door on her future, but theirs too. The elopement would mean that their own freedom to go when and where they pleased would be curtailed. They would, in fact, be made to suffer for her crime. Already their mother had lost her trust in them. It was almost as if she expected them to do a disappearing act too, as if they would elope any minute. Thinking back, Farina and Nadia realised they had not been out of doors since yesterday afternoon.

Neither girl could bear to think of the social repercussions. Friends and relatives would be pointing accusing fingers at them – referring to them as 'the sisters of that girl'. They would be in the unwelcome limelight, and each and every action of theirs would be scrutinised and criticised.

If their father found out – each sister shivered at the thought – why, he would never allow them out of the front door! What had too much freedom brought them? he would roar. Nothing but shame and disgrace! They would bear the brunt of his anger. The girls felt sorry for their father. From being a very respectable member of their community he would become the victim of the community's gossip; of their pity for him having fathered such daughters.

Their mother too was a bag of nerves. She had not eaten or slept since yesterday. Last night she had paced around the house, keeping awake in case Rubiya turned up. From nine o'clock this morning she had not left her seat by the window. If the telephone rang she shuddered but did not have the nerve, however, to go and answer it herself. Her girls understood. She would not know what to say to Rubiya, if it was her. She did not want to speak to her. Mentally, she had already cast her out as her daughter. No love remained in her heart for this child, only a burning contempt.

Since yesterday afternoon their house had become a shambles. The everyday routine of washing and tidying up had been neglected. The girls still marvelled at themselves, for despite what they were going through, they had managed to cook the evening meal, albeit in silence, and to act as normally as possible when their father came home for dinner yesterday afternoon and last night. After staying with their parents for what they felt was an adequate time so as not to arouse their father's attention, Farina and Nadia escaped to their rooms. At some time or another they had dropped the hint that Rubiya was upstairs in her room. During the rest of the evening they waited nervously, expecting any minute for their father to blow his top. Flicking through some paperbacks, they waited, trembling, until ten o'clock. Everything, however, appeared as usual downstairs. They even heard their father laughing at something. Both felt sorry for their mother's predicament.

When their father actually came upstairs and went to bed, their hearts stood still with relief. They couldn't believe their luck. He did not know! They marvelled furthermore when he did not notice Rubiya's absence at breakfast-time too, the next morning.

Tonight, however, was going to be different. Their father was bound to notice that his daughter was missing. What if he took it into his head to go and see Rubiya – check on how she was doing? They'd mumbled something earlier about her having a headache. They had lied. The next time, it would have to be the dreadful truth!

At six o'clock when their father came home, the girls felt very edgy. They did not know what to do with themselves – how to behave; what to say. All they seemed to be doing was exchanging silent glances with one another.

Mother and daughters waited on tenterhooks for him to mention Rubiya. In Nadia's head, a plan was already forming. If her father wanted to visit his daughter in her bedroom, then she'd sleep in Rubiya's bed and pretend to be her — and hope that he wouldn't wake her up if he saw her fast asleep.

They'd toyed with their meal, very much aware of the tension mounting up in the dining room. It was almost tangible; they were sure they could slice their way through it with a knife.

Back in the living room, after the meal and the clearing up in the kitchen, television held no interest for them. Usually Thursday evening found the girls glued to their TV set, especially for *Top of the Pops*. Today, however, when their father switched onto another channel, they did not bat an eyelid. Their thoughts were elsewhere. They were busy devising ways of creeping out of the room without arousing their father's interest. Haji Farook, an intelligent and perceptive man, couldn't help but notice the mood in the house. At one stage in the evening he commented on the fact that they all seemed out of sorts.

At about nine o'clock he got up and went out of the room. The girls relaxed — too soon. When they heard him climb the stairs, they looked at their mother. Fear was etched on her features. They too were afraid. *What if he took it into his head to look in on Rubiya?* they asked themselves.

Nadia got up resolutely. She knew what she was going to do. Her father was in the bathroom. They could tell by the treading of his feet above. Perhaps she still had time to carry out her plan. She hurried out of the room.

Just then, Suriya heard the back door open and then click shut. *What was Nadia up to?* she asked herself. It was not the day for the dustbins to be placed outside. She waited for her to return so that she could ask her this. At the same time she was listening to her husband's footsteps overhead. Her heart

149

had begun to beat a tattoo again. His footsteps were now in Rubiya's room.

This was the moment they had all feared. Now the whole world would explode. Suriya shrank inwards – she could not cope with this!

Farina was listening to her father's footsteps too, her eyes goggling above at the ceiling.

Neither the mother nor the daughter noticed the living-room door open and a young woman dressed in outdoor clothes enter the room.

When Suriya caught sight of her, she almost leaped out of her seat. Farina's mouth fell open; she was unable to believe her eyes. It was almost as if they were watching a Shakespeare play at the Royal Exchange Theatre.

"Rubiya . . ." She whispered the magical word. Surely her eyes were playing tricks on her. For there stood Rubiya, looking worn out and dishevelled. She was apparently struggling to stick a brave and confident expression on her face, but without much success.

Not daring to look at her mother, she addressed her sister.

"I came round the back way," she said quietly as if in explanation of how she had got inside the house. She held the key out to her sister. As the steps thudded down the stairs, three pairs of eyes turned to the door. Rubiya swivelled a desperate look at her mother. Suriya stared back, her face expressionless. She was already thinking ahead – and in control once again. She was the puppeteer now, not Rubiya, her daughter.

On entering the room, Haji Farook noticed his eldest daughter standing there. A baffled expression settled on his face. He looked at his wife and his youngest daughter, Farina, for an explanation. He then turned back to look at Rubiya.

"I thought you had a headache," he said. "Nadia just told me you were asleep." He noticed for the first time the outdoor summer jacket that Rubiya was wearing and the handbag she was clutching to her side. Where had she been?

Suriya had already decided upon her answer a minute ago.

"Rubiya went to Jamila's house just before you returned home. Your sister wanted her to sew a kameez for her. Nadia did not know about this. Jamila has just dropped her off . . ."

"Go to bed, child," her father told her. "Why, you look worn out. You should not have gone there if you had a headache." With a wave of his hand, Haji Farook dismissed his daughter. Then, unaware of the charade-like nature of the situation, he settled in his seat to await the *Nine O'Clock News* on BBC1.

Rubiya could not believe her luck. He did not know! Damn that other man! *Damn him!* she cursed, and then grieved. She would never be the same again. What a fool she had been.

Her head held high, she muttered her "Good night," to no one in particular. As she left the room, however, she felt her mother's and sisters' eyes boring into her back.

Last Train to Krakow

Auschwitz-Birkenau Complex, Poland; Budapest, Hungary, January 1943

Woken by a fierce cramp in her stomach, Karolina knew that she needed to visit the latrine. Terrified of waking the three other women who shared the top bunk, she prised her aching body from her twin sister Ilana's arms. Then, slipping her hand under Ilana's dress, she carried out the routine check to see if she had wet the bed: thankfully, the straw on which they lay was dry. As she did this, Ilana's head accidentally knocked against the bony shoulder of the fifty-one-year-old Ewa.

"Shift yourself, you stupid cow!" Ewa groaned in her sleep. Her hollowed eyes remained closed while a scrawny hand reached up to scratch her lice-infested scalp. Once, Ewa had been a proud hairdresser in Krakow's main square with a cap of glossy auburn curls; now her cropped hair was greasy and heavily beaded with rows of shiny louse eggs.

Another stomach cramp, more urgent than the first, had Karolina climbing down to the floor of their barrack. She and the other inmates were all women from the Krakow Jewish ghetto.

The cold dawn air chilled her bare legs as she squatted over a hole in the sewer slabs; by now, the sight and stench of human waste from hundreds of prisoners no longer revolted her. The devilish tornado in her stomach did its job well, flushing out the remains of cabbage soup and stale bread eaten the previous night. When some droplets landed on her bare ankles, Karolina grimaced in disgust. Lifting her dress up, she hobbled over to the communal sink to wash her hands and legs. Then, standing on tiptoe, she peered through the soot-grimed window.

Outside the barracks, some Polish and German Kapo guards stood on duty; others lounged against the wall or took turns to rest on wooden chairs.

The young woman's gaze flitted to the imposing building in the far distance. Its tall chimneys were still belching out a pungent dark smoke, scarring the early morning blue skies. Last night, before clambering into bed, she had watched that smoke hovering over the buildings in the neighbouring camp – Auschwitz – before the wind ruthlessly directed it towards their huts and the woodlands beyond, now swathed in snowflakes.

It was the start of another wretched day in Birkenau. Petrified and starving, Karolina and her twin sister were still waiting to learn their fate.

The Hungarian freight train, on schedule and straining with its human cargo, clattered through the icy forests of Poland. Inside the carriages, women, the elderly and young children were crammed together, some standing, others semi-squatting on top of their suitcases or holding onto their beloved children and babies. Limbs and hands ached from clinging on to their precious possessions. With only a few inches of space between them, everyone nervously avoided touching the others or making eye contact in the dimness of their surroundings.

Nine months pregnant with her first baby, twenty-four-year-old Hela's waters had just broken. Her frail mother Janina, face pinched with worry, held on to her as Hela lifted up her long velvet skirt and woollen coat with its yellow Star of David. Her stomach heaving from the pain of the next contraction, she vomited into the latrine bucket. Mortified by the disapproving looks on the faces of the two women standing nearby, Janina wiped Hela's sweat-dotted forehead with the end of her small cotton napkin.

The fervent Hebrew chanting by the older women had begun. "O Lord help us! Let us find peace in our new homes in Krakow!"

Some wondered if the Judenrat, the Krakow Jewish council, would really be able to help them settle in Poland. Others were too exhausted by the rigours of the journey to chant. They merely echoed the same prayer in their heads – for God to provide them with a new home, safe from abuse, humiliation and danger at the hands of Hitler's ruthless followers.

Thousands of them were heading for the Jewish quarter in the Kazimierz district of Krakow. Fear of the unknown was visible on all their faces, along with tears of grief, a longing to be back in their original homes, leading their old lives in the country they had left behind – their homeland.

Hela's fear was of a more immediate nature – of giving birth here and now, in these nightmare conditions. The labour pains had begun the moment the German SS soldier had hauled her up onto the train after she went to relieve her bladder behind the bushes. She had lost her step and fallen, screaming in agony when another woman tripped over her, pressing Hela's abdomen down hard on the dirty wet floor of the cattle truck.

The journey had been traumatic. The Nazis had set up a system: after three days of energetic racing through the

Hungarian countryside and into Poland, the trains would eventually come to a noisy halt. Their raging hot engines would have but a few minutes' respite to cool down before heading back to Budapest to pick up the next round of two thousand Hungarian Jews. Each cattle truck was intended to carry between thirty and forty people but was regularly packed with up to eighty passengers. And then the trucks were locked, with no access to water, food or ventilation apart from the cold air coming through gaps.

The Jewish passengers were told that this was the last train to Krakow. It had set off from Budapest at one of the collection points in the city: the imposing synagogue in Dohany Street – a beautiful, majestic building and the largest synagogue in Europe. It was here that the women had camped for one day, anxiously awaiting their turn to board the train to join their menfolk, who had left a few days earlier. Prior to that, they, like many other Jewish families, had been herded at gunpoint out of their homes and taken to the camp in Pest, ready for resettlement in Poland.

Their minds were numb with apprehension, but their hearts refused to believe the rumours circulating that their journey was part of the Hungarian and German initiative, the *Entjudung* – the deportation process organised by two hard-line Jew-hating Hungarian officials, Baky and Endre, in collusion with German officials. When the train with their menfolk had departed for Krakow, the anxious women had been assured that they were being taken to oversee the arrangements for the family accommodation.

In this particular carriage, food and water had run out after one day on the train. There was only so much the women could carry with them. Nor had they been informed properly of how long the journey would take to reach their destination. By dawn of the next day, the Hebrew mourning prayers had begun. One toddler and an eighty-year-old woman died gasping for air in the arms of their loved ones.

The mother was hysterical, cradling her small son to her chest. The daughter-in-law of the old lady named Leah wept quietly, clasping the wizened body in her arms. She was deeply affronted by the averted gazes and the manner in which others had sidled away from her, even though there was hardly any space to move.

In the semi-darkness, Hela's mother clung on to the holdall of baby clothes; inside was a blue woollen suit with matching hat and mittens that she had knitted in the last four days whilst preparing for the journey.

When there was a loud thud on the truck from outside, everyone became alert, and then the doors were noisily dragged back. Exhausted eyes blinked at the rays of light filtering into the carriage. Sounds of deep breathing could be heard, as the passengers welcomed the fresh but chilly morning air. All got ready to get off the train, groaning in pain from stiffened limbs and knee joints. The sharp order, '*Herauskommen!*' had an immediate effect.

Gathering their belongings and children, the women scrambled down from the train, ready to crowd into the buses that were no doubt assembled to take them to the Kazimierz district of Krakow. Those with their dead, however, were in no rush to leave, too stunned by grief to care what happened next. Hela and her mother stayed with this group, waiting for Hela to be taken straight to a hospital to deliver her baby.

But as the passengers stepped down onto the platform, stumbling over luggage items, they gaped in bewilderment at their surroundings. Was *this* the city of Krakow? Surely this could not be the main railway station? There was no sign of

157

urban life: no plaza, streets, shops or cars in sight. Just two railway tracks, desolate-looking rows of barracks in the far distance and an expanse of open land, fringed by snow-coated woodlands.

Near the railway tracks were two blocks of buildings; the tall chimneys from one of them were puffing out large volumes of thick black smoke. The air, they noticed, was heavy with the smell of ash, and the ground near the railway track was covered with a layer of soot.

Children began to whimper, shivering in the cold. Mothers pulled the little ones' woollen hats down over their ears, as well as tightening their own scarves around their heads.

Tall, smartly uniformed German SS men and women were waiting to receive them. Hooded blue eyes watchful beneath the peaks of their grey caps, they assessed the new Hungarian intake. To the delight of most of the passengers, they were informed that they must first refresh themselves by taking showers before continuing their journey into the Krakow district. Faces lit up at the word 'refresh'. Surely that meant they would be offered food and drink too?

"This way! *Schnell!*"

When ordered to leave their belongings on the platform, some were reluctant to abandon their worldly goods out in the open for fear of loss and theft, even with the guards supervising everything. Others meekly followed the orders, too weary to care and eager to wash off the filth and the stench of the train.

When the name of Dr Gyorgy Havas was called out, a white-coated man materialised in the midst of the SS officers. The women were then ordered to get into two groups. The younger, stronger women – immediately assessed as the 'usable' ones – were directed to assemble on one side of the track, whilst the rest, including some old men, were led into the buildings. On the road parallel to the rail tracks, five trucks were waiting to carry out their allotted duties. They had arrived, as planned, the moment the empty freight train had departed.

Hela looked around, hoping to catch a glimpse of her husband Laszlo, desperate to be with him at the time of the birth of their first child. Exhausted children were squealing for food and water. Distressed mothers gently shushed them, reminding them that they would get something to eat soon. As if reading their minds, two SS women handed out candies to the little ones, eliciting wan smiles on the faces of their mothers.

One woman, anxious to both feed and wash her nine-month-old baby, insisted on taking her bag with the baby milk powder and clothes into the building. The child's non-stop crying on the train was due to the stinging rash on his bottom from a heavily soiled nappy. The SS men sternly admonished her, pointing to the floor. Mouth quivering and eyes large in her strained face, the Rabbi's daughter handed the bag over, looking beseechingly at her fellow passengers for some support. Helplessly, they looked away.

Dr Havas, meanwhile, was busy with his task of assessing the remaining newcomers from his vantage point a few yards away. Catching his eye, Janina alerted him to her daughter's plight. Hela was by now a heaving mass of labour pain. A wry smile touched the face of the man in the white coat as he walked swiftly towards her through the crowd of people.

Standing by Hela, he debated which side he should assign her to: should it be to the right or to the left? To go with her mother to the showers or be transferred to Dr Josef Mengele's experimental medical ward? In the end, the older woman decided for him. In both Hungarian and German, she pleaded that he take her daughter away to deliver her baby.

159

Hela, however, insisted on washing herself first, desperate to get clean before giving birth. Switching his bemused gaze from mother to daughter, the doctor came to his decision. Shrugging his shoulders, he made the appropriate signal to the SS officer in charge. Hela would remain in the line with her mother.

The older men and women, and mothers with children, were made to file into the building. The group of young women who were left looked wistfully over their shoulders at their relatives, as they were marched off in the other direction.

Inside the building, the new arrivals were herded into a cold, unfurnished hall where they were instructed to undress before entering the showers. All were given individual number chits to place on their pile of clothes and were asked to memorise them. "So that you can all easily identify your clothes later." Those were the reassuring words of one Kapo who was in charge of overseeing their arrival and stay.

Most women stood horror-struck at the prospect of revealing their nude bodies to others. They had expected some level of privacy like individual cubicles, not hundreds of women disrobing at the same time, in the same hall. And in front of eleven elderly men!

The deadpan faces of the German SS staff matched the aggressive expressions of their minions, the Kapo – Polish prisoners entrusted by the Germans to carry out various unpleasant duties for them. The Kapo did their overlords proud in their demonstration of ruthlessness. New arrivals quickly learned the importance of the Kapo staff's role and the fact that they had to obey the latter, otherwise they would be shot or hurt.

Alarmed and fearful mothers began to fumble with their children's buttons, collars and shoe laces, wrenching off shoes and hurriedly stripping away three days of travel-stained clothing. When it came to baring their bodies, those with children stood them as props in front of their bodies, shielding their private parts. Ashamed, those without children held one arm across their breasts, whilst their other hand remained protectively over their pubic areas.

There was no interest in the bodies of others, only shame at showing one's own. The women did not care to note whether the breasts of others were upright or sagging, small or large, or with pointed or inverted nipples. For everyone was in the same humiliating predicament. Young children began to wail, still hungry, thirsty and shivering from the cold.

The appearance of large pairs of scissors and shaving equipment in the hands of the Kapo staff frightened the women into a stillness. They listened to the brusque announcement informing them of the need to have their hair cut before showering. Dazed and distressed at the thought of having their hair shorn off, the women meekly began to pull out the pins from their buns and chignons, and to unwind their braids. The Orthodox married women wearing sheitels – marriage wigs – reluctantly removed them, revealing their own natural hair. Long plaits, neatly sheared away, fell on the concrete floor, and curly tresses were caught in large bags by the Kapo staff. Then the brutal shaving of heads began. Traumatised, but too afraid to utter a word of protest, the women bowed their heads to their new ordeal.

Bemused, Hela watched the scene around her, swaying under the strain of another tumultuous contraction. Her pregnant torso appeared monstrous above her long, thin legs. Janina, standing naked and shivering by her daughter's side, tugged at the arm of the woman Kapo and pointed to her daughter's abdomen, expecting her to understand.

"First the shower. Then the doctor," snarled the woman in accented German.

A tall female Kapo with a large pair of scissors was heading towards Janina, her gaze sweeping over Hela's head and then down to her pregnant belly. Hela's body contorted with another contraction, just as the Kapo grasped her mother's wiry grey plait, tied in a circlet around her head. The ten-inch-long braid was snipped away. The next minute, the same callused hands were on Hela's head, wrenching it upright and cutting away the soft, shoulder-length brown curls.

"Much easier to wash," muttered the scowling woman Kapo, confronted with Hela's condemning look.

The other women tentatively felt their scalps with trembling hands, recoiling from the short tufts of hair. The remains of their crowning glory were carelessly shovelled away into bags by Kapo staff, scurrying around with brooms.

Hela, who was in too much pain to care about her hair, ignored her mother's gaping mouth. The word 'why?' never left Janina's lips, however, as the SS women briskly shepherded the naked and shorn women and children into a line, to lead them into the large 'communal shower hall'.

Hela just wanted to lie down on the cold floor of that hall and give birth to her baby, there and then. The heavy pressure on her pelvic floor had pushed the baby's head right down, fully opening up the neck of her cervix.

Her mother, holding onto her arm, whispered words of encouragement. "Hold on, my Hela!"

Hela nodded, squeezing her eyes shut, recalling the filthy conditions on the train. She had to hold on, so she could shower and get clean before bringing her baby into the world.

"Ready?" commanded the German SS woman, facing the line of naked women and children. "Remember the number for your clothes!"

Hela with her mother had been given the number 65. Another contraction hit her. Holding her arm against her chest to hide her ageing breasts, Janina hurried over to the older SS woman directing women into the shower hall.

"My daughter is about to give birth! Please call the doctor!" she implored.

"Shower first!" hissed a female Kapo.

Hela staggered by her mother's side, the last ones in the queue of women shielding their naked flesh behind the bodies of others. The cold from the damp, flaky walls and the concrete floor shot through everyone's tender bare soles.

Doubled over in agony, "Mother! I need to lie down!" Hela cried urgently, letting out another howl of pain.

The Kapo women ignored her but continued to usher everyone into the shower room. Hela was the last to enter it, leaning heavily against the wall, hugging her baby mound with her arm.

Everyone looked around nervously, eyes feverishly seeking shower cubicles. There were too many people packed in one shower room. How would they all wash themselves in such a cramped space? And where was the soap they so desperately needed?

Janina looked away from the sight and smell of unwashed naked flesh, the trim bodies as well as the sagging aged flesh, the protruding breasts and waistlines, the flat and the rounded buttocks. The children nervously clutching at their mothers' hands, swamped by tall adult bodies. A four-year-old girl whimpered in pain, nearly crushed between two overweight women. Her mother, desperate to wash, merely shushed her, too weak to pick her up and carry her in her arms.

Sounds of human panic echoed around the shower hall. This was intolerable. Something was not right. Fear spread from one person to the next.

Janina pressed against the wall near the door, worried that the water spray would not reach her and Hela's body; the nearest shower head was a few yards away.

"Mother!" Hela screamed. The primitive urge to push the baby out had become overpowering. Weeping, her mother held on to her.

Others in the shower room were intent on waiting for the gushing sound of hot water to spray their bodies. They did not hear the muffled sounds of booted feet on the floor above, nor see the ripping off of the lids of large sealed aluminium cans. Upstairs, thick leather gloves were pulled on and masks hastily donned. There was to be no dilly-dallying: there were three more shifts to be got through on time. Two other trains were expected that day. The men, quick and experienced in their tasks, worked fast and efficiently.

Down below in the shower hall, people jostled for better position, elbowing others for space to stand directly under the shower heads.

"Go on! Push, my darling!" Janina urged, squatting down on the floor beside her daughter. From behind she heard gasps of horror. She turned. Necks were craned, all looking up at the ceiling, eyes wide and mouths parted.

Janina too looked up, her heart coming to a sickening halt. There was no water. Instead, smoky fumes were curling down from the holes in the shower heads, creating a yellowy canopy over their heads, screening the shower heads from sight.

"It's gas!" someone shouted.

Terrified, women fought each other in an attempt to reach the door. Some fell, and were crushed under the weight of others. Then the screams and coughing began – hands clamped against mouths. Mothers pressed their children's faces against their bodies, desperate to protect them from the thick curtain of fumes now snaking around them and stinging their eyes.

Janina, standing beside the door, clawed at the handle, but her feeble efforts were to no avail. Other women joined to pull at it, knocking their fists on the door, shouting, "Help! Help! Please open the door!"

On the other side of the wall, standing at a distance, away from the adult screams of agony and the children's weaker cries, four SS women calmly studied the clock face, timing the gassing process, pleased that they were on schedule.

In the shower room, Janina fought for space and life, battling with the deadly fumes tearing at her throat whilst cradling her newborn granddaughter's body in her arms; her hand in blessing on the baby's mucus-coated head. Eyes closed, Hela was unaware of what was going on around her. Her only mission – to push the baby out of her body – she had at last accomplished.

"God have mercy on us!" The fervent Hebrew and Yiddish chanting continued as the deadly fumes tore at throats and nostrils. The physical agony was now combined with the raw terror of dying.

They all knew.

No longer could they deny the truth. There would be no resettlement in the Kazimierz ghetto in Krakow. Instead, they were the 'raw material' shipped on purpose to the death factory, deported for annihilation, for *Entjudung*. The gas chamber was their ultimate home, their graveyard.

The SS officers, snug in their long, navy greatcoats, stepped out to take a short break – to smoke a cigarette and drink coffee. To enjoy a brief respite, before supervising the next arduous task: the shovelling and shifting of the bodies from the gas chamber into the adjoining building for the next phase of the process. Over a dozen men were even now waiting patiently for a signal from their superiors to wheel their empty trolleys into the building and get on with the job.

A short distance away, outside the prison barracks, the daily '*Appell*' – the roll call, the counting and recounting of prisoners gathered in rows – was about to begin. With frozen feet and empty bellies, the Polish women prisoners faced the Kapo guards.

Karolina nervously leaned her twin sister's body against her own to make her stand upright, tightly holding onto her arm. Ilana, blissfully fearless and unaware of her surroundings, was about to throw one of her periodic tantrums, demanding to be taken back to Krakow, to the room they had shared with another family, overlooking the square in the Jewish ghetto near the old synagogue. Head lowered, she kept muttering, "I want my knitting needles, Karo." She had never quite mastered the purl and knit sequence but loved weaving the woollen thread over the needles. "In out, in out," she chanted, as if practising the purl stitch.

In their prison dresses, the women shivered in the morning chill. The order to stand up straight made Karolina pull at her sister's arm again.

"Ilana, please stand up properly," she urged, and then was horrified as she saw her sister withdrawing her hand smeared with blood from under her dress.

"Karo, I'm bleeding again," Ilana said, afraid of the sight of blood.

"Hush, I'll clean you up later, my darling." Karolina glanced at the reddish-brown stain on the back of her sister's dress, stiffening at the spiteful sniggers from the row behind.

Two more men joined the guards. One was shorter, very formally dressed, and wore glasses. The guards stood up straight and saluted him. It was Dr Mengele. His gaze, however, was drifting over those assembled. Then his eyes hit on the special pair he had had transported from the ghetto. Coolly, he signalled to the guards before strolling back to his office in the medical block.

Karolina was trying to soothe her sister, who was distressed by the mocking whispers coming from behind her.

"Look at that loony! She's simple-minded, isn't she, and her poor sister has to take care of her."

Then, without warning, the guard was upon them. "You two come with me!" he barked.

Meekly, Karolina followed, putting her arm protectively around her sister's cold shoulder. She herself was sweating in the chilly weather. Where were they going? Terror gripped her. One of the women prisoners had whispered that as they were twins, they would be sent to the medical block. The pebbles on the road between the prison blocks at Auschwitz-Birkenau camp dug into their shoes.

In one room in the medical block, the artist waited, standing between his two easels, sharpening his pastel crayons and neatly lining them up on the little wooden stool by his side. A tall nurse, dressed in the prison guard uniform and with a starched cap fixed on her golden-brown shoulder-length hair, stood gazing out of the window, watching people entering the block. When she nodded, the artist perched himself on his painting stool, ready to start work.

After a knock on the door, the guard entered with the twin sisters, Karolina and Ilana, behind him. The nurse addressed him in Polish, making an effort to smile at the two bedraggled young women, obviously sisters, but nobody could tell that they were twins.

"We need to take a copy of the shape of your heads, as part of our Dr Mengele's medical study. To draw your scalp properly, we need to shave off your hair." The nurse paused, averting her eyes from Karolina's shocked gaze. She then grasped a handful of Ilana's hair and began hacking at it with a pair of scissors, trying not to inhale the stale smell of menstrual blood that was caked on her dress.

Karolina watched, mortified, wanting to stop the woman. Ilana squealed in discomfort at the feel of the sharp razor and the cold air on her naked, egg-shaped scalp. She began whimpering like a child, as the artist, stony-faced, led her to perch on the small wooden stool before the easel to the right.

"Sit still," he commanded, annoyed at her twitching movements, afraid of her toppling over. The nurse was working on Karolina's head now, reducing her cap of short, blonde hair to a shiny, white scalp, whilst the artist transferred the shape of Ilana's head onto the canvas. He sketched it from the side position, attempting to show its elongated shape.

Every so often he glanced at Karolina's face. Tears were leaking from her eyes.

When the phone rang, it startled everyone in the room. The nurse reached to answer it.

"Yes, Dr Mengele," she said. "I will bring them in soon. One is done, the other still needs to be sketched. No, they are not identical twins." There was more talking, then the nurse told him, "I'll go and check myself. I'm sure someone mentioned a pregnant woman from that trainload last night from Pest."

Karolina listened, her heart stopping with terror. If only she could swap places with her sister, to lose herself in the world of simplicity and knitting needles.

In the gas chamber which Hela had entered with her mother, the Kapo guards were busy with the checking and removal of items from the piles of corpses, including the brutal ripping out of gold teeth from the victims' mouths, as well as pulling off rings, earrings and gold chains.

"Hey, look – a baby hanging out of the mother!" The men crowded around the two women lying in an embrace of death, with a newborn infant resting on the thigh of the younger one. Many had gasped their last breath in the arms of their loved ones, making it difficult for the guards to prise some bodies apart.

One guard sniggered, suggesting, "Let's take the mother and baby to the medical block. Dr Mengele may reward us for this."

Outside on the platform, some Kapo staff were shifting sacks of hair and the belongings of Hela's group – their suitcases, bags and bulging baskets – onto the waiting trucks destined for the warehouses. Hela's little black leather suitcase with her two dresses, small trinkets of jewellery, her mother's shawls, blouses and two skirts was thrown into the truck, along with Janina's holdall containing the baby clothes. An unworn baby mitten, affectionately crocheted by Hela's elderly Christian neighbour from her old house, before they moved into the 'yellow star houses' in the ghetto in Pest, forlornly lay on the railway tracks; the men walked over it, unseeing.

A short while later, the shrill siren of another goods train from Hungary with its human cargo of more followers of 'the faith of Moses' had the SS men and women hurrying out onto the platform to continue with their mission of *Entjudung*.

In the distance, the crematorium chimneys burned on, angrily belching out great clouds of pungent black smoke, adding another layer of sooty film to the snow-coated white landscape.

The Journey

New Delhi and Kot Badal Khan, India; Lahore, Pakistan, August 1967

Poor Raju was having the same dream again. In it, he was once more the boy he had been, aged seven years old.

"Water, water!" he demanded in his child's piping voice, tugging at the man's arm. A hand clamped hard over his mouth, blocking his cries. Desperate for air, his small hands clawed uselessly at the adult fingers. The man tightened his hold, staring ahead in the dark.

Raju sat up in bed, his heart pounding. Drenched with sweat, his muslin nightshirt clung to his body. The last time he had had the same nightmare was three months ago. This time, it would prove an apt beginning to what lay in store for him that day.

When he returned from taking a shower, Raju's eyes fell on the crisply pressed shirt laid out for him on his bed. Love for his mother welling up, he went looking for her in the kitchen where she was making his favourite breakfast of potato parathas.

"Namaste, Mata ji," Raju greeted her, giving her a hug from behind.

'Namaste, my son," Kumari Patel replied, lathering his paratha with extra ghee.

As Raju waited in the dining room, he read the note his father had placed on the table before leaving the house early to open up his chinaware shop.

Dear Raju,

If you have today decided to do what you've long set your mind on doing, Bhagwan will help you. I wish you luck, my dear son. Just remember that we love you very much. We will always love you, my dear son, no matter what happens.

Your loving Pita ji.

His mother entered and placed two hot parathas and dal before him. Normally they sat together to eat. Not today. Too distraught, she hastened back to the kitchen to hide her wet cheeks and leaking eyes.

Kumari Patel stood sobbing over a simmering pot of milky tea. She had tried so hard to be fair about this, reminding herself many times that she should have faith in her son . . . but the jealousy for an unknown woman continued to torment her.

Nervous energy building up in his stomach, Raju dipped chunks of his paratha into the dal bowl. After he had finished eating, he called out to his mother.

Hurriedly dabbing her eyes with the corner of her sari fold before entering the dining room. Kumari paled at the sight of his suitcase. Despite having packed it herself, it symbolised her loss. She kissed Raju hard on his forehead. He, in turn, bent down to respectfully touch her feet. He couldn't leave without uttering the poignant words.

"I love you, Mata ji."

"I love you too, my son. May Bhagwan take care of you and help you succeed in your mission. Have you got the address?" she fussed before hugging him.

"Yes. It's here in my diary." Raju pointed to the hidden pocket in his coat.

Kumari wanted to say more, but stopped herself.

Picking up his suitcase, the young man turned once more and said, "Goodbye, Mother. I will return."

"Goodbye, my Raju," she said quietly. Time would tell if he returned, but she had no right to keep him. She watched from the front doorway, until she lost sight of the taxi. Once inside, she cried as if her heart would break.

At Attari station, Raju took the Samjhauta Express, showing his first-class ticket to Lahore in Pakistan, and settled into his compartment. On the platform, vendors carrying savoury snacks in overflowing baskets stacked on their shoulders hastened to the train windows, chanting, "Garm samosas, garm pakoras." The satsuma and banana sellers energetically vied for the passengers' attention too. Raju waved them away from his window. Five minutes later, the train shrilled into action, speedily puffing its way towards the Wagah border, separating India from Pakistan.

Raju sat thinking of what was ahead of him and about the people he was likely to meet. What would they be like? What would *He* be like? Raju quickly switched his thoughts to *Her*. Would they resemble the blurred shadows in his mind? And how would they react to his arrival on their doorstep?

He then dozed off and was woken by the train coming to a halt at the Wagah border, where customs and immigration clearances took place.

When the train entered Lahore station in Pakistan late in the afternoon, Raju sat up, a tingle of excitement coursing through him. Yet, peering out of the window, he noted that it was a replica of any other Indian station: the same style of buildings, the same bustling atmosphere and ambiance, with vendors keen to sell their goods. People were everywhere, of the same colour as Indians.

In the taxi, Raju gazed out of the window, letting the scenes of midday Lahore city life roll before his eyes. The taxi rode past the imposing Victorian red-brick buildings of the Lahore Museum and the old University of Punjab campus. The driver skilfully manoeuvred his taxi through the traffic jam of motorcycles, rickshaws, trucks, minibuses and cars, to reach the neater lanes of Mall Road heading towards the airport and the army cantonment area, popularly known as 'Kent' by the Lahorites.

The taxi finally came to a halt in a large street lined with modern shopping plazas and villas. Raju, who had been chatting with the driver about cricket, stopped abruptly, his heart thumping. The driver pointed to an elegant two-storey villa with a white and peach tiled facade, and a wrought-iron balcony circling the upper floor.

Raju paid the driver with the Pakistani rupees he had exchanged in Delhi. The taxi disappeared in the midst of late-afternoon traffic with schoolchildren returning home. Unable to slow the rapid beating of his heart, Raju stood with his suitcase by the side of the house, not quite ready to ring the bell beside the imposing gate and meet its inhabitants.

On the other side of the road was a cafe. Raju walked across and ordered a couple of samosas and a cup of tea. Remembering his mother, he had opted for vegetable samosas. As an orthodox Hindu, she forbade the eating of meat in her household. However, she turned a blind eye to the fact that her son and husband often treated themselves to roast chicken in restaurants.

Raju sat near the window, eyes resting on the house. The muezzin's call to prayers from a local mosque startled him. Some men in the cafe left for their prayers, heading in the direction of the minarets towering behind a row of plazas. Raju's cup of tea remained poised in mid-air, for the gate of the villa had opened and a man of average height had stepped out. Dressed in a traditional white shalwar kameez suit, and with a prayer hat on his head, the man set off in the direction of the mosque. Raju's eyes followed the man until he disappeared around a corner.

Unaware of the interest he had aroused in the young man sitting in the cafe across the street, Sarwar Hussein walked briskly to get into step with his friend, who was keen to sit in the front row of the prayer congregation.

The mosque was full with men sitting in neat rows. Sarwar Hussein took his usual place at the rear end of the prayer congregation. A few minutes later, the prayers ended. Most men departed, to get back to their work, home or business. A few stayed behind, sitting on seats or on the plush carpet, offering their personal du'ah to be heard by their Almighty Allah.

Sarwar Hussein was one of these men, his hands raised in front of him with tears pouring down his weathered brown cheeks. People had stopped asking him why he always ended his prayers with tears. Too reticent and sensible to pry, they left him alone with his sorrow.

Always the first words of Sarwar's personal prayers were, "Forgive me, my Almighty Allah, for I have sinned . . . and in such a way that no man can carry a heavier burden on his shoulders than the one I've been carrying for the last twenty years."

In the mosque, memories of the past tortured him. There was one scene in particular which he could never get out of his mind – when he had accidentally choked his beloved young son to death!

This was the tragic secret which had eaten away at his soul for the past two decades and made his wife a nervous wreck. Their eldest daughter had been too young to remember. They had fled India with other Muslim refugees in 1947 when India was divided into two parts and Pakistan was founded as a state for Muslims. They had never shared their painful story with their new neighbours and friends in Pakistan.

They now had three children: one daughter from India, and a son and daughter born in Pakistan. Neither parent ever forgot their eldest son, whose body they had left behind in India, without even burying him. His wife, Zarine, never forgave her husband for what happened that night.

With his eyes closed, Sarwar Hussein suppressed a moan as he let the memories from that fatal night haunt him again. Reliving those memories was a daily ritual and a welcome form of punishment.

August 1947

In Kot Badal Khan near the district of Nakodar in India, Zarine sat huddled with her two small children in the rear storeroom of their house. Numb with terror of being attacked by Sikhs or Hindus, she had switched off all the lights and was feverishly chanting *Surah Yasin* verses under her breath.

It was as if the whole world had gone mad. With the famous 'Mountbatten Plan' in place and the 'Radcliffe Line' drawn on the map, India had been carved into two parts, with Pakistan

176

in the north for the Muslims. Neighbour had turned against neighbour; friend against friend. All in the name of religion. No one was to be trusted. With increasing communal riots, fear and mayhem reigned. A few months earlier, it was an inconceivable thought that something like this could happen in a civilised state. Overnight, millions had been made refugees.

What neither the Indian nor the British decision-makers had anticipated was the fragility of humankind and its easy slide into hatred.

Anger raged. Whole districts – the local malas where Hindus, Sikhs and Muslims had lived side by side with shared walls, balconies, animal compounds, courtyards, communal cooking and washing areas – had become no-go areas. Houses and shops were ransacked, looted and set on fire. Muslims and Sikhs in particular were at loggerheads. The Sikhs' animosity towards the Muslims was inflamed by the Khalistan issue. The Muslims had gained Pakistan. What about the Sikhs? They too deserved a state of their own – their Khalistan.

News of people slaughtered on trains coming from and going to Pakistan terrified those fleeing from their homes with their belongings in oxcarts, with the old people carried on makeshift palanquins to the safety of the Delhi Red Fort, the Purana Qila camps.

Anxious friends and local leaders of different religious groups urged their dear ones to save themselves, to forget about their houses, farming land, cotton crops, animals and jobs. There was only one option: to flee to the part designated for them. Muslims headed north to the new state of Pakistan, with Lahore, the old Mughal capital of India, on its side. Hindus from the north, the tribal mountainous Swat region, and from the city of Peshawar, and Sikh Pathans from Punjab, fled south to the Hindu state of India, Hindustan.

The province of Sindh in Pakistan, with its large port of Karachi, became a popular destination for the refugees, the Muhajirs. It was the home city of Mohammed Ali Jinnah, who with a group of people had founded the state of Pakistan.

For all those who had fled to Pakistan, an equal number of Muslims remained in India: they headed for Kerala, Lucknow and Hyderabad. This was when the madness of home exchange schemes came into action, with Muslims taking up the abandoned houses of the Hindus, whilst the Hindus were given the vacant Muslim homes. The messy minor details of reciprocity would be dealt with later. If one family's home was bigger than the one they had left behind, they had to make arrangements to pay the difference and vice versa.

When the famous 'Radcliffe Line' was drawn on the map, dividing rivers, towns and cities, people were in a state of utter disbelief. They woke up the following day in either India or Pakistan. With so much at stake, people had at first merely waited, biding their time, crowding around their radio boxes, anxiously listening to the news updates by the hour. After all, it was no trivial matter to abandon one's entire way of life and just flee. From having been thriving businessmen, shop owners, wealthy farmers, government employees, civil servants and respectable members of the community, the people became first fugitives and then refugees – that is, if they reached their destination safely. The Muslims who lived in northern cities like Lahore, Montgomery and Lyallpur congratulated themselves on their good fortune in living in that region. Their Sikh and Hindu neighbours, however, within hours and days had fled with their families to the southern part, leaving behind their beloved homes, belongings and friends. There was heartache, anxiety and chaos.

Sarwar Hussein was one of those who had lagged behind, uncertain whether to leave or stay. His two siblings living in

Nakodar had already left to join some relatives living in Lahore, an obvious destination for his family. But like thousands of other fellow Indians, he was reluctant to believe that he had to leave his home!

However, his Hindu schoolfriend and neighbour, Lal Mehra, seriously brought home the message to him that he was endangering the lives of his young family by staying in India. Zarine's relatives, living in the nearby town of Phillaur, had already fled to the north in the buses provided.

"You're my dear friend, Sarwar ji, and I love you very much, but I can't stop anything happening to you or your family. The situation here is really very bad with the riots, my brother, believe me. You must get out of this region! If I help you, the mob will burn my house down. No one is to be trusted now. You do understand me, Sarwar ji, don't you?"

Yes, Sarwar came to understand that situation well when he went to phone his brother from a local post office late in the evening. His brother had advised him to buy tickets from Phillaur to reach Jullundur railway station and said he would meet them there. On the way back, riding on his bicycle, Sarwar passed the small town of Banga, inhabited by Sikh families. He slipped off the main road and hid behind a tree after witnessing the scene of a young Muslim man being ambushed by a gang of Sikh youngsters. Terrified, Sarwar remained crouched on the ground.

In the scuffle, the young Muslim man knocked one of the Sikh boys to the ground; the boy hit his head on a large stone and died on the spot. In a rage, the others savagely turned on him and one stabbed him in the neck. His cries for help as he bled to death deafened Sarwar's ears. Petrified with fear, Sarwar crept away into the sugar-cane fields. With nausea churning in his stomach, he remained there for hours. His mouth was parched, but he was afraid to drink the pinkish water from the well near the field, knowing it might be disinfected to stop the spread of cholera.

The incident had taught him that travelling through Banga was not an option for his family now. They couldn't risk being attacked by a mob out for revenge. Heart thudding like a tabla drum, he retrieved his bicycle and stole back home in the darkness of the night, cycling hard and out of breath, constantly peering over his shoulder in case someone was following him.

"Allah Pak," he whispered, "Lal ji was right. If this is the reality of living in India now, then we can't stay another minute. Not that we want to leave. I love this country, my home, the Sutlej River. This is my birthplace. How can I desert my parents in the old cemetery? Abandon my grocery shop, with its stock piled high up to the ceiling? All our savings that I've invested in the goods? But we can't take anything with us, apart from money and gold jewellery. The way things are, we'll be lucky if we manage to leave our area safe and in one piece."

By the time he reached his front veranda porch, he had come to a firm decision. They had 80 kilometres to cover before they reached Lahore, but it would be too dangerous to go there by major roads or by train. Instead, they would travel stealthily through the village fields. Sarwar reckoned this would be the safer route to Jullundur from where his brother had made arrangements to take them by bus. However, he seriously doubted whether they could make it with two young children, and with only one bicycle as the means of transport. There were no taxis, or horse-driven carriages, tongas or the buffalo carts to hire at night-time. How would they manage to walk for hours on foot?

All the lights were out in the Muslim households in his Mahallah; the only lights visible were in Lal Mehra's home and the homes of the three Sikh families. His own dwelling lay in pitch darkness. Even the courtyard's dim oil lantern was not lit. Pulling off his muffler from around his face, Sarwar softly knocked three times on their front door and waited.

Then he called quietly, "Zarine, it's me."

Immediately the door was pulled open and his wife ushered him in. He sighed with relief. It was so good to be back in the safe haven of his home – but for how long? What if somebody decided to attack them in the middle of this night? Hindu and Sikh neighbours knew which houses belonged to the Muslims; apart from Lal ji, nobody could be trusted any more.

He hastened after his wife into the windowless storeroom at the rear. Zarine switched on the light, and they sat down at each end of the old charpoy, where their two children were sound asleep. There was no need for an anguished debate now; their fearful, silent glances confirmed to both that it was time for action – time to flee. Where Sarwar had witnessed a live killing, Zarine had heard of the carnage on the trains, and fires in the Powadra and Talwan area as well as the shooting of a Muslim family just two streets away. One member of that family had reacted and killed a Sikh man and then fled in the night.

"Did you get the tickets, Sarwar ji?" Zarine anxiously asked, scrutinising her husband's face. There were no more arguments with him to stay put; by now, she was ready to abandon her home and leave empty-handed. Their house, shop and her brother's cotton fields no longer mattered. Only their lives.

"No, Zarine, it's too dangerous to travel by train," he told her. "Terrible things are happening out there. We can take the train from Jullundur." He was reluctant to share the details about what he had witnessed in Banga.

"In that case, what are we going to do then?" she demanded, noting her husband's sweat-beaded forehead and the nervous tic in full action in his left cheek.

"We're leaving tonight, travelling on foot and with the children on my bicycle – and taking very little with us." He let the words sink into her mind.

"What? All that walking – are you joking?" She rose to her feet, agitated and angry.

"It's no joking matter, Zarine! There's no other way," Sarwar explained. "It's too dangerous to go as a family by road; we'll be easy targets. If we go by night it'll be safer so there's no time to lose. Please get your things together and secure your gold jewellery in the large breast pocket of the under-slip that you were showing me last week. Make lots of parathas and take a jar of mango pickle. That should last us for some time. Fill the water bottle and choose some warm clothing for the children, as it will be cold outside. That's all we can take. I will help you, but we must hurry!"

As Zarine set about hastily preparing the dough for the parathas, Sarwar went through the rest of the house, looking for something precious and small enough to carry in his shoulder bag. Common sense prompted that with two children to carry, as well as the required food, they couldn't take much with them. Unlike other families they had no buffalo cart at hand to transport their goods.

"But *everything* here is precious. This is our home!" Sarwar mourned, a sob rising in his throat as he removed his family's sepia photos out of their frames. He could not leave his memories behind; they had to go with them. His mind refused to dwell on the following day when their neighbours would discover they had fled in the night. For how long could Lal ji be expected to safeguard their home from being looted, stripped of everything and left empty for any Hindu or Sikh refugee family from Pakistan to take up abode? He wondered if there would be a similar sort of house waiting for his family in Pakistan. The government had promised a fair system of exchanging houses and land.

Sarwar wanted to thank his neighbour Lal Mehra in person for his long friendship and love, but he couldn't risk it. Sitting down at his desk where he normally did his business accounts, he dipped his pen in the inkpot and wrote a long note in Hindi. Stepping outside in the darkness, he slid the note under Lal Mehra's front door. By the time his neighbour got to read the note they would be far away.

In the dim lantern-lit kitchen Zarine was busy with the parathas. In the storeroom, Sarwar hunted for his children's warm jumpers in a cupboard. Riaz whimpered as his father coaxed his limp arms into the sleeves.

Zarine handed her husband a bag containing a bundle of hot parathas, a small jar of mango pickle and a water container, then rushed into the adjoining storeroom. Opening her silver trunk with the key hanging from her waist by a nala string, she drew out the cotton pouch containing all her gold jewellery. Everything else of value she left untouched. There was no time or luxury for nostalgic tears as she shut the heavy lid on all her old wedding outfits and special items of her dowry lying in that steel trunk, and locked it. She left a note with their name and which city they were heading for, dearly hoping that the family who came to live in their house would be honest people who would return their belongings.

Married eight years ago, Zarine was devastated at leaving everything behind. Sobbing bitterly, she changed into her under-slip with her pouch of gold jewellery tucked inside. God knew, the gold would be needed in difficult times. She put on a warm cotton shalwar kameez suit, and on top of that she wore her outdoor burqa.

Sarwar Hussein too had changed his clothing. Sorting out his money into different bundles of notes, he strategically placed them around his body with a few precious items such as his children's photographs in different pockets of his Punjabi suit and coat.

"This is it, Zarine," he said tenderly. "Ready to say goodbye to your beloved home?"

As she stared mutely at him, her eyes full of tears, Sarwar Hussein felt duty bound to remind her, "Never mind, my dearest, we'll make another home in Pakistan – a much better one than this. And now we must let the children sleep for as long as they can. I know it's going to be difficult for them. You can sit on the bicycle with them and I'll lead it."

Like thieves in the night, they crept out. Sarwar fastened the padlock of their house. He cradled their sleeping son, with one hand pushing the bike. Zarine carried their two-year-old daughter, Tahira, on her shoulders.

Looking stealthily over his shoulder, Sarwar Hussein led his family out of their area, carefully looking down for potholes. He avoided the main road where he knew ditches had been dug and then covered up with hay and animal fodder to lure an unwary traveller or enemy vehicle to fall into them.

For a couple of hours, Zarine sat on the cycle too, precariously holding onto both her children. When it became too uncomfortable, she got off. Sarwar then hopped on and began to pedal, holding his children and two bags tightly in front of him.

To Zarine's aching legs, the few miles they had covered seemed like hundreds. The backs of her shoes were digging into her heels, making them sore. She begged her husband to stop and rest, but Sarwar insisted that they persevere for another couple of hours and try to reach the city of Jullundur, where hopefully his brother would be waiting for them.

It was past midnight when Riaz whimpered, waking up in his father's arms "Daddy, why are you carrying me on the cycle?" he asked sleepily. He tried to slip out of his father's arm, gazing up at the night stars. Sarwar gently lifted him down to walk beside him, slowing his own pace. His mother and sister took their turn on the cycle, with his father leading it.

They had walked for half a mile when Riaz began saying that he was hungry.

"Zarine, I think it's time for Riaz to rest and eat something. How about if we take a short break over there?" Sarwar pointed to the bushes at the side of the road.

Zarine was only too glad to comply. She limped towards the bush where she gently laid her sleeping daughter on her shawl spread out on the ground. With Riaz sitting beside him, Sarwar Hussein shared out the food. The parathas and mango pickle had never tasted as good as they did in that strange environment, under the stars.

They were halfway through their meal when the calm silence of the night was interrupted by the sound of male laughter. Zarine and Sarwar froze, the food between their fingers forgotten, fear etched on their faces.

Sarwar peered from a gap between two bushes. To his dismay, it was a group of young turbaned Sikh men, drunk and singing lewd songs. Two of them carried guns. Another two swaggered from side to side, sharing dirty jokes. Cold fear washed over Sarwar's body. The men were drawing nearer.

Unaware of the gravity of the situation, Riaz came up to his father. Tugging at Sarwar's coat sleeve, he demanded in a clear, loud voice: "Water, Daddy, water. I'm thirsty!"

The men heard and turned, cocking their ears in the direction of the bush. Petrified, Sarwar stared down at his son. Riaz was about to repeat the request. Sarwar clamped his hand hard over his son's mouth. Riaz began pulling at his father's arm, but Sarwar remained oblivious to his son's struggle as he watched the men pass right by the bushes where they were hiding.

Sweat was pouring down Sarwar's temples; unaware of his wife's urgent hands clawing at him to pull her son from his vice-like grip. It was only when the men had passed, that he became aware of what he had done. Glancing down in horror, he dropped his hand. Riaz fell to the ground, lifeless.

"Oh, my God, Sarwar ji, what have you done?" Horrified, Zarine knelt beside her son, shaking him and rubbing his cheeks. No sound, no breath came out of Riaz's mouth.

An anguished scream burst through Sarwar's throat, but before it could pierce the night's silence, he strangled it by shoving the end of his woollen muffler into his mouth and biting hard on it. He had killed his son while trying to save their lives, but if his scream was heard by those drunken men, not one but all four of them would be dead.

Kneeling beside his son, Sarwar wept. Zarine too, was sobbing, rocking her son to and fro in her arms, beseeching him to wake up. Around them were the cotton fields. Their little daughter was now wide awake with the sound of her parents' distress. Shivering, she too began to cry in the night's darkness.

Sarwar didn't know for how long they vented their grief and wondered what to do with their dead son. Should they take him with them, or leave him behind and hope that some kind person would bury him? Zarine was out of her mind at the thought of abandoning her son. Sarwar begged her to understand their predicament.

"We have to leave . . . we still have so many miles to travel. How can we carry our son's dead body with us? Please understand, Zarine. Some compassionate soul will find our Riaz and bury him," he appealed to her.

The thought of leaving their son there, however, was too much for Sarwar Hussein. He didn't know where he drew his strength from as he wrapped up his firstborn in Zarine's shawl and placed the limp body on his bicycle.

In the end, he literally had to drag his wife away from the bush area. They stumbled, half-senseless, into the next village. In one home, lights were still on and music was blaring. It could only be the home of a Hindu family, who had no need to fear or flee from their home and were still celebrating. The couple laid Riaz's body outside the door then rang the bell and stepped aside so as not to be seen.

A few minutes later they saw a woman in a silk sari come out and find the child on the doorstep. She removed the shawl from Riaz's face.

"Patel ji, look here! A child . . . sleeping. He's not dead, is he?" She called to her husband who came running to the door and peered over at Riaz. Lifting the child, he took him inside. Riaz's parents watched their son's body being taken into the house.

"Zarine. We won't have to worry about him now," Sarwar comforted her. "The copy of *Surah Yasin* we left with him will tell those people he's a Muslim. They must and should bury him. Let us leave this place now, Zarine."

Inside the house, placing his ear near the child's chest, the woman's husband listened for a heartbeat. Nothing. Pushing the shawl aside, he gently puffed air into the boy's mouth.

Kumari Patel stared in amazement at what her husband was doing. Had he gone crazy? He was now pressing on the child's ribs and puffing air into his mouth. Then, as if their Bhagwan had heard their prayers, her husband detected a slight heartbeat and jumped back in joy.

"Kumari, the boy is alive!" His wife beamed with happiness, holding out her two hands in prayer to her Bhagwan. "Quickly, let's take him to our doctor." As she tenderly cuddled the child in her arms, her husband went to wake up their driver.

In the doctor's surgery, much to the astonishment of those around him, the boy coughed but remained unconscious. Riaz only came fully awake a day later in Kumari Patel's home. His hands were clawing at his mouth, and he kept saying the words, "Water, Papa, water!" His eyes anxiously sought his parents. Where were they?

Kumari, with no children of her own, rejoiced in her newfound happiness. God had blessed her with a child at last, literally delivered it to her door. She wanted to adopt this blessing of a son, believing that his own parents had abandoned him and therefore had no claim over him. Whether they were in Pakistan or in India, she was not interested in tracing their whereabouts.

It was only many years later that Kumari Patel's conscience bullied her into admitting that they needed to find out about her son's biological family.

When the child Riaz was fully conscious and found himself in a new home with a Hindu family, in his child's mind he deliberately blocked out his own mother, his baby sister, their home – and *Him*, the father who had nearly choked him to death.

Mama and Papa have left me! His young mind struggled to come to terms with what had happened. The last scene he remembered was eating with them in the night amongst the bushes somewhere. Where were they all – and why had they left him behind? In anguish, he sought solace in the arms of his Hindu foster mother.

By that time, his natural parents had reached their destination. They had first gone to the city of Jullundur where they could not find Sarwar's brother, but managed to get on a bus to the city of Lyallpur's refugee camp in Pakistan. After a few days, their relatives came for them from Lahore.

Sharing their tales of woe as refugees with their loved ones, Sarwar and Zarine omitted to mention how Riaz had died. Instead, they offered a fabricated tale of their son dying of a fever, just before they left their home. As to the burial of their son, they dared not utter a word. It became their shameful secret. Zarine never spoke about it, but neither did she forgive her husband for that terrible night and the loss of their son. In her eyes, he had killed their beloved Riaz and then abandoned him on the doorstep of total strangers.

They settled down in a home vacated by a Hindu family who had fled south to India. Sarwar started a new business with the gold jewellery they had brought with them. Zarine gave birth to two more children in Pakistan, but she never forgot her beloved Riaz. Life went on, but they were always tortured by the thoughts that would never go away. What had happened to their son? Had the family who took his body inside buried their son?

On his way home from the mosque, Sarwar Hussein was unaware of a pair of dark eyes boring holes into his back as he entered his home.

His heart beating wildly, Raju stood up. The hour of reckoning had come. It was time to meet the ones who had deserted him, leaving him for dead. Raju left his suitcase with the cafe owner, as he did not want to put his host off by his luggage. After all,

189

they didn't know him. And he had no idea whether that man who entered the villa was his father.

Gathering his courage, he pressed the buzzer at the outside gate. A young man led him into the front garden. Was this his brother? Blushing, Raju greeted him, "Assalam-a-Alaikum. Can I meet Sarwar Hussein, please?"

"Walaikum Salam. Please come in." The young man led Raju through the open porch and into their reception room. Asking the guest to be seated, he then went to call his father.

Raju waited apprehensively. It was all so surreal. He had seen dramas of family reunions in Bollywood films starring Amitabh Bachchan or Shahrukh Khan, but had never imagined himself as the protagonist. His eyes glided over the furnishings of the room, which celebrated the Islamic faith of the family, from the woollen tapestry woven with the Al-Kaaba design and the names of the prophets, to the hand-painted glazed plates with verses from the Holy Quran, to the large family portrait in their Ihram clothing taken after they had performed Hajj in Mecca. The high-quality furniture indicated to him that his family had done well for themselves, considering that they had abandoned everything in India and started from scratch.

Just then, he heard a female voice and the sound of approaching footsteps. Raju felt a thrill run down his spine and the hairs on his arms stood up. When a middle-aged woman with greying hair and a silk chador draped over her head entered the room, he gazed at her in wonder, bade her salam and stood up.

"Walaikum Salam, my son," she innocently returned, a greeting she normally used for all young men entering her home.

At the words, 'my son', something leaped in Raju's chest, and his eyes filled.

"Sarwar ji are having their lunch, they'll be with you shortly. Please feel at home." Out of respect for her husband, she always referred to him in the plural.

She was about to leave. Raju stepped forward. This was the moment and he wanted it to be with her only and not *Him*.

"Mother," he uttered softly behind her back.

Puzzled, Zarine turned, her forehead creased with perplexity at the young man's peculiar use of the word 'mother'. Raju poured his soul into his eyes.

"Mother," he repeated with emotion. "I am your son, Riaz."

Zarine stared, as the meaning of his words hammered at her brain. Her mind screamed, *Is this a hoax?* Her Riaz was dead. She began to sway. Raju reached forward to hold her.

"But my Riaz is dead," she whimpered, her eyes huge in her face.

"Yes, Mother, you left me for dead, but I was only unconscious . . . I was alive." He waited for his words to sink in. When they did, she could not contain her utter joy and excitement.

"Sarwar ji, Tahira, Javid, Saira – where are you all? Come here!" Zarine called at the top of her voice from the doorway.

The family came running from different parts of the villa, wondering at the commotion. Her children stared at her in amazement. What had happened to their normally subdued and serene mother?

Pulling Raju into her arms, she hugged and embraced him as if she would never let him go. Her family looked at each other, alarmed at her behaviour. Had she gone out of her mind, to be kissing a total stranger?

Zarine turned to Sarwar Hussein with tears streaming down her cheeks. She sobbed, "Sarwar ji, you'll never have to curse yourself again. Your son is alive! Look!"

As Sarwar Hussein continued to blankly gape at her, Zarine rushed up to him, tapping him on his chest.

"Look, Sarwar ji, our Riaz . . . whom we left behind in India!"

Clutching his chest, Sarwar stumbled out of the room. The doctor had said that shock of any kind was not good for his heart. Seeing this, Tahira, his eldest daughter, rushed to her father. She called for her brother Javid, who ran to her aid. They led their father to a sofa for him to lie down and were about to call the doctor, when Sarwar told them he was fine, just needed a few minutes' quiet. He sat up, the pain in his chest forgotten, and held out his hands in prayer to his Almighty Allah Pak. Later, he would offer his special thanksgiving Nafl prayers.

Sarwar then lay down and fell into a deep sleep of relief and joy. No more would he be tortured by that terrible memory of killing his son and then leaving his body behind. But he was not ready to face his son or talk to him, just yet.

Over the next hour, Zarine forgot her family, so engrossed did she become in her eldest son – her firstborn child lost to her for so long. Her other children looked on with bemusement. Tahira was cynical about her mother's reaction. The man who claimed to be their long-lost brother was a complete stranger, and from another world, India, their arch-enemy, the land from which she and her parents had fled twenty years ago in 1947, in order to save their lives.

Zarine, who was in high spirits, asked Tahira to lay the table for dinner. Holding onto his arm as if he would disappear if she let go, she took Raju around their house. Her other children followed silently behind her. They hadn't quite got used to the idea of acquiring another brother – an older one at that.

In awe, Raju silently moved from room to room. He was struck by the thought that this would have been his home, living with his two sisters and a brother. Oddly, he felt nothing for them. Even Tahira, his baby sister who was born in India, kindled no feeling. They were, quite simply, strangers. He was acutely aware of his siblings' scepticism, if not outright hostility, regarding his arrival.

At Zarine's request, the dining room was opened up. The large, marble veneered table was soon covered with various dishes – some hurriedly prepared by their cook and his mother. Fried fish was brought in from a local restaurant. Raju began to eat with the others. Zarine watched each and every movement of his, noting that he did not use a spoon for rice. He ate the way they used to in India, scooping rice with their fingers. She had not had time to quiz him about all those years away from them. Nor was she in a hurry to learn about the people with whom he had spent most of his life.

Later, after dinner, while they were sipping hot cups of tea and munching on warm, sweet jalebis, Zarine decided it was time to confront her son's past and hear about the people who were part of his world now. Raju shared everything his adopted parents had told him – about how they had found him on their doorstep and, after discovering that he was still alive, had taken him into their household. They now lived in New Delhi, where he worked as a manager in a reputable publishing firm.

Zarine was eager to know how he had managed to trace them to their home in Pakistan. Raju told her how, as a child, he had mentioned the names of his real parents and that of their neighbour, Lal Mehra, as well as the name of their town. Within the first few weeks his adopted parents had visited that area and discovered that his parents had left for Pakistan.

Later, when Raju was older and determined to discover the whereabouts of his real parents, his adoptive parents went back to his former house and met the neighbours, asking for information about his parents. Lal Mehra had shown them a letter with a Lahore address that he had received from Sarwar Hussein many years after they had left India. Raju's adoptive parents did not mention anything to Lal Mehra about Raju being Sarwar Hussein's son, but said that an old Indian friend wished to visit Sarwar and his family in Pakistan. Lal Mehra had happily handed over the letter with the address.

"And so with Bhagwan's help I'm here now," Raju ended emotionally.

Zarine's hand froze on the cup she was holding at the mention of the word Bhagwan – the Hindu word for God. Riaz hadn't said Allah but Bhagwan.

Raju caught the uneasy look in her eye. He did not fail to note the change in her demeanour. His steady gaze made hers falter. Surely his mother would accept the fact that he had adopted the religion of his adoptive parents? Did it make that much difference? After all, he was still her son. He had missed out on their lives and they on his. It was a sobering thought. He had embraced the life and faith of his adoptive parents as his own.

He smiled at the thought of his mother, Kumari Patel, waiting for him in Delhi – and missing her all of a sudden, he momentarily forgot the strange woman sitting in front of him, the one who had given birth to him.

Whilst her eldest son tried to get to sleep in the guest bedroom, Zarine stayed awake for a long time thinking about him. The word Bhagwan kept tapping in her head. Bitterly she wept. It was on religious grounds they had fled from her beloved home in India and it was religion now which had crushed her joyous feelings about her son's homecoming.

Zarine was angry with fate, the injustice of it all, and the suffering of her family in having lost Riaz. And all those years her poor Sarwar had tortured himself. Why did those people not try to trace them earlier? Why leave it till his adulthood?

Riaz was not her Riaz, but a stranger. It was the last straw for Zarine to know that her firstborn, for whom her family had excitedly distributed laddoos around in Phillaur on the day of his birth, was now called Raju, and had become a Hindu. Zarine thought of his Hindu mother, wondering what she should feel about her. Was she jealous of her for looking after her son all these years?

Zarine glanced at her husband fast asleep beside her. For once she didn't envy him his sleep. He deserved it. For him nothing else now mattered, only that his Riaz was alive. She prayed for her husband's health and that of her three children. No, not three children but four, she automatically corrected herself.

The next day passed in a flurry of activities for the entire Hussein family. Raju was taken sightseeing, to view Lahore's historical monuments: the Shalimar Gardens, the Gurdwara and the Badshahi mosque, as well as touring the walled city with its many doors, and the Anarkali bazaar. He met some of his Pakistani relatives, who were totally puzzled by his appearance, but happy nevertheless for his family.

Before arriving in Pakistan Raju hadn't given much thought to how long he was going to stay in Lahore. Perhaps a week or a month he had thought, depending on how his visit went. By the third day, however, he began to feel homesick and restless and decided that it was time to return home. He promised his mother Zarine that he would return again soon.

Sadly, Zarine reconciled herself to the fact that her Riaz could never be a permanent member of her household. Raju gave them his Indian address and the telephone number in Delhi, and requested them to visit his other family. Sarwar remained in the background. His guilt kept him there. He lovingly watched his son from a distance, realising that they both, father and son, needed time to bridge that gap between them.

At ten o'clock in the morning of the fourth day, Raju left for Delhi. His family hugged him and saw him off at the Wagah border with mixed emotions. Zarine rained kisses on his face, reluctant to part with him. She did not know how to handle this separation. Subdued, his family returned home, knowing that their lives would never be quite the same. Riaz would always be in their thoughts, but never theirs fully. His two sisters and brother were ambivalent about their sibling's intrusion into their lives. They didn't know whether they felt happy or sad when he left.

Raju's immediate thought as he settled comfortably in his seat on the train was that his life's mission was accomplished. He had discovered his birth family. He still felt no affection for his father, but he had learned from his mother their version of the story, about how petrified they were of the drunken men, and how that had resulted in the tragedy of his being accidentally suffocated.

In Delhi, Kumari Patel was sitting in front of their altar. With her eyes closed, she was praying for her son Raju's well-being. When the outside door creaked, she opened her eyes, surprised. Her husband was supposed to be at a business evening meal.

On catching sight of her son, Kumari flew into his open arms, the folds of her Banarasi sari flying behind her. Raju rested his head on her shoulder, filled with emotion. Finally, he whispered, "I've come home, Mata ji. Bhagwan has returned your son to your arms."

She heard the joy in his voice. He knew where he belonged. Too overwrought, Kumari didn't reply. Instead she took his face in her hands, showering it with kisses, starting with his forehead and moving down to his chest. When she eventually released him, Raju bent to touch her feet. Joy rippled through Kumari Patel's being. Her dark eyes glowed in her face.

There was a lot to be said, and a lot to be heard, but she would leave it till later. She let go of her son, telling him to bathe and change into his favourite blue kurtha and matching pyjamas. She then returned to the altar and bowed her head for a special prayer, with her hands firmly pressed together in front of her favourite goddess for a long time. She thanked her Bhagwan for her son's return. Four days ago, she had lost hope of holding onto him, mortally afraid that his Pakistani family would keep him with them.

Her Raju called from his room whilst he unpacked the presents from his other family. "Mata ji, you can now call Neeta's parents and tell them to go ahead with our engagement. I now know that I'm ready to marry and start a family of my own, after visiting my other family. And I am going to tell Neeta the truth about where I have been. To Pakistan, not Dubai."

After getting their Indian visa three months later, Sarwar Hussein and Zarine visited Riaz's Indian family. They too arrived by train. He and his parents went to receive them. It was a strange and awkward meeting. But both sides were thankful. Riaz's parents were grateful to his adoptive parents for saving their son's life and for raising him so well, and also for taking the trouble to trace them back to Pakistan. And Raju's adoptive parents were thankful that he had come into their childless life as their beloved son, and delighted that he had not deserted them to join his biological family.

His parents only stayed for two days. Zarine watched her son and his mother from afar, painfully aware that Kumari adored their Riaz and that he was, indeed, their son. She hugged and kissed him as she left, but gracefully accepted the fact that her Riaz belonged to the other woman. She was simply profoundly glad that he was alive. The regular phone calls continued, and the bonds were gradually deepening between the two families.

Six months passed and Sarwar Hussein and his whole family arrived in Delhi for their Riaz's wedding. It was a first-time visit to India for his siblings; the Indian Hindu wedding was a weird and unique experience for them. Sarwar and Zarine somehow managed to hold onto their composure as they watched their son circle the wedding fire with his bride Neeta, with wedding garlands around their necks. Both of his families were in tears.

However, Kumari Patel and her husband had a surprise for them. They had also invited an Imam to perform the Muslim Nikkah ceremony. After all, their shared son belonged to two faiths. The two mothers stared at one another, delighting in each other's happiness. It was at that moment, watching the tears in the other's eyes, that the two mothers found a deep joy in sharing him.

Riaz for one, Raju for the other.

The Concubine

Cusco, Peru, 1539

Poised over the steaming pot of red dye, the two sisters Bachue and Cava stared at one another.

"He's going to *her!*" Bachue whispered, raising a well-arched eyebrow at her beautiful older sister before dipping another skein of raw, creamy-white alpaca wool into the dye pot.

Together, they turned and watched Ayar Manco, Cava's husband, sauntering across the large communal compound towards them. The sisters' eyes rested on his new *manta*, the fine woollen shawl that his mother, crouched in front of her weaving frame, had painstakingly woven for weeks and which he wore for special religious festivals, such as the Festival of the Sun. Tall and handsome, his shoulder-length raven-black hair was sleekly combed back, and there was a gleam in his eye.

Ayar Manco held the important and responsible role within the community of maintaining the *quipo* – a complex device made from woven cords and knots on which was recorded the history, transactions and activities of the tribe.

The young man had come across to the dyeing quarter of the compound to say goodbye before leaving for the town of Cusco in south-east Peru. Bachue did not need to say anything more to her sister, for Cava's expression revealed her feelings of loss about the imminent departure of her beloved husband. Her usual smile had been whipped away as if the Apus, their sacred mountain divinities, had in a fit of rage punished them with a violent storm, instilling fear and casting a shadow over their day.

But Cava valiantly fought back. She would ignore her younger sister's suggestive innuendoes and refuse to allow her to meddle in her relationship with Ayar Manco and come between them. Changing the mood, she mischievously dipped a mud-baked drinking beaker into another pot of tepid dyed water and flicked the liquid at her sister. The antic reminded them both of their fun-filled childhood days. Bachue immediately retaliated, splashing her sister back with some cold dregs, giggling. Then they sobered, grimacing at their reddish-stained tunics. There was a lot of work to get through that day, due to the burial of a cousin who had died during her labour, with the baby still inside her womb: a tragic double loss for the family.

The sisters dipped two more skeins of wool into the dye pot simmering over a blazing log fire. With sturdy wooden poles they stirred the mixture to ensure a good consistency of colour for the wool. Over the smoky pot Bachue's eyes continued to taunt, but Cava took no notice. Her keen ears were following the sound of her husband's flute growing fainter as he strode down the stone-cobbled village lane to where his horse was tied to a tree next to his mother's hut. Today, there was an energetic pulse to the tune. Cava recalled how she had watched him the previous night meticulously dusting his woollen hat. Ayar Manco had carefully picked out the remains of the berry leaves from his hat, instead embellishing it with the three elegant condor feathers that she had playfully thrown over his head.

Looking uncharacteristically evasive, her Ayar Manco — named *the most successful one* — had delivered the information in a matter-of-fact tone: "I'm not sure how much work there'll be in the Casa Don Antonio, nor am I sure when I'll return — so don't wait for me, please. I'll have eaten with the casa staff."

As she hung the soggy, steamy skeins of dyed wool to dry under the warm morning sun on a wooden frame, Cava thought about her husband's journey. Having visited the casa twice herself, she was able to time it well, predicting when he would reach the magnificent building, the home of the Spanish General, Don Antonio. Cava wondered who would be there this morning. More significantly, who would be monopolising his time the most today. Would it be Don Antonio — or Doña Isabel, his Spanish wife, newly arrived from Spain . . .

Brushing this disturbing thought aside, Cava joined the group of women weavers in the compound. Wearing warm alpaca wool hats with earflaps, their shoulders draped with woollen shawls, the women sat on rugs in a circle in front of their weaving frames and chatted whilst they diligently worked away. Squatting in front of her mother's old frame, Cava concentrated hard. There was no time for gossiping today as she had to sort out the various funeral activities for her poor cousin.

In the city of Cusco, capital of the Inca empire and popular settlement site of the Spanish explorers — Francisco Pizarro and his army — the streets were alive with various activities. Vendors were eagerly hawking their goods as llamas laden with packs of supplies trotted by and artisans toiled in their workshops around the main square, the Plaza de Armas. The sounds of the native Incan Quechua language intermingled harmoniously with that of the Spanish invaders and their employees working in and around the monumental church they had built on the foundations of the Incan Temple of the Sun.

In the casa, Don Antonio was still at home; his horse was tied to a tree outside. The moment he stepped into the courtyard, Ayar Manco heard raised voices coming from the master chamber on the top floor. Alarmed, he sprinted up the wooden stairs. Then, fearful of intruding, he discreetly stood outside the bedroom, on the terrace. The Moorish-styled balcony overlooked the square courtyard, with its central fountain and mature alder, cedar and weeping willow trees. Ayar Manco peered down to see if anyone else was listening to the argument between the Señor and his wife, Doña Isabel.

Just then, a maid with her hair neatly plaited into a thick braid emerged from the arch of the kitchen area, carrying a wooden platter of clay beakers and *chicha* – corn fermented drinks – for all the casa staff. Catching his eye, she smiled up in understanding, squinting in the sun.

"What's happening?" Ayar Manco called quietly.

The young woman dropped her gaze, afraid to divulge. Then ventured to share: "They are fighting . . ."

Ayar Manco heard Don Antonio's steps in the master chamber. Noiselessly he sprinted back downstairs and hid behind an elegantly carved wooden screen on the veranda. From the small gaps in the design he watched Don Antonio stride across the courtyard, his brown hair still wet from the morning bath, and dismissed the errand boy holding open the door for him with a brusque wave of his hand.

Ayar Manco remained standing behind the wooden screen, lost in thought. Then, heartbeat racing, he slipped silently back upstairs. Without knocking, he gently pushed open the imposing bedroom door, surprising Doña Isabel. Still in her night clothes, and with her back to him, she wore a white linen chemise and a matching Spanish underskirt. Her coils of bronze ringlets, freed from the night pins and ribbons, fell in sensuous waves to her waist, and the sleeveless chemise showed off her creamy shoulders. Very rarely had Ayar Manco seen their Señora like this. Doña Isabel always stepped out of her room formally attired in her long dress, with her shoulders discreetly covered. Her hair was always elaborately piled in a coronet around her head, providing a becoming frame for her delicately featured, heart-shaped face.

Startled, Doña Isabel turned, pinning their household manager with a look of condemnation in her blue eyes. No one dared to enter without knocking or calling out first! This tall Incan native from the mountain area, a Keeper of Memories, had rudely trespassed into her private domain. The fact that she was in her night clothes made her look and feel vulnerable; not at all the figure of authority as mistress of the casa that she normally presented to her Incan staff.

Blushing, Isabel became conscious of the firm thrust of her full breasts behind the chemise. Warmth rushed through her body and cheeks. Snatching her night shawl from the bed, she draped it around her shoulders. Fringed with exquisite cotton lace and purchased in Madrid by her Aunt Maria, Isabel loved it and used it all the time. This native had no right to see her like this. Then she was alarmed by his question in Spanish.

"*Que pasa, Señora?* What's wrong?" His eyes rested on her tear-stained cheeks. Ayar Manco dared not use her first name, fully aware that he had trespassed into a marital minefield.

Still reeling from her husband's callous words, Doña Isabel mutely stared, unable to interpret the expression in Ayar Manco's dark grey eyes. His mouth parted, ready to speak, to burst out with speech – but her look held him back.

Then it became too much for Isabel, with Antonio's terrible admission continuing to sting her ears: "*Yes, Rumi is mine – my son. Are you satisfied now, you foolish woman!*" She fell against the magnificent four-poster bed, her bosom rising and falling with her anguished sobs.

Watching from the doorway, Ayar Manco could not help himself. He padded across the cool room, with the window shutter fully open, revealing a view of the city's grand cathedral and beyond it, in the distance, the mountains with the terraces of potato crops and yellow and purple corn.

Ayar Manco stood in front of Doña Isabel, breaching the social etiquette of communication between the Spaniards and the native Incan people. Alarmed, she glanced up, feeling his warm hand on her arm. Her eyes were wide in her face, and her soft pink lips quivered in distress. Only a few inches of space separated them.

She was about to reprimand him when a loud female Spanish voice sounded from the courtyard below. Doña Rosa had arrived on time for her morning visit with Doña Isabel.

Ayar Manco's hand fell to his side. Eyes guarded once more, he stepped back and walked out of the room. Head reeling, Isabel could still feel the warmth of his hand on her arm.

In Doña Isabel's world, Ayar Manco was a mere native worker. In his Quechua tribe, he was the revered Quipu Keeper, trained to chronicle and record the local and national Incan events, customs and rituals, through the knotting process on his quipu, an artefact laboriously worked on to archive events for eternity. A highly intelligent man, Ayar Manco carried out this role with both integrity and humility. In turn, he elicited deep respect and was held in awe by his fellow tribesmen and beyond.

In the eyes of his wife Cava, he was simply her Apu, even Ataguchu, the god who created heaven. Just as her tribesmen worshipped the mountains, their Apus and Maya their 'Mother Earth', she worshipped her good-looking and god-like husband, Ayar Manco.

Cava had grown up in the same clan as Ayar Manco. As a child she was his faithful shadow, scrambling up behind him on the food terraces of the sacred valley's mountains. As a blossoming teenage maiden, Cava coyly eyed him over her weaving frame, often cooking food for him and his mother. She loved pairing with him for the religious and festive dances. As a young woman passionately in love with Ayar Manco, a man equally adored by all the other young tribeswomen, including her younger sister, Bachue, Cava frequently suffered the deadly pangs of jealousy.

"Ayar Manco is mine and mine alone!" were the words she repeated over and over again to herself as she triumphantly lured him with her beauty and adulation.

And when, after months of courting and co-habiting in their own hut, Ayar Manco officially asked her father for her hand in marriage, Cava was transported into the heavenly world of the Sun. Ecstatic, she had fallen into her mother's loving arms and wept with joy.

Cava was at the ripe age of seventeen − a tall, beautiful young woman who had quickly ascended the hierarchy of skilled weavers to become a master weaver − which enabled her to supplement her family's income well. Quick-witted, she sketched and replicated the designs for herself and other weavers, adding her own flare and creativity to them. Where other women normally took two months to complete a *manta,* she spun it in a month, earning herself the title of master weaver. This accolade made her the target of resentment and envy by her sluggish sister Bachue, who loathed everything to do with weaving; she was better with the herding of the domestic animals and other related tasks. Cava was also in popular demand for helping with many religious and healing ceremonies, the mummification of the dead and the preparation of the ayahuasca medicine.

Ayar Manco, an only child, lived with his widowed mother in a large hut, a lane away from Cava's compound. In the tribal hierarchy, his quipu role had elevated him beyond the normal life of farming, fishing and herding of the alpacas. Whilst alive, his father, Sayani, had been highly ambitious for his only child, who was blessed with an extremely sharp memory. From a very early age, Ayar could recall and retell, retaining minute details, all the stories of their ancestors as well as those relating to their divinities.

Ayar Manco was extremely well-versed in burial and shamanic religious rituals. Like Cava, he had mastered the art of mummifying corpses in the sitting position in jute woven baskets for their burial in the mountain crevices. And like Cava, he too actively took part in the annual ritualistic washing of the remains of the dead in their burial baskets.

Ayar Manco was regularly consulted by his fellow tribesmen, and those from as far away as the Machu Picchu mountains. His vast knowledge was impressive and his opinion mattered. In addition, his manly person, good-looking face, his courteous and kind manners drew men and women to his side. He was popular with the Spanish invaders too.

His mother did not have to bother with the growing of potatoes, the rearing of guinea pigs or herding of the alpacas. Their food basket was always full and their wooden table was often piled high with offerings from those who had benefited from Ayar Manco's services. Above all, their house was never short of yellow and purple corn cobs.

Ayar Manco, however, was ambitious. His gaze, vision and thoughts went beyond his own tribe, and the Incan civilisation. He was not only angry with but was also curious about the Conquistadors who had landed on the Andean shores, killed thousands of Incan people in a battle, including their emperor, and settled around the revered city of Cusco and up north, in the Quito region, enslaving men and women. Over the years, Ayar Manco saw the number of Spanish men and women in the Cusco region increase.

From afar he tasted the Spanish way of life, absorbing their customs, religious rituals, beliefs and practices; all so different from those of his proud Incan warrior race of people. He deeply resented the way the Incan ancient palaces had been plundered and their gold treasures looted. He hated how a cathedral, the Spaniards' House of God, had been built over their revered and ancient Temple of the Sun in the main square of Cusco.

Francisco Pizarro, who led the Spanish invasion of Peru, had encouraged some of his men to stay in the city, providing them with enforced local labour. Thus, the invaders' army had settled well, leading flourishing lives. Some were later joined by their wives and families.

Whilst intrigued by these strangers, Ayar Manco grieved over the fatal impact of their arrival on the Incan civilisation. Some tribes had been wiped out completely due to the dreadful disease, smallpox, which the foreigners had brought with them. These invaders from beyond the seas had not only taken over their world but were slowly treading upon their Incan customs and religious beliefs. He saw racist incidents, and heard racist talk by the Spaniards towards his people. He was deeply offended by their derogatory comments about their divinities, which the invaders dismissed as mere mountains. Seething, he watched the patronising Spanish eyes mocking their shamanic rituals.

Ayar Manco's agile mind enabled him to quickly master the language of the 'conquerors' and also observe their way of life, including learning how they sat at tables and ate with metal tools of different shapes. Innate wisdom informed him that the fair-skinned strangers were not only fleecing their land of its wealth, minerals and gold, but at the same time they also provided ample opportunities for employment for his people. Ayar Manco watched the slow migration of his tribesmen to the outskirts of the city of Cusco. Many abandoned their farming, the rearing of livestock, relishing the feel of money in their palms from their Spanish employers. Some reckoned that their traditional system of reciprocity was no longer sufficient. The Incan men soon became potters, builders and horsemen for the enemy.

Pizarro's army needed men for the building of houses and military barracks. They needed food brought from the mountain terraces and the Sacred Food Valley, and fish from the clear waters of the sacred Willkamayu and the local Tullamayu rivers. The big houses like his master's needed servants. Women found employment by caring for young children and carrying out domestic chores.

Some became the concubines of those Spaniards who were either single or had left their wives back in Spain. Even

Pizarro, over fifty years of age, had taken a young concubine, Cuxirimay Ocllo Yupanqui — sister of the Incan Emperor Atahualpa whom they had killed — and with whom he had two children. The attitude towards the results of such relationships — the children of mixed race born to the concubines — was matter-of-fact. Very few husbands or lovers of the Incan women spoke openly about what went on behind the walls of the casa or barracks. It was all stoically dealt with; the women's families accepting that men, no matter of what race, needed the welcoming warmth of female flesh. If the invaders paid the women handsomely for their amorous services, there was no grievance on either side.

When a lighter-skinned baby with fine hair appeared in their midst, the child was absorbed into their communal way of life. No one referred to the issue of its paternity or pointed an accusing finger at the mother. However, no one knew or openly discussed what happened inside the compound huts, between the spouses where the wife had lain with a Spaniard, whether there was anger, shame or rancour. No one cared. If there was gossiping amongst the women about who slept with whom, it was light-hearted and without malice.

The hardship suffered by Ayar Manco's tribe of thirty people after a bad crop of purple corn left them destitute and forced the young men and women to seek work elsewhere. A deep gash on his mother's thigh, the result of an accident with a thorny cactus plant, compelled Ayar Manco himself to head to Cusco, to seek the help of a Spanish doctor. This brought him into contact with the invaders' world and caused him to stray from his quipu work, for he found himself employed within the household of a wealthy Spanish general, Don Antonio from Cadiz. Ayar Manco had little idea of where that place was in Spain, merely guessing it to be far away across the vast ocean.

The one-hour trek on his horse from his home village at the base of the mountains near Ollantaytambo, the city of the Temple of the Sun, to Cusco became a stark reality for Ayar Manco as he took on the job of managing Don Antonio's household and supervising the five Quechua domestic workers. Don Antonio was preoccupied with his army duties for which he was rewarded well by his leader Pizarro and country of origin, Spain. He spent his wealth on his casa and local workers. Ayar Manco had never been inside a building of such size or splendour. It was like being in a dream, he thought as he walked around the house, noting the animal quarters and workers' compound that had been built at the rear. He was impressed by the delicate carvings on the ceilings, the elegant wall alcoves with their miniature oil paintings of scenes of Spain and members of his family, the monumental pillars gracefully holding up the veranda and the intricate Moorish-Arab design of the window galleries, neatly copied from those in Córdoba and Seville in Spain.

To Ayar Manco's eyes, the entire casa was breathtakingly exquisite: the central courtyard with its Moorish fountain and Spanish tiled floorscape; the elegant wooden furniture imported from Spain and upholstered in a variety of fabrics — silks, brocades and damask. He was at first intimidated by it all, afraid to sit on the soft couches in case the dust from his clothes soiled them. The four-poster bed and the mirror in the master bedroom were imported ahead of Don Antonio's wife's arrival from Spain. One corner of the salon downstairs was left empty for her musical instruments that she insisted on bringing with her to Cusco.

Ayar Manco was assigned the task of managing all aspects of the running of the household. Learning about the Incan's quipu work, Don Antonio was assured of both his intelligence and his capability and thus happily offered a generous salary for the other man's multiple roles. Don Antonio wanted everything to be perfect for his wife Isabel's arrival. Four years of separation, with dozens of letters in between, had strained their relationship. And then there was the matter of Kukuli, Don Antonio's concubine, and their child, Rumi.

Six months before Doña Isabel's arrival, flowers and bushes were planted everywhere, trailing over the balconies, amply perfuming the house with their sweet aroma. A huge oil portrait of Isabel was hung on the wall facing the four-poster bed in the main bedroom. Spanish ships had imported some of the furniture and her belongings over the months.

That was the first time that Ayar Manco caught a glimpse of Doña Isabel, his future employer. Arrested, he went on gazing at the young woman with the startling blue eyes staring down at him. Mesmerised by her rosebud of a mouth, he could not help wondering which plant the Spanish mistress used to smudge colour onto her lips. *My Cava of course will know which plant was used for that shade of red*, he thought.

Spanish wives and new brides were arriving to join their husbands and grooms. Ayar Manco had seen some Spanish women around the cathedral area in Cusco, and out in the streets, but Doña Isabel had taken his breath away. His eyes had lingered on her luscious curls; the creamy white bosom, half visible in the cherry velvet gown, made his eyes fall and cheeks flame. He had never glimpsed such a pale shade of skin or so much flesh of a Spanish woman before. The ones he came across in public were always discreetly covered, hiding their delicate skin from the hot sun.

One day, his master caught him looking at the large portrait of his wife.

"Yes, Ayar, my Isabel is a very attractive woman – and by Spanish standards too!" He had laughed aloud, enjoying the look of discomfort on the face of his Incan manager. "That's why I married Isabel. Not only for her looks, but she's educated too; she can read and write extremely well. Let me show you her beautiful letters." He went to fetch one from the dressing-table drawer.

Ayar Manco gazed down at the perfumed paper with its elegant, black scrawled writing that he could fully recognise. He wanted to emulate Isabel's style of writing.

Unaware of the thoughts of his Quechua employee, Don Antonio continued, "See her writing? It's superb. Of course, you can't appreciate it as you can't read or write in Spanish."

Ayar Manco had stiffly corrected him. "I can read and manage some basic Spanish writing, sir." Then he proudly added, "I'm the tribe's chronicler. We've our own writing and recording system, sir. Of course, it's different from yours."

"That's why I've employed you, you clever chap!" His master had good-humouredly tapped him affectionately on his shoulder.

When Ayar Manco started to work for Don Antonio's household, he had already mastered the Spanish language through conversations with an Incan chef, nicknamed with a Spanish name, Enrique, who cooked big cauldrons of meat and potatoes for the Spanish soldiers in the barracks.

"I'm hoping to have your mistress join us in the next two months. Isabel will be sailing off soon with a group of women arriving in Lima," Don Antonio had informed his manager one day.

Back in his village, when he lay on the floor rug with his beloved wife Cava, the image of the distressed Doña Isabel in her night attire flashed through Ayar Manco's head. His arms tightened passionately around his wife's waist. Cava turned in his arms, welcoming his embrace.

Ayar Manco woke up to the light streaming through the small crack in the window of their hut. He glanced down at his wife, admiring her classic Incan beauty. Her high forehead and cheekbones. The full mouth, with soft lips always coated with the colour of berries, either from eating or juice deliberately applied for his benefit. Cava carefully plaited her full head of thick hair into many shiny braids, pinning them around her scalp, in the way he loved. He hated it in the winter when she had to wear either a shawl or a hat on her head. Ayar Manco's eyes then lingered on the dusky-pink valley of his wife's full breasts, visible in the opening of her loose tunic.

Hugging Cava, he dismissed the image of Doña Isabel, his mind and heart refusing to compare his beloved wife to the Spanish Señora. Yes, there was beauty – the Incan beauty and the European beauty. But who decided which was the more appealing? In his eyes, both were very attractive. However, some of his fellow Incan men scoffed at the pale skin of the Spanish women, lacking the brown colour of life in the sun.

Opening her eyes, Cava took her fill of her Ayar's handsome face. Like their wedding night, she wanted to go on passionately kissing him, unable to believe that after years of waiting he actually belonged to her. She had aggressively ensured that no other woman entered her husband's life, let alone became his concubine. For that reason, she had been active in introducing young men to her younger sister. She shuddered when Bachue openly flirted with her husband.

Ayar Manco laughed against Cava's warm cheeks, amused at her passion, the possessive love shooting out of her eyes and the way her lips insisted on grinding against his mouth. Giving in to the warm pressure of her breasts against his naked chest, he happily succumbed to their passion for the second time that night. And there was an added reason.

They were married a year ago and had enjoyed a physical relationship several months before that. No child, however, was conceived. Despite the persistent questioning from family and friends, both remained unperturbed, leaving it to their divinities to bless their union. Cava's main preoccupation these days was in pleasing their gods, who would endow her womb with a little one in due course.

As time passed, Cava became defensive about her body and refused to visit or consult their local healer. Then an emotional storm rocked her body – jealousy of other young women around her with children and those in the big casa; of Kukuli with the creamy-dusky-skinned baby rumoured to be fathered by the master and, of course, of the newly arrived white Señora under whose roof her husband worked. Fearful thoughts of her Ayar Manco taking a concubine in order to have children devastated her.

That morning, when she learned from her husband about his child, Isabel had gone down in a numbed state to host Doña Rosa for breakfast in the salon. After setting the table, Ayar Manco had left them alone and went to supervise the work on the building of a new shed for animals. As soon as her guest had left, Isabel had slipped away upstairs, loath to go near the kitchen where Kukuli's mother Sami worked. Isabel knew Ayar Manco would deal with everything.

In her bedroom Isabel looked at her surroundings with a new pair of eyes, recalling the day when she had first stepped on the shores of a foreign land, known to the locals as Piru, Land of Abundance. Everything was so surreal: a foreign woman in a

214

land far away from her home, ready to settle with people of another race and adapt to an alien way of life and climate.

From the main port of Lima she had travelled south on horseback, on bumpy, rocky terrain to Cusco. Her husband, after meeting the two generals Almagro and Pizarro in Lima that morning, was at the port to welcome her and take her home. With three male Incan workers hired from Cusco they transported her four large trunks from the ship onto their horses.

Exhausted and disoriented, Doña Isabel had arrived in Cusco in the middle of the night. Her new home, the casa, was flickering with rows of oil-lit clay jars, to guide her in the darkness. Isabel could hear the sound of running water from the nearby waterfall and shivered, feeling the chilly air from the mountains penetrate the thin material of her gown.

Stepping into the courtyard, Doña Isabel had trodden over a sleeping dog and jumped back in fright. Waiting to receive them, Ayar Manco had reached out with his arm and stopped her from falling. Doña Isabel had given him an alarmed look in the semi-darkness of the courtyard; Ayar Manco's arm abruptly fell.

Inside the casa, an excited entourage of grinning native Quechua workers with lit oil jars welcomed the lady of the house, whose painting they had adored. The sullen cook, Sami, swiftly ushered her daughter Kukuli out into the cooking area, then had to call her back, to bring another oil lamp.

It was at that moment that Doña Isabel stood beside the central fountain, with the stars shining above her. Staring at the slim silhouette of the tall, new mistress, standing in the courtyard with her back to her, Kukuli lost her nerve and slipped away into the darkness of the veranda, the light from the oil jar flickering in her face.

Speaking in Quechua, Don Antonio commanded, "Kukuli, bring the light out here." His wife looked on, listening to the sound of the language of the natives.

Head lowered, the young girl stepped forward into the courtyard. Holding the light away from her face, she guided the master and his wife to their bedchamber. Mouth dry, Isabel followed the shadowy female figure of Kukuli leading them up the wooden stairs, wearing the native traditional skirt and matching tunic wrap, a thick plait hanging gracefully down to her waist.

In the bedroom, Antonio sharply instructed in Quechua. "Kukuli, hold up the light, for God's sake, woman!"

Isabel was disconcerted by the harsh sound of the language coming out of her husband's mouth. Her Antonio was indeed totally at home amongst the natives. She glanced at the dark shadows of the wooden furniture then brightened at the sight of the four-poster bed, a familiar piece of furniture imported from their home in Cadiz, and her portrait by a well-known Catalan artist hanging on the wall opposite the bed. The rest of the furnishing, the richly woven tablecloth and the Incan wall hangings with geometrical patterns, she would see properly in daylight.

Hiding the hurt in her eyes, thanks to the darkness of the room, Kukuli held the oil lamp up to Isabel. It was then she caught a proper glimpse of Antonio's wife: the, soft parted lips, the pale skin, icy blue eyes and the delicate straight nose. Then she turned, hearing Antonio address her again. This time, his tone was gentle and Kukuli melted with it.

"Leave the lamp on the table, my dear," he said, and his eyes roved possessively over her body. Keeping her face hidden in the shadows, Kukuli happily obeyed, wanting to escape from the room and relishing what she heard next.

"Kukuli, go to your hut and rest now. Rumi needs you." The smoothly murmured words 'my dear' had, as intended, performed their magic.

Even in her confused state of mind, Isabel was alert to the charged ambience of the room. She had noted the gentleness of her husband's tone towards the maid, even though she could not understand what he had said, and had caught the look that passed between him and the woman called Kukuli. She had observed the maid's quivering mouth, her coils of dark hair springing away from her brow and the curve of her shoulder before she closed the door.

The tall young man introduced earlier as Ayar Manco now entered with two men carrying her trunks. From the flickering light of the oil jar on the dressing table Ayar Manco too got his first proper look at their mistress. His eyes slid to her portrait hanging on the wall, and in awe he compared the painted woman to the flesh and blood one. Their Apu, mountain god, had blessed his master well, he thought. Nervously, Ayar Manco dropped his gaze as Doña Isabel thanked him with her husband's help, without realising that Ayar Manco already understood.

"Isabel – Ayar Manco is a very important person in our household. He does everything in the casa, manages all the staff. He's also the local record-keeper, recording everything to do with his Quechua people's lives. A very intelligent man. In fact, he's simply indispensable, believe me, my Isabel!" Don Antonio had ended generously, making Ayar Manco blush and his skin darken.

Don Antonio had instructed him to stay the night and go home the following day. There was a lot of work to be done. A welcoming feast had to be prepared in honour of Doña Isabel's arrival, and other Spanish families were to be invited to pay their respects to her.

Ayar Manco was up before dawn to see to the breakfast for their new mistress, and it was then he spoke to her for the first time in Spanish. Pleasantly surprised, her eyes lit up; it would be good to have someone who could speak her language when her husband was not at home.

Kukuli was in her hut in the workers' compound at the rear, impassively getting her baby son, Rumi, ready to leave for their mountain village. Her mother, Sami, who managed the kitchen, gruffly explained to Ayar Manco and the other workers that Kukuli would be visiting some relatives for a few weeks. Ayar Manco merely nodded, and made no comment. He knew everything that went on in the casa and welcomed Kukuli's decision to leave as a most prudent one.

Back in the village Cava knew that her husband was very busy with the arrival of the new mistress in the casa. She herself was absorbed in the planning of the funeral rites ceremony. There were two days to go before their trek to bring back her maternal grandparents' mummified corpses resting in their funeral baskets from the mountain burial sites, for the annual bathing and reburial ceremony.

On top of that, Cava had been tasked with an urgent errand – to take their neighbour's little girl, Killa, to Amaru, their shaman healer, locally known as 'the one who sees and the one who knows'. Six-year-old Killa had complained of a bad stomach ache. The mother was busy nursing a sick baby, so Cava had promised to step in and take her place.

Her arm held protectively around the whimpering little girl, Cava entered the shaman healer's large hut, where scores of different items of religious importance were tidily displayed on a wooden mantelpiece. A dead guinea pig lay ready for the ceremony. Eyes closed, and concentrating hard on the prayers, the healer held the guinea pig near the girl, moving it around her body, chanting prayers to their divinities to make the girl better.

Killa squirmed in Cava's arms. Smiling, Cava held onto her, remembering her own similar healing ordeal as a little girl. She was always frightened when the healer placed things near her body, including rubbing an egg to take away her fear, and now she hushed the child into silence.

After going back and leaving the child with her mother, Cava returned to her loom to work with her sister. Bachue was busy clearing bits of dirt and impurities from the raw alpaca and vicuña wool. As Cava shot her weaving tool through the wool threads, she wondered what her husband was doing in Cusco and when he would return. Lately he had been staying overnight; he had his own room in the casa on the first floor next to the salon and the master's office.

Three months passed. Isabel's husband was away on duty, upon the orders of Francisco Pizarro, to quell an unrest in the Nasca area. The natives were still seething about the loss of their Incan Emperor Atahualpa – killed by Pizarro and his men even after all the gold had been handed over. Pizarro was experiencing difficulties himself with his fellow explorer and commander Almagro. The heated rivalry between the two men was affecting the morale of people like Don Antonio, who worked under Pizarro's command.

Don Antonio was particularly keen for Isabel to see the ancient walled complex of Sacsayhuaman and its stonework whilst he was away in the north. Ayar Manco had guided her around the monumental ruins, arousing her interest with his retelling of fascinating tales of his people and the history behind this place, and of his noble Incan ancestors. He explained how the city of Cusco was planned in the shape of a puma, with Sacsayhuaman as its head and the River Tullumayo that they had walked along earlier as its tail – and with the main square as its belly.

His wife Cava was staying at the casa too for a couple of days. She was on a special business errand – to sell some woollen *mantas* in the square to the ladies there. Cava had joined them on the ruins expedition, walking behind the horse led by her Ayar Manco and carrying Doña Isabel. Unable to communicate in Spanish, Cava spent her time quietly observing Doña Isabel, fascinated by the sound of her voice, her mannerisms, the hat she wore with her ringlets of hair tucked beneath it, the outdoor cape and gown worn over her petticoat. Cava keenly noted the smiles and attention Doña Isabel gave to her Ayar Manco and the ease with which she spoke to him.

Tight-faced, Cava had trailed behind them. Doña Isabel, almost oblivious to his wife's presence, enjoyed Ayar Manco's company, hugely admiring him for having learned Spanish so well. It made communication between them so easy. She just wished that their native female workers too could speak her language – in particular, the sullen cook Sami, who very rarely smiled in her presence and kept well out of her way. What Isabel did not know was that the cook was Kukuli's mother and that the woman deeply resented her arrival. Missing her baby grandson had not only given Sami many sleepless nights but had increased her loathing of Don Antonio's Spanish wife. In her eyes, her Kukuli was Antonio's wife too – and, what's more, had a son to show for it.

Ayar Manco had become the chief translator between Doña Isabel and the rest of the Incan staff. He arrived early from his village, in time for his employers' breakfast before he dealt with his other duties: checking the work of the middle-aged man, Antay, overseeing the repairs carried out by the local masons around the house, and shopping for household goods as well as maintaining the accounts of everything that entered and left the casa. Above all, Isabel relied on Ayar Manco to ensure the efficient management of the domestic workers. Her husband was insisting that she learn Quechua and connect with the workers herself.

It was late evening. Doña Isabel had played the organetto to entertain herself before she went to bed and was ready to write a letter to her aunt. She was still in a buoyant mood, after an exhilarating day spent amongst the local Incan ruins. Isabel was in the salon at her desk writing the letter when she heard a baby crying. Her forehead creased with two fine lines and she put her quill back in the inkpot. As far as she knew, there was no baby in the casa. The sound came from the kitchen area.

Picking up the oil lamp, she went out to the star-lit courtyard. It was then she saw the back of a female worker carrying something in her arms and heading towards the stone archway which led to the rear compound. Isabel was curious about the visitor. How did she enter and who had let her in?

Hearing Isabel's footsteps, the woman turned. On glimpsing the figure of the Spanish wife, she hastened her pace and soon disappeared through the archway. Confused, Isabel remained standing in the shadows next to the archway. Lifting the hemline of her petticoat with one hand and holding the oil lamp with the other, she then followed the woman into the workers' *kancha* where four huts had been built around the cobbled square with its vegetable and herb plots, washing and weaving areas.

Only once before had Isabel visited this part of the casa. It was the workers' domain. Sami, the cook, lived there, along with her two younger helpers and the older man, Antay, who looked after the domestic animals. The alpacas, vicuñas and the chickens were housed in a separate large hut outside the compound. Food was prepared and eaten in the main large kitchen of the casa that Don Antonio had insisted on building to perfection for his household, with windows, shelves and cooking area.

Isabel stood in the middle of the workers' compound, standing near bushes with some washing draped over to dry. From one hut came the sound of two female voices. One she immediately identified as that of the cook.

When Isabel thrust open the door, Sami was standing near her daughter Kukuli, who was sitting with her son on the floor mat, holding a beaker of water to his mouth. Kukuli froze, shocked to see the mistress inside their hut.

Smiling, Isabel came right inside and bent down to look at the baby. She loved children and longed to have her own. Each month since her arrival she had anxiously waited to see if she had successfully conceived. Bitter disappointment followed. Isabel angrily blamed her empty womb on her husband's military trips away from home.

Isabel peered into the baby's face, but when she reached to stroke his cheek, Kukuli pulled her son away and turned her back on Isabel. Imagining that the girl was scared of her appearance in the dark, Isabel apologised.

She said, "I'm sorry," along with a few other words of Quechua that she had mastered. But Kukuli remained with her back to Isabel, head lowered and the baby's face pressed protectively against her chest.

Isabel left. From outside she could hear but could not understand the mother and daughter's heated exchange.

"Daughter, why have you come back to the casa? You stupid girl! I told you to stay in the mountains. Don Antonio has provided well for you. Had a special hut built for you . . ."

"I'm not going back there, Mamay. I'm staying right here — this is where my son belongs."

Her mother gasped. "You are mad, Kukuli. Don Antonio will be livid. Face facts . . . You can't live here any more."

"Mother, I'll not go back! It's cold in the mountains . . . not good for Rumi. I'll not jeopardise his health, come what may! You know there are no proper healers of the kind we have in Cusco . . . My Rumi has been coughing for two weeks. Here in the casa everything is clean, and we get plenty of food to eat, plus the hut is much warmer at night. You know all this, Mother!"

Sami shrugged her shoulders helplessly. The health of her grandchild was important, and Don Antonio should know that. In the meantime, she would find work for Kukuli in another casa, so that she was out of the way during the day with her baby, who she was still breastfeeding.

In the days that followed, Isabel often heard the baby's cries but she never actually came across him in the main casa building. She had addressed Sami once, with Ayar Manco as the interpreter, to ask how the baby was doing. With eyes averted, and a peevish tone, the cook had mumbled, "He's fine."

Blushing, Ayar Manco translated.

It was during the party that Isabel hosted for fellow Spanish expatriate wives that the subject of the baby in the casa cropped up. The women, dressed in their elegant silk robes, were sitting in the courtyard near the marble fountain, enjoying the morning sun and the warm breeze. Isabel was serving them sweetened cheese and French figs when they heard Rumi crying. Isabel smiled — but her Spanish guests appeared discomfited. She explained, biting into a fig, china plate daintily held in her hand, "That's the baby of our worker, who has returned from the mountains."

"Have you actually seen the baby yourself, Isabel?" Doña Rosa, a frequent visitor, ventured to ask. From Córdoba, she had been one of the first Spanish brides to arrive in Cusco. Another woman exchanged a quick glance with her, which Isabel accidentally intercepted. Doña Rosa sheepishly looked away.

"No, I have not," Isabel replied. Head bent over the plate, this time she missed the raised eyebrows and the surreptitious looks going around the group of five Spanish women.

A few weeks later, when she was in bed, Isabel heard the baby crying. The noise came from the courtyard below. Wondering if she could help in any way, Isabel went down to check, draping a shawl around her shoulders over her night chemise.

In one corner of the veranda, Kukuli was squatting on a woollen rug with Rumi in her lap, feeding him. An oil jar was on the table nearby. She did not hear Isabel's footsteps, imagining her to be fast asleep upstairs. It was when Isabel went up to bed that Kukuli was finally able to roam freely around the casa and its courtyard with her son.

Barefooted, Isabel came from behind and decided to make use of her mastery of the Quechua language. She had taken lessons from Ayar Manco, spending an hour every day learning various phrases and sentences, and then would practise them with him by her side with their domestic workers and the local shopkeeper. Ayar Manco, immensely proud of her progress, loved listening to her mispronunciation of the words.

Isabel now confidently asked in Quechua: "Is your baby hungry?"

Kukuli nearly jumped out of her skin. Rising to her feet, she turned and faced her enemy. The light from the oil lamp shone on the child's face and Isabel stared at his green eyes and the light brown curly hair.

"*Dios mio!*" she whispered, taking a step back. Panicking, Kukuli fled to her hut through the casa archway.

Isabel remained standing in the courtyard, face pale, heart beating and thoughts flying in her head. She did not go back up to her room; she could not bear to be in bed with Antonio. As if in a dream she walked to the salon and remained huddled on the couch till dawn when Ayar Manco came searching for her.

Surprised at the look of devastation on her face, he immediately guessed it had something to do with Kukuli and the baby. Door firmly closed, Isabel remained in the salon until Antonio had left. Her husband merely assumed she was around in the casa somewhere.

Isabel spent the day locked in her bedroom, having instructed Ayar Manco that no one was to disturb her – not even her husband – as she had a very bad headache. When Antonio returned, she pretended to be fast asleep, and did not respond to his touch.

It was on the following morning that she confronted Antonio about Kukuli's baby. In reply, he had hurled at her the damning words that confirmed to her that the child was indeed his son. That was the time when Ayar Manco had witnessed her breakdown into tears.

Isabel never recovered from that shock. Something died inside her. Feelings of shame, betrayal and humiliation were eating her up. She recoiled from the knowledge that all the Spanish families knew about the baby, and tasted a new feeling in her life: hatred for her husband, hatred for the young woman called Kukuli, and, more importantly, for that lovely young baby with her husband's eyes. And above all, she hated herself for harbouring these poisonous feelings. She was normally a kind person with an optimistic soul.

What was going to be her future and that of her children, with Kukuli's son in their midst? she asked herself. And what would become of Antonio's relationship with Kukuli? Isabel trembled at the thought of meeting again the woman who had lain in her husband's arms.

On that day, too overwrought to get up and face the world, Isabel had remained in bed. Only Ayar Manco was allowed into her personal domain. His perceptive gaze took in everything, but he did not share his thoughts or what he knew about the master and the mistress's row with anyone, not even with his beloved Cava back in the village.

Four days later, Don Antonio left the casa for his military duties, this time with General Almagro. He had to spend several months, spread out over the year, in the northern region, in Lima. Antonio departed without bidding his wife goodbye. Ayar Manco had become the reluctant go-between for the husband and wife, and was saddened by Isabel's personal pain. He had advised his employer that it would be best if Kukuli and the baby lived in another place, away from the casa, and Isabel.

"Sir, it will make it easy for everyone if you consider the home situation. At the moment, Doña Isabel is not going anywhere near the kitchen and workers' compound area in case she meets Kukuli . . . When the baby cries, she grows anxious."

Don Antonio was annoyed at first, but then upon reflection he realised that what his manager had said made sense.

"Very well. Whilst I'm away, go and find a small newly built house for Kukuli and her mother. Remember, they can't go back to the mountains. I'll not have my Rumi made ill for Isabel's sake. Why does she not see what it's like for Kukuli? You know the situation, Ayar. I can't turn them out – I can't be callous like some of my countrymen, who turn their backs on the native women the moment their wives arrive. I refuse to do that. The child is my son and my responsibility. Kukuli has been looking after me whilst Isabel was in Spain all those years. I can't just abandon them . . ."

He stopped, afraid to discuss the emotional welfare of the two women in his life in Cusco, their jealousy, the angry, betrayed looks both women shot at him. Both saw themselves as victims, but it was worse for him. His love for Rumi and his mother, as well as human decency, demanded that he could not abandon Kukuli now that his lawful wife, Isabel, had arrived. Kukuli had made a considerable sacrifice: she had given up the prospect of marrying someone from her own clan by staying with him. He owed it to her mother, Sami, who had generously allowed him to co-habit with her daughter. His wife's jealousy and bruised pride did not merit abandoning three innocent people at one go.

In order to reassure Kukuli and her mother that he was not going to treat them differently now that his wife had joined him in the casa, Don Antonio spent a whole afternoon with Kukuli in her hut the day before he left for Lima, enjoying the warmth of her eager and loving body. Neither cared whether it could result in another child. It was the afternoon when his wife was away on an expedition with fellow Spanish women to the Machu Picchu area. Sami, with her grandson cradled in her arms, sat under the shade of the alder tree and guarded the compound.

Seeing the healthy glow return to Kukuli's sun-bronzed cheeks, Antonio had ardently promised her that she still remained his dear and beloved concubine.

"Kukuli — you're the mother of my son, so how can I forget you? I know you don't say anything to me . . . but your huge, beautiful eyes are very expressive, my dear. They say everything to me, my darling . . . I know you're unhappy . . . I'm going to buy another house where you, your mother and our Rumi can live. I can visit you there whenever I want to, without worrying about anything or anyone. Would you like that?"

Kukuli had happily nodded, blossoming under his warm, green-eyed gaze, revelling in his possessive touch, passionate kisses and the thought of frequent future intimate moments like this with him in her new home. Her anxious thoughts and misgivings were quashed there and then. Kukuli was immensely proud of her sensual power over Don Antonio, which had ensured that his eyes had never strayed to other local women. She did not know about the Spanish women friends whose company he might occasionally enjoy or of other cities he visited — nor did she care. Now with his lawful wife in his home and bed, jealousy stung Kukuli day and night.

"Luckily my son is my blessing and saviour, my solid bridge with Don Antonio. Master Antonio adores his son. He'll never forget about us," Kukuli fervently reminded herself several times a day.

Before Isabel had arrived, Don Antonio went around his casa with his son in his arms, she recalled. Their Rumi and her enticing body would ensure that Antonio remained part of her world. That afternoon, Kukuli took great care to dress in a new garment, to braid her hair into an attractive style, and she smudged deep berry colour over her lips, making them appear more luscious.

When Isabel caught sight of Kukuli the following morning, she knew straightaway that something had happened at the casa whilst she was away on the expedition. It was that daring and becoming shade of colour coating Kukuli's lips combined with the confident, sensual sway of her brightly skirted wide hips that had signalled to Isabel that she had a deadly rival in the casa.

Isabel trusted Ayar Manco enough to ask him later whether Master Antonio had been in the casa whilst she was out with the ladies on their trip to Machu Picchu. Ayar Manco had first looked away and then glibly lied that the master had been out all day.

For Isabel, however, the nagging, sinking feeling remained. That night, she kept to her side of the marital bed, squeezing her eyes shut on the image of Kukuli lying in her husband's arms, feeling so alone and betrayed. Inside her head, thoughts came and fled. She was the virgin bride. No other man apart from Antonio had ever touched her.

Ayar Manco quietly observed the emotional goings-on in the casa. He understood the cause of Doña Isabel's loss of appetite, the reason why she remained withdrawn and had started to shun the social events organised by the local Spanish families. Doña Rosa and her other female friends were no longer invited to the house. All was silent in the casa.

One afternoon, a few days later, when Ayar Manco returned from his village, Isabel called him over and asked: "Ayar Manco, where's the baby? I can't hear any noise from the compound." She was sitting under the veranda, enjoying the cool mountain breeze passing through the courtyard and working on a new embroidery design for a tablecloth.

"The baby has gone with his mother . . ." Then he paused, reluctant to reveal more.

"Where?"

"Perhaps back to the village."

"Are you sure?" she persisted.

He shrugged his shoulders and left the casa on another outdoor errand. Isabel returned to the salon to read again a letter newly arrived from Madrid, from her maternal Aunt Maria who had raised her as her own.

The following day, Doña Rosa arrived uninvited, and was only too happy to inform her of the whereabouts of Kukuli.

"You do know that Antonio's native concubine Kukuli or whatever she's called has moved to the other side of the city, behind the ruins."

Isabel's heartbeat stopped. Fortunately, the entrance of a maid with refreshments gave her the excuse to ignore the comment. She turned instead to news of the arrival of another Spanish wife in Cusco.

"We've to look after Mercedes as she's fresh from Spain," Doña Rosa remarked, then lowered her voice to add: "As everyone knows, her husband Hernando not only had an affair with Sofia, José's wife, but also has an Incan concubine in Lima with child."

Isabel's eyes widened in disgust.

It was when Antonio left for Lima a few days later that Isabel insisted that Ayar Manco take her to the place where Kukuli lived. Horrified, he pretended ignorance at first.

"There's nothing you do not know of what goes on around here, Ayar," Isabel had reproached him. "You're the local Quipu Keeper — it's your job to collect information . . . I'm sure that you are helping with the errands for Kukuli. I know Antonio is devoted to his son . . . I expect him to look after them . . . Please take me there," she wheedled.

Unhappy at taking her without the master's permission, Ayar Manco was thrown into a dilemma. And Don Antonio was too far away to be reached. Ayar's beloved Cava was in the village and he could not consult her as to whether he was doing the right thing. It was Sami, Kukuli's mother, who cynically instructed him that it *was* the right thing to do.

"Take her," she said. "What's there to be afraid of? It's better she comes to terms with our Kukuli and Rumi's existence in Master Antonio's life. They're not going to disappear into the mountains or oblivion as she would like them to do, but are here to stay. *She* can go back to where she has come from, or better still take a lover herself in revenge if it bothers her too much," the woman had ended caustically.

Reddening, Ayar Manco turned away, not wanting to hear any more. Soon afterwards, Ayar Manco reluctantly accompanied Isabel to the other side of the city of Cusco. Her face pinched, Isabel had stood outside, staring at the newly built hut, with a small compound at the back to grow vegetables.

When Kukuli opened the door, with her son in her arms, Ayar Manco held out the goods that he had brought for her.

"Your mother has sent these from the casa." He then asked, "How are you?"

231

"I'm fine . . . Has the master gone?" When he nodded, Kukuli's expression dulled, imagining weeks going by without her master's visits.

Ayar Manco went inside with her, giving Rumi a cuddle and asked, "May I take him outside for a few minutes for a bit of fresh air?"

Surprised by the request, Kukuli agreed, trusting him. Ayar Manco had kept his promise to Doña Isabel, who had wanted to catch a glimpse of the baby again. It was a last-minute nervous request before Ayar had knocked on the door.

Isabel was hiding behind a tall bush at the side of the hut. Ayar Manco carried the child to her. Isabel had a good long look at him, noting that the shape of his nose and the colour of the baby's eyes in daylight straightaway showed the resemblance to her Antonio. Her natural love of children had her longing to caress the baby's plump cheeks, but stinging jealousy kept her arm at her side. It was then Kukuli came out, looking for her son.

On spotting her rival, the mistress of the casa, peering into her son's face, she dashed over to Ayar Manco, yelling in Quechua: "You did not tell me about her! Take her away!"

Face pale, Isabel turned and walked away to the horse that was waiting for her.

"Doña Isabel just wanted to see him," Ayar Manco offered lamely.

"Tell her to keep away from my son! I've left the casa, as she wanted – is she now going to hound us here too?"

Ayar Manco shook his head in exasperation and ran after Doña Isabel. He helped her up on the horse tied to a tree, holding out his hand. Isabel took it without hesitation. He saw the wretched, tearful look upon her face and quietly turned his own horse around, whilst holding onto the reins of hers.

Isabel kept her face averted, aware how perceptive he was. The silence continued all the way back to the casa, where Isabel once more shut herself away in her bedroom. The women workers gossiped about her. It was only when he took the oil lamp to her room that Ayar Manco saw Doña Isabel sitting slumped in her chair, in a pose of utter despair.

She had but one question for him, and needed the answer very badly. Ever since Doña Rosa had mentioned Lima, her mind had been in a torment.

Voice shaky, Isabel asked, "Does Antonio have another concubine in Lima?"

Ayar Manco froze with the oil lamp in his hand, staring at her across the room.

In Ayar Manco's village, Cava had finished sweeping the floor of her hut. Since her husband had started working in the casa in Cusco, she did not bother much with her cooking pot but ate her meals with her mother and sister. As his absence continued, her hut became better furnished. Ayar Manco always carried back something he had purchased from the central square with his earnings. Also, Doña Isabel was a generous woman, always rewarding the workers with some gift or other which she had brought from Spain. In Cava's home, small attractive items began to add Spanish character to their living space. The latest gift was a silk, lace-trimmed money pouch. In a fit of rage, Cava had thrown it out on the Kancha floor, where much to her husband's horror it landed in a small puddle of dyed water. Ayar Manco had arrived late again and then had handed her another gift from the Spanish Doña of the casa.

"I want you, not these knick-knacks from that white madam!" Enraged, Cava had cried.

In the evening darkness, from their compound archway Cava gazed at the dark, swollen clouds, ready to burst and pelt the majestic mountains and the fertile food valley with rain. Out in the lane Cava headed out of the village, wanting to climb up the hill leading to the food terrace where the corn and potato crops were growing. Once there, she perched herself on a moss-encrusted old rock to rest. Then, kneeling on the ground and facing her body in the direction of their Apu, Cava broke down with the anguish of the last few months and her desperate longing for a child.

"My dear lord, put my mind and heart at rest," she prayed. "Please bless my womb with a baby soon. I can't bear it any more!"

Cava was deeply unhappy about her mood changes and the negative thoughts plaguing her mind about people and things. It was seriously affecting her relationship with other people and her artistic creativity. Crouched in front of her loom for hours on end, her vivid imagination and artistic skills resulted in exquisite floral designs for rugs and traditional items that the Incan women wore to carry goods and young children behind their backs. That morning she had made many mistakes.

Cava was adored by the village women for her multiple skills and the fact she was quick to lend a hand for any domestic or wool-related chores. For that reason she was readily called upon to work on the four-post loom with three other women. Moreover, Cava was very knowledgeable about the different sources of the dyes they used. Cava knew exactly where to locate them. For example, for the carmine dye she sought the cochineal – the purple beetle – from the cactus plant. Similarly, she was adept in the speedy picking of the leaves from bushes in the woodlands for the minty, green colour. Her long, sturdy arms came in handy with the rinsing of the heavy skeins of wool.

Cava was so ashamed; for the first time in her life she had refused to help their neighbour with her weaving that morning. At one point, she had angrily accused Mother Earth herself for not listening to her anguished prayers.

Cava was full of hate. For her husband, for often being absent from home. For her sister Bachue, for flirting with her Ayar Manco. Cava shuddered at the chilling thought of their Bachue becoming her Ayar's concubine and bearing him children. She despised herself for becoming so possessive about Ayar. When he returned home she remained by his side most of the time.

Her erratic mood swings had begun with her overhearing a conversation between Bachue and their mother, whilst they scrubbed their dirty clothes in an open stream running behind the compound.

"Our Cava still has not produced a child, Mother. They've been sleeping together for over two years . . . If Ayar Manco decides to take another woman to become his concubine, and bear him children, then I'm going to be that woman, I'm telling you Mamay! And don't look so surprised . . . It's better that it's me than another woman, surely . . . He's not going to sit around without children for ever, is he? No matter how much he loves our Cava! His mother won't let him anyway."

Rooted to the spot, something clutched fast at Cava's heart; her breathing grew ragged. Loathing her sister, Cava had withdrawn into her hut.

The following day, Cava's eyes refused to meet her sister's. After two days of being ignored, Bachue enquired, smiling, "What's wrong?"

"You, Bachue! You'll never be my Ayar's concubine," Cava had bitterly turned on her sister.

Taken aback, Bachue sensibly withdrew without responding.

Now, the dark clouds above suddenly burst, pelting Cava's head and shoulders with heavy drops of rain. Within seconds her clothes were soaked, and she began shivering in the thin, mountainous cold air. Was the storm a positive signal or a bad omen from their gods? Cava could not tell.

Between anguished sobs, she vowed: "Mother Maya, protect my Ayar Manco. For he's mine!"

This time it was not Bachue, her sister, who was in her head, but Doña Isabel, the beautiful Spanish wife.

In the casa, Isabel's question to Ayar Manco hung heavily between them.

Isabel stood facing him in her chamber. Antonio would be in Lima for another two weeks, and Ayar Manco had been given strict instruction to station himself for most of that period in the casa to support the mistress and to manage everything. Ayar Manco was supposed to go home for a two-day break that night and his wife Cava was waiting for him in his home village.

It was a stormy evening. Isabel was afraid of Ayar Manco and his horse being caught in the wild wind and rain, making her feel anxious. She had kept him busy all day with different tasks, including accompanying her to Kukuli's home. The visit to her husband's concubine's home had turned her life upside down. Bereft, she was reflecting on her uncertain future in this land of the Incan people.

In the flickering light from the oil jar Isabel scrutinised Ayar's face.

"Is there another Kukuli in Lima too, Ayar Manco?" she quietly repeated, looking him straight in the eye.

Outside, the wind continued to howl against the wooden window shutters; the sound of thunder had everyone in the casa rushing to their huts. What had made their gods angry?

His face tight, Ayar Manco looked away.

Isabel waited. She was dressed in her night chemise, with a linen shawl draped around her shoulders and ringlets of hair falling freely down to her waist. Bare-footed, she stepped in front of him.

"Please tell me," she urged. Ayar Manco was not her employee any more, but a dear and trusted friend. A begging expression in her blue eyes pierced his soul. His heartbeat quickened but his mouth remained stubbornly sealed.

At last, "I don't know," he muttered, head down.

Her bosom behind the shawl was rising and falling, her lips were parted. "You don't know, Ayar? You? Who know everything?" She grasped his arm and implored, "Please tell me!"

Time stood still for them both. They were lost in each other's eyes. His grey-black eyes were pained; her blue ones afraid. Finally, Ayar Manco dutifully obliged her with the truth.

"There might be." The words hung heavily in the air between them.

They simply crushed Isabel. The image of another Kukuli had tears stinging her eyes. First there was one; now there were two rivals. Two native women amorously involved with her Antonio. *He's in her arms right now!* The words screamed in Isabel's head. She just knew.

Ayar Manco watched helplessly, falling into deeper waters; unwittingly, he had added more distress to Doña Isabel, who had become a dear friend, had begun to share her life with him and treated him with the utmost respect.

He had not said, "There is . . ." Instead, he had opted for the word 'might', wanting to protect her and spare her further pain.

Then Isabel froze as another alarming thought flashed across her mind. Mouth dry and dreading the answer, she asked, "And is there a child too?"

Ayar Manco barely heard the words, closing his eyes. Finally, he opened them and stared down into her eyes, which sought truth whilst desperately demanding a denial from him. Trapped, he carried on looking at her, debating whether to tell her the truth and destroy her. Or to hide it and prolong her suffering.

He had watched and studied Doña Isabel as a person from the moment she had arrived. She was now a totally different woman from the one who had curiously looked around her surroundings and home with enthusiasm, treating everyone with a smile and genuine kindness. A woman who had made a real effort to fit into her new surroundings, to adjust to an alien life.

She had blossomed in herself and in her new home. He was able to observe her closely as he had to communicate with her several times a day on household matters such as deciding on the menu, doing the shopping, and supervising the building of a new bathing area for her in one corner of the inner courtyard. As he could speak Spanish, Don Antonio had requested that Ayar Manco take her on sightseeing expeditions, to view the Incan historical monuments. They had spent many happy times together; she telling him about her Spanish world and he about his upbringing in an Incan village.

As the weeks and months passed, a special rapport had developed between them, with Isabel treating him as an equal, learning from him the Incan traditions, the shaman rituals, about their gods and traditional way of life. Ayar Manco felt valued and treated with respect by both his employers. As Antonio was out of the casa most of the time, it was Doña Isabel he had to refer to for all matters.

The day Isabel saw the baby in Kukuli's hut in the workers' compound, things had begun to change. No more did the sound of laughter issue from Isabel's mouth. She took to going to bed before the master had arrived. The rift grew between husband and wife.

Don Antonio had even left for Lima without informing Isabel when he would return. There were no goodbye hugs or fond looks. She hung around the courtyard, but at a distance, to bid him farewell. All the workers knew it was for appearance's sake only. Ayar Manco had stopped the staff from gossiping in Quechua, in case Doña Isabel understood.

"Ayar — *is there a child too?*" Isabel bitterly demanded; her voice had risen. She dreaded the answer, but she still had to know.

Pressed, Ayar capitulated and replied, "Yes." He had seen the baby girl, named Illari, the previous year when he had accompanied Don Antonio on his visit to Lima. Antonio had spent the night with little Illari and her mother before Isabel's ship had arrived.

Isabel swayed with the image of another mixed-race child burned in front of her eyes.

Her animal-like wail shook the room. She stumbled back and fell against the bedpost. Before she sank to the floor, Ayar Manco rushed to her side and caught her in his arms, supporting her. Isabel wept bitterly, forgetting where she was and with whom.

Ayar Manco was afraid to touch her, but her ringlets were tangled around her face and on his thigh.

She wailed in agony in her native tongue. "Is this what I have come to, his bastard children and concubines? May God help me!"

Ayar Manco wanted to console her but did not know what to say. He lifted her up and laid her on the bed. Outside, the mighty wind continued to howl, rattling the window shutters. Down below, in the compound huts, the workers huddled in their warm bedding, trying to sleep.

In Don Antonio's bedchamber, Isabel lay vanquished on her four-poster Spanish bed, eyes staring unseeingly at the damask canopy above her. The anguished sobbing continued. Ayar Manco remained sitting by her side, distressed at watching her lose control. Finally exhausted from the sobbing, Isabel lay quietly, still staring into space.

Outside, lightning struck again and thunder rolled menacingly; the wind continued to roar. Ayar Manco was unable to leave her. He thought of his Cava waiting for him in their hut. But she must know he would not come home on a night like this.

The flame was flickering in the oil jar. Ayar Manco was about to rise, to go downstairs to fetch more oil, but Isabel's hand stopped him. Ayar glanced at it, the creamy whiteness of her hand against the sun-kissed bronze of his own skin. As he stood, her hand tightened on his arm.

She was now looking at him. Cheeks wet, damp ringlets spread around her on the pillow. "Please don't go," she whispered.

The appeal, and the pain in her eyes, grieved him. He sat down on the edge of the bed and held onto her hand. She closed her eyes. Then once more she breathed, "Please stay with me, Ayar. I need you."

Ayar Manco looked down at her, yearning to say so much, wrestling with his thoughts and emotions.

Then, as the tears rolled down her face, he leaned over and finally nodded his head. With reverent fingers, he brushed away her tears then let them trail down her flushed cheeks. Isabel's hand rose to his face, letting her naked eyes say it all.

Acknowledgements

I am immensely grateful to my dear friend, Dr Manorama Venkatraman, PhD, for her sterling initial editorial work on my stories.

I want to thank my publisher Rosemarie Hudson for her enthusiasm and Joan Deitch, my dear editor, for her helpful suggestions and editorial expertise.

A warm thank you goes out to the following people who provided me with invaluable guidance and helped with my research – in particular, in the checking of factual and cultural details.

Rudolf Rau from Germany for the story *The Slave-Catcher*, set in Boston, USA. Dr Marisa Menchola, PhD from USA and Peru for *The Concubine*. Qazi Marzia Babakarkhail for my story *Our Angel*, set in Afghanistan. Marilyn Berg, Rabbi Warren Elf, June Rosen and Jonny Wineberg for my story *Last Train to Krakow*, set in Poland and Hungary. Abaidullah Naeem for my story *The Journey*, about the Partition of India.

I am grateful to Ruth Edmark, whom I met on a writers' retreat in Peru, for introducing me to Dr Marisa Menchola.

My thanks also go to Leanne de Cerbo for her wonderful summary of my stories, and to Moein Ilyas, for all administrative work relating to *The Concubine* and *The Slave-Catcher*.

I am deeply thankful to my fans and friends for their inspiring contributions of ideas and for their spirited reading of my stories: Sabiya Khan, Nadira Mirza, Farkhanda Hussain-butt and Dr Sandra Decard, my former German neighbour.

I am indebted to John Shaw, my personal assistant for several years, Dr Akbar S. Ahmed (USA), Dr Abdur Raheem Kidwai (India), Dr Karin Vogt (Germany), Jane Camens (Australia), Dr Mohammed Ali, Nikki Bi and Professor Lynne Pearce, and Dr Afshan Khwaja, my dear sister-in-law, for their support, guidance and celebration of my writing over the years.

Last but not least, my most profound gratitude goes to my wonderful family: my husband Saeed and our sons Farakh, Gulraiz and Shahrukh for their unwavering loyalty, patience and love – as always.